Zekious Starbo: The Rise of Magic

Zekious Starbo, Volume 1

James Dellwo

Published by James Dellwo, 2024.

ZEKIOUS STARBO: THE RISE OF MAGIC

First edition. May 30, 2024.

ISBN: 979-8227006813

Written by James Dellwo.

Table of Contents

To JJD

May you never stop being curious. Always keep learning.

Chapter One

Twenty thousand years ago, during the last ice age, there was an advanced worldwide civilization of about two million people. Civilization was very adept with many sciences, including astronomy, astrology, mathematics, and engineering. This ancient civilization had access to a special technology. One of those citizens was a was tall, muscular man in his late teens by the name of Zekious Starbo, and he wanted to spread that special technology to everyone.

Zekious was a bright and brave young boy. He preferred to be outside. His parents had a few books that they used to teach Zeke to read and write. He was also very curious. No matter what he was doing, he always tried to figure out the how and why of things. Zeke's life had been anything but orthodox.

As far as he knew, Zeke's life started out ordinary. His family had a small farm and raised a few livestock. Occasionally they would go hunting or fishing. They lived in a small hut, far away from any settlements. What they could not grow themselves, they could get from nature. Zeke never knew anything different. What he did not know, though, was how strange his life would turn out.

When he was a child, strange things had always happened to him. One time when he was five years old, he had gone fishing with his dad. He was not having any luck catching fish, so he was getting angry and let down. On three different occasions, fish jumped out of the river and would hit Zeke and land, flopping at his feet.

Another time when he was six years old, he was playing in his mother's garden. A butterfly fluttered around and landed on Zeke's nose. When the butterfly landed, he got very excited. The more excited he got, the faster all the flowers in the garden began growing. More butterflies came and started fluttering around and landing on him.

Zeke and his parents were aware that these things were strange. However, none of them realized that it was Zeke making these things happen. Every time another of these strange circumstances took place, Zeke and his family were very intrigued. Eventually, they got used to these strange things happening.

At ten years old, Zeke and his parents had gone on a hunting trip to get some deer, or some other kind of meat. It was starting to get cold earlier than normal. They were expecting a long, hard winter, and would need meat to survive the winter. They had traveled west from where their hut was located.

Zeke and his parents had been hunting for two days. They were camping along a stream and were settling down in the late afternoon. They had been successful, and had harvested three whitetail deer, and several small game animals. They heard a rustling in the willows next to the stream. Zeke's father stood and grabbed his bow and some arrows, preparing for what might come out of the willows.

It was a large male short-faced bear. It had come to steal their meat. When the bear saw Zeke and his family, it stood on its hind legs and roared. When it stood, the bear was more than twice as tall as Zeke's father. The roar was so loud that Zeke went partially deaf for several seconds. The stench was bad enough that Zeke almost vomited.

Zeke's father stepped in between the bear and Zeke, drew back, and released his bow. By the time the arrow was released, the bear had already dropped to all fours, and began charging. In a flash of brown fur, the bear had traversed the thirty yards to Zeke's father. With a single swipe from its massive arm, Zeke's father had been hit by the bear and was flung into a tree.

Zeke's mother had picked Zeke up and began trying to run away. Before she could take five steps, the bear had slashed his mother's back. In the attack, his mother had dropped Zeke. He landed face first on a pile of jagged rocks. The rocks had cut open his forehead and left cheek.

Zeke rolled over and saw the bear was standing on top of his mother. When the bear saw Zeke sitting up, it began slashing at the ground, knocking up dust. The bear began slowly advancing on Zeke sitting on the ground. The fear, sadness, grief, pain, and confusion all hit Zeke at the same time.

Being overwhelmed, having just seen his parents killed. The bear was now going to kill Zeke. Zeke wished the bear would die. He wanted it to die the most horrible death imaginable. As the bear drew closer to Zeke, it mysteriously caught on fire.

The bear stood on his hind legs again and began trying to rip into itself. It dropped back to all fours and began thrashing and rolling around on the ground. When the bear was unable to get the fire out it tried to run away. It only made it about three steps before being killed by the fire.

After watching the horrific events of the last couple of minutes, Zeke was unable to move. All he was able to do was to sit there and hope that it had all just been a nightmare that he would soon wake up from. After nearly twenty minutes, he was finally able to stand. He knew there was nothing he could do for them, but he approached his parents.

Zeke's mother was laying face down. He rolled her body over and folded her arms across her chest. He knelt down beside her and began to talk to her as if she were still alive. He promised her that he would always be kind, and to always help others whenever he could. She had aways been kind and loving to everyone she ever met.

Zeke's father had landed in a contorted position after hitting the tree. Zeke moved his father's body next to his mother, also crossing his arms over his chest. Kneeling once more, Zeke promised his father that he would always be brave, and that he would never stop learning.

After he said his final goodbyes, Zeke began burying his fallen parents. He used large stones from the nearby streambed to cover them up. Blinded by the pain of grief, Zeke failed to notice that large stones were floating by themselves from the stream to where his parents lay. He was nearly finished when he realized that the stone he was carrying was far lighter than it should be for its size. When he looked up, he saw other stones placing themselves on his parents' graves.

After he buried his parents, Zeke began to cut up the bear. The hide was no longer useable, but the meat was still good. When the bear meat was cut up and stacked on his family's wheeled drag cart, he left for their hut. Even though it was now dark he needed to leave that place. He could not spend another second in that horrible clearing next to the stream.

With his drag cart now filled with meat, and Zeke being alone, the cart was very heavy. It had taken him nearly three full days to return to his hut. He did not sleep, he continued walking. He would only stop for short breaks before he continued to push on.

Even though it was fall and getting cooler, Zeke decided to dry the meat. The meat would stay edible much longer. The deer they had gathered along with the bear meat, Zeke was sure he would have enough to survive the upcoming winter. When all the meat had been cut in thin sheets and cooking over several fires, Zeke crawled into bed to sleep.

Zeke slept for a day and half. Over the next couple weeks, he did his best to fend for himself. He tended to his mother's garden, and his father's crops and livestock. Until winter settled in felt like it was there to stay. Winter turned out to be the worst he had ever seen, it was really long, hard, and cold. The cold and deep snow lasted into late spring. By the time the snow had melted, Zeke had run out of food for the livestock, and had almost run out of his own food. Eventually, all of the livestock died due to cold and lack of feed.

Late winter, Zeke had run out of wood for fire to keep his hut warm. He needed to go to the tree line to gather more, but it was blizzarding. After a day and half of no heat, and no signs of the storm letting up, it was time. Zeke donned an extra deerskin cloak and headed for the door.

After Zeke had taken five steps out of his hut, could barely see it behind him. He grabbed the wheel cart from next to the door and headed for the trees. It took him over an hour to walk through the deep snow to the tree line. He found a small pine tree that he would be able to chop down by himself.

When the tree was cut down, Zeke began chopping off all the limbs. The branches and pine needles would make good fire starter. With the branches cut off and piled in the wheel cart, he lifted the main trunk on top of the cart. When his firewood was loaded, he began the walk back to his hut. When he was back, at the hut he would cut the wood into a size that would fit in the fire.

It was nearly two hours later, and Zeke had still not made it back to his hut. He was beginning to wonder if he had missed it and walked past. He stopped and began looking around. All he could see was white. Looking at his cart, he could not even see the top of the tree he had cut. He could have been more than five feet from his hut and not seen it.

Zeke began getting very scared. He was lost in a blizzard. He was going to freeze to death if he did not get inside soon. He was angry with himself for going out in the blizzard, and not tying himself to garden fence. Until his strange luck showed itself again.

It was as if the storm let up just between him and his hut. His hut began glowing bright gold, so he could see it. Fifteen feet to his left. He turned and headed for the door. Once inside, things did not improve much. He broke some small branches and placed those along with some pine needles in the fire.

The kindling was still far too wet to be able to light. Just to stay warm he began chopping the tree trunk. When he had gotten three or four sections cut and chopped in the proper fire size, his axe handle broke. Tired and freezing, Zeke got back in to bed. He knew that if did not get a fire started soon, he would sure die.

Zeke felt as though he slept for several days, when he woke. He was having a dream that all his wood was cut, chopped, and stacked along the wall, next to a burning fire. It was only a dream. When his vision had returned, and he was fully awake, there was no fire. The tree was still uncut, and the axe was still broken.

Feeling very hopeless, fearing this was the end but refusing to give up, Zeke picked up the axe head. He used a section of tree trunk and began shaving it down with a knife and the axe head to make a new handle. Every slice with the knife blade seemed to be perfect. The first time he checked the fit with the axe head, it was a perfect fit.

When the axe was repaired, Zeke went back to chopping the tree trunk. His strange luck struck again. Every swing of the axe cut all the way through the trunk. In a matter of a few minutes, the wood was all cut and stacked. He hoped he could get his fire started now.

His first strike with his flint produced ten very large sparks. The sparks instantly started the small branches and pine needles on fire. After adding a few more, larger pieces of wood, Zeke had a nice hot fire burning.

Sitting in a chair next to his fire, Zeke began reflecting on his past several months. His parents. The bear. The winter. His luck, both good and bad. Every time something strange happened to him, it still intrigued him. Finally warm, and safe for the moment, he drifted back to sleep.

The remainder of the spring and into mid-summer was colder than normal as well. Zekious had no seeds to plant any crops. His livestock had all died during the winter. He knew that he could not survive another winter like that.

He spent several weeks trying to figure out what he could do to survive on his own. His father had always said that the farther south he had gone the nicer it was. Zeke figured he should head south. Maybe the winter would be easier if he was farther south. It could not be any worse, he thought.

Zeke's father would travel south to go to a village to trade. The village was south of a large raging river. Zeke had never been further south than the river. The river was a day's walk from the hut. Every time his father had gone to the village, he was gone for several days. The village must be a couple days past the river.

Zeke had made up his mind. He would travel to the village. Someone there would take in a lost, orphaned child. He could live there and have others to survive with. He would not be alone; he might even find some friends his age.

Zeke made a makeshift pack. He loaded a bed roll and some extra clothes. The only weapons he had were the stone axe and knife, and his father's bow. He only had a few arrows but could make more. He filled the rest of his pack with all the dried meat he could fit. The next morning, he set off.

When he had reached the river, he could not cross it. It was so wide that he could not have shot an arrow to the far side. As he was standing there with a myriad of emotions, wishing he knew a way across. It was as if his prayers had been answered. Sticks and mud from the shore and water started forming a small rickety bridge. That was the first time he had realized that strange things happened because he had been very emotional. Did he make that happen? How did he do that?

When he reached the small village, it had been abandoned. There was no one around. It appeared that everyone had left before winter hit. He searched the huts for food and supplies. All he found was a few arrows. It was not much, but at least it was a start. He also found a few animal hides that he could use for more clothes. He was beginning to outgrow the ones he was wearing. Remembering his promises to his parents he forced himself to keep moving.

Chapter Two

As Zeke continued to wander the wilderness, he kept trying to hone and control this strange skill he had. After eight years on his own, living off the land, he had learned that he could only use his power when he was emotional. The only time that he had ever managed to get his power to do what he wanted, was when he had a dire need for it. He could not just want it, but he had to need it. Most of the time when strange things happened, he was not even trying to make them happen. Zeke normally used other tools. Along with a bow, Zeke had also made two more stone axes that he carried with him.

Living off the land by himself since he was eleven, Zeke had grown to a very strong and muscular young man. Zekious was now six foot four inches tall, was very muscular, and had dark unkempt hair with short bangs, a large forehead, and a scruffy beard. He had a rounded chin, hard jaw line, and yellow eyes. He also had three vertical scars down from his forehead over his left eye to his cheek, left over from hitting his face on the rocks during the bear attack.

One late fall night, it was snowing, and he could not start a fire due to everything being wet. Zeke was sitting by the campfire he had been trying to start, shivering uncontrollably, and twirling the stick he had been using to start the fire in his hand. Out of sheer desperation, he pointed the stick at campfire and yelled the word for fire in the language of the holies, "HAMATU". He was not sure why he used the language of the holies, but it was all that came to him at the time. Several blue sparks traveled along the stick and out the end of it into the campfire. Instantly, the kindling he had gathered burst into flames. The stick he was holding had also burst into flames.

Curious, Zeke pointed his finger at the fire and said "hamatu" again. This time he only emitted one small yellow spark out of the tip of his finger. The spark burned out before making it to the campfire he was pointing at. Zeke picked up a branch of birch and tried his experiment again. This time two large blue sparks flew out of his stick. The tip of the stick was only slightly singed, and the sparks spread apart but did not land exactly where he was pointing.

The next morning, when Zeke was getting ready to set out again, he pointed his birch stick at the fire and said "hebu". A small spout of clear water ran out of the end of the stick and doused the fire. The stream of water was spread out and erratic. Zeke spent the next several days trying different types of wood. Zeke found he was drawn to length of ash heartwood. The stick he had found was twelve and a half inches long, was a medium brown in color, and a slight twist. When Zeke first picked it up, he felt a tingle in his fingertips.

When Zeke lit his fire the next night, with his new ash wand, the blue sparks went exactly where he wanted. The wand responded so fast it was as if it knew what he wanted before he even said it. When he used it, there was a slight vibration in the wand. Zeke used his stone axe blade to shave off the knots and bumps from his wand. He then used some small rocks and sand inside a piece of leather to smooth it. When he was finished, his wand was smooth and sleek looking. He found sap on a nearby tree and rubbed it into his now smooth ash wand. When the sap had dried his wand had a nice sheen to it along with a protective layer.

After he smoothed and polished his new wand, the vibration was less but it was still there. The wand needed something else to make it perfect. Zeke was not sure what that was yet, but he was determined to find out. Zeke was also determined to find out what else he would be able to do with his newfound power.

With his fire good and warm, Zeke laid down and tried to get some sleep. He awoke a few hours later to a faint scream some distance away. The scream was definitely an animal of some sort, but not an animal he had ever heard. It sounded as though the animal was hurt or scared. As quietly as he could,

Zeke followed the scream. After sneaking through the forest for almost a mile, Zeke saw what was screaming. The animal was the size of a lion, but the front half of the body and the head was that of an eagle, the back half of a lion, with long retractable claws, and a long tail, and large wings. Instead of hair the lion body was also covered with feathers. The body was brown and black brindle in color, and the wings were brown with gray spots. A griffin. Zeke had never seen one, but his father used to tell him stories about them. They are very fierce and mean-spirited creatures.

This one seemed to be trapped in some sort of net. The net had large rocks tied to the bottom. Someone had set a trap to catch animals. As Zeke approached, the griffin saw him, and began to really fight, both from fear and anger. As softly and calmly as he could Zeke said "Nehtu. Calm. Nehtu. Easy"

As Zeke got close to one of the rocks the net was tied to, he grabbed his wand, pointed it at the net where it was tied to the rock. Out of desperation he said the first thing that came to his mind. "Naharmutu" was the word for dissolve in the language of the holies. As he did so a wisp of light blue smoke flew from the end of his wand. When the smoke contacted the net, the net dissolved, freeing that corner of the net from the rock. Zeke made his way to the next corner of the net and again pointed his wand and said "Naharmutu". Again, the net melted away. The two corners that held down the net over the griffin's head were now loose.

Zeke slowly continued around towards the griffin's rear, still trying to calm the griffin by saying "Nehtu, Nehtu, Easy, Calm". As he got to the third rock and cut the net, enough slack had been created, and with Zeke standing to the rear of the griffin, it was able to move forward and escape the net. As soon as it was free, the griffin took off into the air and disappeared into the night.

Zeke made his way back to where he had camped for the night. While he was sitting awake by his campfire, Zeke kept thinking he was hearing the flapping of wings. Then after a few moments, he did not hear it anymore and was able to calm down. He finally laid back down to try to get a few more hours of sleep before daylight.

There it was again, the gentle flapping of large wings off to his left. This time he heard the flapping descend towards the ground then stop followed by a thud. Zekious jumped up and grabbed his wand, preparing to defend himself from the griffin that had obviously came back to kill him. Zeke waited in silence.

Then through the darkness Zeke saw the griffin slowly approaching. When the griffin was about twenty feet away, it folded its large brown and gray wings, and bowed its brindle-colored head. Zeke lowered his wand and returned the bow. The griffin raised its head then sat on its haunches. Zeke rose and slowly approached the griffin. When he got close enough to touch, he raised his left arm, with his wand still in his right. He slowly reached out and tentatively began to pet the griffin on the beak. He then rubbed it behind the ears. As he did so, the griffin's eyes went soft, and its long black tail began to gently swish back and forth on the ground.

While Zeke was petting the griffin, he still had his wand in his other hand, and as he was touching the griffin the ash wand completely stopped vibrating. That was it. The griffin was the key to completing his wand.

"I wonder if I could have one of those feathers?" Zeke thought to himself. Then aloud he said, "Why did you come back, if not to kill me?" Knowing full well that the griffin would never understand what he was saying, and if he did not want to be slashed by a four-inch-long talon, it was best to not just take one. As he said that, the griffin raised its left wing and brought it forward over Zeke's head. Zeke looked up and could see that on the underside of the wing, a feather was loose and about to fall out.

Zeke looked at the griffin and said, "You have a loose feather. Do you want me to take it?"

The griffin looked down at Zeke. It was as if it was smiling. Zeke felt as though the griffin was telling him that it would be okay if he took the feather, as thanks for rescuing it.

Zeke reached up and grabbed the loose wing feather and pulled it free. After he had grabbed the feather, the griffin folded its wing back down. Zeke went back over and sat next to his fire trying to figure out how to get the feather attached to his stand. While he was pondering his construction project, he took the large hare that he had killed earlier and cooked that evening off of the spit over the fire. He tossed what he had not eaten over to ground in front of the griffin. "Here you can have this, I'm not much for hare."

The griffin took it and laid down as it began to eat. Zeke did not get any more sleep; he spent the rest of morning until dawn contemplating how to attach the feather to his wand. He did not know why but something told him that the feather needed to be inside of the wood to be perfect. The wand needed a core.

When daylight came Zeke went to find some more ash branches, he had an idea how to get the feather inside his already formed wand. When had come back with an armful of ash branches and twigs the griffin was gone. Zeke had hoped that they would become travel companions, maybe it had gone off to go hunting. Maybe it did not be companions with a human and would not return.

Zeke grabbed his wand and picked up another ash twig. Pointing his wand at the center of the end of the twig and said "Naharmutu". The whole twig dissolved into nothing. Zeke picked up another twig, this time he tried "Naharmutu Mislu". Again, the whole twig disintegrated. He repeated with a third stick, this time changing the words around, "Mislu Naharmutu". Perfect, the center half of the stick dissolved, leaving the outer edge untouched.

Now Zeke needed to use a different stick to put the hole through the center of his wand. He found the one that gave him the best results other than his own wand. He pointed the stick at the back of his wand and repeated the phrase, "Mislu Naharmutu". There now was a perfect hole drilled through the center of his wand.

Zeke fed the feather from the griffin into the hole through his wand starting at the point. Now he had a new problem, the hole was still through the wand and the feather may fall out. Again, he pointed the stick at the back of his wand, this time he used the word "serdu". The hole in his wand was now filled in, encasing the griffin feather inside. When he held the wand in his hand the vibration was gone completely. It was as if the wand was breathing with Zeke. They were in perfect harmony.

It was midday and the sun was high in the sky when he finished revising his wand. This was a good spot to camp for a while. There was an abundance of kindling for fire, and several species of small critters to hunt for food. Zeke wanted to practice his new talent and see what else he could do. But now was time to go get some supplies. Zeke set off to find some lunch and gather more kindling. When he had returned from gathering supplies, the griffin returned and there was a dead deer lying next to campfire.

Zeke processed the deer and cut up some steak strips. He put the steak strips and some wild onions he had found on a stick and fried them over the fire. After he fried up the food, he offered some to the griffin. The griffin looked at the rest of the deer carcass lying on the ground. Zeke figured the griffin must prefer its meat raw. Zeke went over and cut the hind legs off the deer and tossed them over to the griffin.

While they ate, Zeke wondered how long the griffin would stay with him. Zeke was also wondering if there were other people out there like him. Others that had this gift. Zeke wanted to stay here for at least a few days to try other things and learn more about his abilities. While he had never been there, he knew that there were cities with thousands of people all over. After he learned more, he wanted to travel. He wanted to go see these cities and hopefully he could meet others that had the same gift, or possibly, read to learn more. His parents had taught him to read from a few books about the holies. He had only seen those few books his parents had, but his father had told him that some cities had large libraries full of books. He wanted to see these libraries, he wanted to learn all that he could.

The next day, after some more steak and onions, Zeke began smoking the rest of the meat to save for later. While the meat was smoking, Zeke continued practicing using his wand to make other things happen. He was able to produce ice by saying the word mammu, however the ice was not consistent like the other things he had tried. It was erratic and kept sputtering from the end of his wand. Getting frustrated, Zeke began to flourish his wand angrily. The movement had made the flow of ice emanating from the end of the stick in his hand better, but still not strong and steady like the other things he had made happen.

Another realization set in, it was not only the word that needed to be spoken but sometimes there was a certain movement that he had to make before, and possibly during, whatever he was trying to accomplish. Zeke found out that his best attempts at producing ice were after he had twirled the wand in a small counterclockwise movement. When he stopped making the small circles the flow of ice would scatter and stop. Zeke had to keep making small lefthanded circles with wand for as long as he wanted the flow of ice to continue. He also noticed it came to a nice clean end if he made a small flick with the tip of his wand, downward and to the right.

Learning to do all that he could do with his abilities was going to take unending practice. For the best results, the correct word, spoken in the language of the holies, had to be used. When he tried to say the words in his own language nothing would happen. The proper wand movement, and great concentration were also needed. Zeke was hoping in his travels he would find more people that could teach him or at least writings that he could learn from.

Chapter Three

After spending a few more days in the same spot and trying to learn what else he could do, it was time to move on. Zeke was unable to find anymore word and wave combinations to get any other skills. It was evening, Zeke and Longtail the griffin, were sitting near the fire. Speaking aloud, but knowing that Longtail could not understand him, Zeke said, "I wish I knew where some of those large cities my father used to talk about were and how to get there."

Longtail perked up his ears and stood and flapped his wings excitedly.

"Can you understand me?" Zeke asked aloud. Longtail seemed to nod his head and smile.

"Do you know where some are?" Zeke asked. "Would you show me?"

Longtail swished his tail, flapped his wings, and started prancing around in a circle. Apparently, Longtail could understand Zeke.

"Have you seen any large cities in your travels?" Zeke asked.

Again, Longtail swished his tail and flapped his wings happily.

"Okay, tomorrow can you show me? Would you let me ride you?" The griffin gave Zeke a piercing look and nodded his head again.

The next day, after Zeke cleaned up his camp, it was time to learn how to ride a griffin. Zeke approached Longtail, who laid down and allowed Zeke to swing his leg over and sat on the griffin's strong back, just behind his wings. Longtail stood up, flapped his large brown and gray wings. They took three steps, and they were airborne.

Longtail climbed steeply until they were far above the grove of trees that they had been camping at for the last few days. After leveling out, Longtail took Zeke in a large circle around the area then started flying west towards the mountains. Riding this large powerful creature was exhilarating. Zeke had never had so much fun. It was as if Longtail, not only could understand Zeke when he spoke but could also read his thoughts.

As they were flying west over the mountains, Zeke looked down and saw a small cave on the side of a cliff. He wondered to himself what was in there. At that moment Longtail banked down and to the left, heading for the cave. Longtail landed just inside the mouth of the small cave. Zeke hopped off the griffin and walked around. The only things in the cave were some old bones and an old bird's nest. A condor had once called this home.

After a quick look around, and seeing there was nothing of real interest, Zekious got back on Longtail's back. With a strong shove of his powerful legs, Longtail jumped out of the cave entrance, spread his wings, and started flying again. They climbed above the mountains again and continued heading west.

Zeke had no idea where Longtail was taking him. It was late in the afternoon when Zeke saw the ocean. The griffin began a steady descent toward the beach. They had covered about a thousand miles in a day. After they had landed, Zeke began unpacking his supplies to set up camp for the night. Longtail took off again toward the ocean.

Zeke walked the beach gathering driftwood to build a fire. He pulled out his wand, using the word "Gisgallu" and pointing at the sand, Zeke made a small pedestal out of sand, good enough for something for Zeke to sit on. He was sitting on the stool made of sand reliving the adventure of flying on the back of Longtail when the griffin returned.

Longtail had caught a large fish in his sharp talons and brought it back. When the griffin landed, he stretched out his front leg, handing the fish to Zeke. Zeke took the fish and began to clean it. When the large fish had been cleaned and filleted, he cut it in half. Zeke gave one half to Longtail and put the other half on the skewer over the fire to cook for himself. When they had finished eating, they sat there listening to the waves lap on the shore as the sun set into the water.

After a good night's sleep, Zeke woke up just after dawn, the sun was not even the width of a finger above the eastern horizon. Longtail stood and yawned, then looked at Zeke, giving him a huge smile. Zeke was still feeling full after the large fillet of fish from last night. He quickly packed up his things, tied his pack to his back and mounted his winged companion once more.

As they took off again, Longtail stayed only about a hundred feet from the surface of the water and headed west and a little south. The sun was just starting to set when Zeke saw a small island at the edge of the western horizon. The sun had set by the time they landed on the small island.

The night was clear with a large, nearly full moon, even the stars seemed brighter than they had ever been. The water was so clear and calm that it reflected the stars and moon. The island was so peaceful Zeke did not want to disrupt that by making a fire. They sat in silence and watched the stars and water, even Longtail rolled over onto his back to watch the stars.

The next morning, Longtail was the first one awake, and stood with a large cat like stretch and a flap of his wings, waking Zeke. Expecting another long day, Zeke quickly gathered his things. He swung his leg over Longtail, and they took off again. This time angling north rather than south. Zeke assumed Longtail had made this journey across the ocean before and knew where the islands that he could make in a day's worth of flight were. Late that afternoon, Zeke saw the large island they were heading for. But it was not just an island.

This island had a shipping city. The city had tall stone walls, a seaport on the southern point, and a large stone circular tower in the center of the city. The tower was two hundred feet tall and fifty feet in diameter, with a domed roof. There was a light on the top of the dome that was blinking. The light was bright enough that Zeke could see it in the light of the late afternoon. Zeke had a feeling that he was about to make an entrance that no one in the city would soon forget. He had his doubts that many people were accustomed to seeing someone riding a griffin.

Longtail landed outside the city walls in an empty section of beach next to the port. Once Zeke had climbed down, Longtail took off immediately, heading east. Zeke looked at the walls and port in awe. The walls of the city were thirty feet tall, made from granite. The stone was polished, smooth, and blue. The port was massive, mooring shipping vessels over a hundred feet long.

Zeke approached the main gate to the city, coming from the port. The gate was open, and people were traveling freely between the city and the port.

As he entered the city, he heard the dull roar of citizens making small talk and the vendors advertising the wares they had for sale. Zeke also realized two things. One, finding out more information about his gift was going to be more difficult than he had expected, he did not understand anything anyone was saying. Two, Zeke was glad he did not live in a city, he preferred the silence and serenity of being by himself.

As he walked along the cobble stone street leading from the gate towards the tower at the center of the city, there were many different vendors. There were people selling clothing, sails, different foods, and beverages. There were also several different stoneworkers and smiths. Zeke heard someone holler, "You. Stranger. You are most definitely lost; you are not the normal sailor we see come through here."

Zeke looked around to see who was talking. He saw a man, smaller in stature and a few years older than himself waving and pointing at him. The man was thin but not starving, stood five foot five inches tall, had short gray hair, a short gray curly beard that was taken care of, and green eyes. The man had brown pants, the legs were torn off mid shin, and a brown shirt with no sleeves. On his feet the man wore a piece of thick leather that was tied to his feet with some sort of rope. He was a stark comparison to Zeke, who was wearing leather pants, a leather tunic tied together in the front, and leather moccasins. All were made from deer skin. Zeke had never seen anyone wear anything except leather. Of course, he had only met a handful of other people, all of whom were nomadic drifters who lived off the land and kept to themselves. Looking around, Zeke saw most everyone else was dressed very similarly to this man who had gotten his attention.

Zeke walked up to the man and said, "No. I have never been here."

The man said, "My name is Barmor Woodheart. Where are you from? Who are you sailing with?"

"I am called Zekious. I come from the western grasslands east of the mountains. I am not sailing with anyone. I am by myself." Zeke said as he pointed to the east across the ocean.

Barmor looked confused, and asked, "Western grasslands? East of the mountains? How did you get here if you were not sailing with someone? Are you sailing by yourself?"

Zeke could tell this man had never heard of the western grasslands. "Well, you probably will not believe me, but I am not sailing. I am flying. On a griffin." Zeke was hesitant to tell him about his powers.

Barmor's eyes got wide. "A griffin! I have seen them flying, but have never seen, nor heard of anyone riding one. How did you manage to catch and train a griffin?"

Zeke told Barmor the story of how the griffin was trapped in the hunter's net. How he had cut the griffin free. Zeke changed the details to cutting Longtail free with a stone knife, instead of with his powers, for now. At this point, Zeke was not sure how much he wanted to diverge until he knew more about Barmor.

Zeke also told him about his travels, over the mountains and ocean. He told about growing up by himself after his parents had been killed by the bear. Then Zeke asked about the people there, and why everyone's pants and shirts were not made of leather. Zeke asked about the things on Barmor's feet. Zeke was really curious about the new things he was seeing for the first time.

Barmor told Zeke about how they were able to make clothes from different materials, about the sandals on his feet. He told Zeke how they were able to work with and make metal tools. They discussed the other coastal cities, and how things get shipped between the cities on the ships in the port. Then when those ships reached the ports how the goods were transported to inland cities by either mammoth or Pegasus. There was a worldwide network of trade.

Zeke asked about how the walls and large blue tower in the center of the city were built. That was when Zeke started to get some of the information that he originally set out to learn. Barmor explained that all around the world there was great knowledge about mathematics and engineering. There were also a lot of people who had special powers.

Some people could make large stones float in the air, like a ship in the water, with a wave of their hand. Some people could talk to some or all sorts of animals. Others still could topple buildings or start fires. Some were more powerful than others. Some people had no powers. It typically ran in families, if one or both parents had an ability, the children were more likely to use magic.

Barmor explained, even with the diversity in the population most people got along. Most people wanted to live in peace and grow as a society. However, there were still those that sought to gain control and power.

"Are people with these gifts, or powers, rare?" Zeke asked excitedly.

"No. No, not really. Probably one in five people have some sort of power or special ability." Barmor answered.

"Have you ever heard of someone who has more than just one special ability? Are there some more powerful than others? Has anyone ever tried to gain more ability, or learn more about the powers in general?"

"Oh sure. Most people who have a power try to learn more about it to become more proficient. Some, yes, do have more than one thing that they can do. And yes, some are more powerful than others."

"Do you have any special powers? Do you have a special word for the power, or for someone who has a special power?" Zeke asked.

"I do have a special power." Barmor answered. "I can manipulate wood. I can make a piece of any wood grow, shrink, or take any shape I wish. If a piece is too big to carry, I can make it weightless. Comes in handy, I am a ship builder by trade, just like my father and family for generations. We call it magic. People who can use magic are called magicians. I am guessing, by your interest, and your line of questions, you are a magician as well."

"I am." Zeke answered. He had become more trusting of Barmor and felt comfortable telling him more about his use of magic. "It started when I was younger, but only when I was in need. Since then, I have learned to control it when I want to. I eventually found out that I was particularly drawn to a piece of ash wood. The wood helps channel it in some way. I am not limited to one aspect of magic; I am only limited by knowing the correct word for what I am wanting to do. Certain things also require me to move my ash, wand, as I call it, in a specific way. I have found, when I am trying to do something, the word must be spoken in the language of the holies, my parents had taught me some before they were killed."

"I am intrigued." Barmor said. "May I see your wand? I would like a demonstration of some of the things you can do, if you do not mind?"

"I would rather not." Zeke replied. "Not here in the open. I am already a stranger here, getting odd looks by how I am dressed. I would rather not draw more attention to myself. Possibly, if you had somewhere more private."

Barmor smiled. "Say no more. Follow me." He motioned toward the gate leading to the port. When they had exited the gate, Barmor turned right, heading west along to beach in the direction of a handful of huts near the shore.

Chapter Four

Barmor lead Zeke past the huts to the very last one. The hut was a little smaller than the rest with a lot of pieces of different wood strewn around the hut, with zero organization. Barmor had his own private dock, that stretched several hundred feet into the ocean. His dock looked as if it was made from one piece of wood. His hut was also made from a single piece of wood. Zeke was not surprised, after hearing Barmor's magical power was manipulating wood into any size and shape he wanted.

As they reached the hut, Barmor waved his hand and turned two stumps into chairs next to the unlit fire pit. Zeke took out his wand, pointed it at the fire pit and started a fire with his word "hamatu". Two bright blue sparks flew from the end of his wand and into the firepit. Barmor jumped in surprise. He turned and looked at Zeke. Then he saw the wand held in Zeke's right hand. Barmor reached slowly, almost hesitantly, for the wand.

"May I?" Barmor asked.

Zeke was reluctant to let anyone else touch his wand. Although it had not been very long, the smooth branch of ash felt as though it was a part of his very being. However, Zeke let Barmor look at it.

Barmor took the wand gently. He turned it over in his hand. Slowly, he studied every inch of the wand. When he was satisfied, he handed it back to Zeke. After Zeke took his wand back, they both sat in the chairs Barmor had conjured next to the fire.

"It's not solid. Your wand." Barmor stated more than asked when they were both seated.

"No." Zeke replied. "It did not feel right. It felt like something was missing. When I would use it, it would vibrate in my hand. Not a lot. Just enough to let me know that it was not yet perfect. Then after I rescued the griffin, he came and found me. To thank me, I think. The griffin let me pet him, and when I did, the vibration subsided some but not completely. The griffin let me have a feather from under his wing. I used another ash stick to bore a hole in this one, and I inserted the feather into the hole, as a core. When I did that, the vibrating stopped entirely. Now it's as if the wand breathes along with me."

Barmor was silent for a moment. "That is absolutely fascinating. What other things can you do?"

Zeke gave Barmor a short demonstration of the things he could do, which at this point was very limited. He explained that his parents' knowledge of the language of the holies was limited. They were farmers and were not very well traveled. Barmor suggested using the common language. The language of the holies was all but extinct, and Outlander, Zeke's first language, was not a well-known dialect. Even if the common language would not work for magic, Zeke knew it would be good to know, because Barmor said it was spoken worldwide.

"Try igniculus." Barmor suggested.

Zeke pointed his wand at a piece of birch bark laying at his feet and said, "Igniculus." Two white sparks flew out of the end of Zeke's wand, instantly igniting the bark. When the bark burned out, Barmor suggested trying to call an oak branch to his hand. Barmor indicated what branch he meant by making it raise off the ground with a wave of his hand.

"Use the word, 'sublego.'" Barmor said.

Zeke pointed his wand at the oak branch and said, "sublego." The branch twitched but did move toward him at all. Zeke knew immediately, there was a wand movement he needed to use as well. At first, he tried a simple downward flick. It did not change the outcome. All the branch did was twitch. Next Zeke tried an upward flick, for the same result. He had an idea.

Holding his wand out, pointing at the branch, with his palm down. Zeke rolled his hand over, so his palm was up, then flicked his wand tip up and back toward himself. As he made the wand movement, he said the word, "sublego". The branch lifted off the ground and flew to Zeke's left hand, and he caught it. Zeke wanted to try it on something other than wood, and something farther away.

Zeke saw a rock a little bigger than his fist about two hundred feet down the beach. He pointed his wand at the rock. He rolled his wrist over and flicked the tip of his wand again, while saying the word "sublego". The rock flew toward him, and he easily caught it with his left hand. Both Zeke and Barmor were very excited.

As they continued talking, Barmor told Zeke that he had never heard of anyone using a wand like Zeke did, nor had he heard of anyone having such a wide range of abilities. He was sure, though, most would be able to do more if they had the drive to learn more about it like Zeke. Zeke asked if he would like to try to make his own wand. Barmor was excited about trying to learn more.

Zeke asked Barmor if there was ever a wood that he felt particularly drawn to, or specifically liked working with more than others. Barmor told Zeke that he had always found white oak was the easiest for him to manipulate.

"Like this one?" Zeke asked. "Try it out." He said as gave Barmor the branch he had drawn to his hand earlier.

Barmor took the branch and held it in his hand.

"Do you feel anything? Do you feel like you do not want to let it go?" Zeke asked.

"It feels as if there is an energy charging through it." Barmor replied. "I have never noticed that before. Maybe, because I was always thinking about it as a supply, not a tool.

"That was what it was like the first time I had picked up a piece of ash. I had only started using wood because I was trying to start a fire. I had a stick in my hand, and my kindling was wet. I waved the stick at the fire pit in desperation and said the word hamatu. The fire started, but the end of the stick was singed, when I tried it without the stick, my hand tingled and felt weird. The first time I tried ash, it seemed to call to me as soon as I picked it up, but I could tell something was missing. I was not sure what was missing until I had my wand in one hand and touched the griffin with the other. Do you feel as though something is missing?"

"Yes. There is something else needed." Barmor answered.

"What do think might be missing?" Zeke asked.

"I have a guess what it might need." Barmor said. As he spoke, he stood and walked into his hut. He returned a moment later. He did not talk again until he sat back down. "When I was about fifteen my father, grandfather, and I were hunting way up north, by the ice wall. We were attacked by a sabretooth. My grandfather was killed first. My father and I fought it, he sacrificed himself so I could kill it. I have the fangs right here."

When he was done talking, he unwrapped two teeth that were about six inches in length. They had a slight curve to them and came to needle like point.

"You can make the hole in the oak branch." Barmor said. "You are more practiced than I am."

"I may be more practiced in different aspects of magic; however, you are the one who knows more about wood. I also think it is important to make your own wand. It has a piece of you in it that way." Zeke suggested.

Barmor understood what Zeke was saying and held the tooth in his left hand and the oak branch in his right. He made the branch turn into a thin sheet. He then wrapped the sheet of wood around the large tooth. When he was done the oak branch now looked sleek and smooth. It had a curve to match that of the sabretooth. He turned the wand over in his hands and examined it.

When he was finished inspecting it, Barmor held the wand out in his right hand. As he did so, Zeke could tell the wand felt complete to Barmor.

"How does that feel now?" Zeke asked.

"That feels amazing." Barmor answered.

"Try it out." Zeke said excitedly.

Barmor used "igniculus" to light a piece of bark on fire. Then he used "sublego" to pull a rock to his hand. He picked up a piece of wood from a cherry tree. He took the piece of cherry wood to the end of his dock, Zeke followed him. When he got to the end of the dock, Barmor threw the piece of cherry out as far as he could. When the wood bobbed back to the surface, he pointed his new wand at it and said "ligneus".

As he did so, a wisp of red smoke trailed out of his wand to the piece of wood floating thirty feet off the dock. The piece of wood transformed into a large ship. The ship was over a hundred feet long, forty feet wide and seemed to be carved from a single piece of wood. The ship was solid cherry. The ship was the most elegant looking ship in the port.

"That is a beautiful ship, Barmor." Zeke said.

"Thank you, I think it is the biggest and best I have ever made." Barmor replied as they returned to the chairs by the fire pit. "I feel like I can make anything I want with this wand."

"Me too." Said Zeke. "That is why I want to learn everything about magic that I can. I think, with practice, patience, and knowledge, anything is possible."

"Maybe, we can learn together." Barmor suggested.

"Sounds like a good plan." Zeke agreed. "Eventually, we could possibly even teach others. First, did you mention something about different clothes, it is pretty warm here to be dressed in deer skin."

"Of course." Barmor answered and got up and disappeared into his hut. He returned a few minutes later with some lightweight cloth pants, a shirt, and sandals similar to the ones he was wearing. "Here. Now, I want to know more about the griffin."

"Other than when he leaves to go hunting, he has been by my side since he found me after I rescued him from the net. He dropped me on the east side of the gate and took off toward those small sand bars to the east of the port. I got the feeling he does not like crowds of people much. I call him Longtail, his tail is as long as his body. The first time I called him that he seemed to perk up and smile at me."

"Do you have to call him, or does he return on his own?" Barmor asked.

"On his own." Zeke answered.

As if it had been on cue, Longtail dropped in from the northwest, and landed just on the other side of Barmor's hut, carrying a large swordfish in his beak.

"I think he can read my thoughts." Zeke answered before Barmor even had a chance to ask. Zeke went over, relieved Longtail of his catch and began cleaning it, while Barmor stared in awe at the beautiful, black, brown, and gray creature that had just landed there.

The swordfish was more than big enough for all three to enjoy a large meal. Zeke gave half of it to Longtail, raw the way he preferred his food. The other half Zeke began cooking over the fire that was burning in front of the hut. When Barmor was done staring at Longtail, he entered the hut and came out a few moments later with a large pot, some potatoes, onions, and other vegetables. He used his new wand to pull some larger rocks into a circle and made another fire pit. On the second fire pit, he put the vegetables in the pot and added some water to make a stew.

After they had eaten their fill. Barmor suggested that they travel to a place he had heard of from sailors that had passed through the port. A place called Cortis Mundi. It was said that they had many powerful magicians there, and many large, beautiful structures that they had constructed. He had heard generally where it was located, but not exactly.

The stories he had heard, the trip by boat was long and treacherous. The trip would take about two months and a couple possible ways to get there. The shortest and quickest way would take you through the Strait of a Million Islands. A place that had very rough seas, filled with islands and sand bars, and shrouded in a thick fog. It was very easy to get caught in a swell or lose your route and run aground. It was also a known area for pirates to wait for merchants to come through.

The other way was to stay in the open water. That way took you a lot farther south, and another month of travel. The open water was not without its perils either. First, the deep, open water was the home of the largest of sea creatures. The kraken and the mammoth shark were very abundant in the South Sea.

Zeke had never been a strong swimmer and was not very interested in either of those routes. He preferred to fly. He wondered if Longtail knew of another griffin that would allow Barmor to fly on, or if Longtail himself could carry both men. From the look Longtail had given him, those options were a last resort. There was a third option.

"How about magic?" Zeke asked.

"What?" Barmor repeated. "What about it?"

"Well, I bet we can find a way to travel to Cortis Mundi by magic. Just like our wands. We can make something that will fly. Or maybe we can come up with a way to just appear there. You just made a large, beautiful ship out of a piece of cherry wood that size of a cup, we can figure out a way." Zeke said excitedly.

Chapter Five

Barmor liked the idea of a ship that could fly. That way, they could be comfortable during their travels. They would also have a place to keep supplies, and a place to stay when they got to their destination. Zeke had another idea; they may be able to build a sail that contained the power of the wind. The wind would always be at their back. With both men in agreement, and a plan made, they go to work making it happen.

First, they needed to figure out how to make the ship float in the air. Zeke found out that if he pointed his wand at something he wanted to pick up, with his palm down, roll his wrist up, with the incantation "volito", the item would float off the ground. As long as he kept his wand pointed at the item slowly pointed his wand higher, he could lift even the biggest stump in Barmor's yard as high as he wanted. When he stopped, pointed the wand at whatever he had lifted it would stay where he had left it.

With the incantation "secondo" and the reverse of the "volito" wand movement he could set it down gently on the ground. Next, he needed to try it on something bigger. Zeke had to see if it was possible to lift the large ship out of the water into the air. Zeke walked to the end of the dock by where the ship was moored. He pointed his wand at the ship, made the wand movement, and repeated the incantation "volito".

The ship lifted out of the water with a splash. Zeke raised his arm until the ship was a hundred feet off the surface of the water. He put his arm down and the ship stayed where it was at. Zeke left the ship float there in the air overnight. The next morning, the ship was still in the same exact spot. Zeke set the ship back into the water with the "secondo" incantation.

Zeke boarded the ship and tried "volito". He was able to get the ship to lift out of the water but could not get it to get more than a few feet off the surface. He must not have been able to get the right angle to lift the ship higher while on board. Now Zeke needed to figure out how to get the ship to raise and lower while on board.

With further investigation, Zeke found out that once something was lifted off the ground with "volito", he could use "sublevo", with his palm facing up and repeatedly flicking the tip of his wand up, he could make it go higher and higher. Adversely, pointing his wand at a raised item, with his palm facing downward, while repeatedly flicking the tip downward, and using the incantation "demitto", a raised item will descend.

Zeke went back to the ship and tried "sublevo" and "demitto". He got it. He had to use "volito" first. Once the ship was floating in the air, he could use "sublevo" to raise the ship up, and he could use "demitto" to set the ship back down. Now that he had up and down figured out it was time to go see if Barmor got the sails figured out.

When Zeke got to where Barmor was working on the sail, Barmor gave him the report. He had been practicing on piece of cloth staked to ground. He could produce wind but when he lowered his wand the wind stopped. Zeke asked him if had tried using the words forever or everlasting. Barmor told him he had not and would try the work for everlasting, sempiternus.

When Barmor tried "sempiternus ventus" nothing happened. So he tried "ventus sempiternus", and all he got was a puff of wind and some purple smoke. Now they had to find the correct wand movement. With both young men trying different swishes, twists, and flicks, Zeke finally found a complicated set of moves to produce a strong wind on the piece of cloth. While pointing the wand at the cloth, he had to make a medium sized horizontal oval in a clockwise direction, followed by a larger circle in the counterclockwise direction, and finish with a flick towards the target.

This produced a puff of wind and purple stream of smoke, and the point where he had pointed the wand was being blown by a wind. When he lowered his wand, the wind persisted. The incantation also produced a couple of problems. The first problem was when they folded the piece of cloth the wind was still blowing. The second problem was the wind was only blowing at the point where he had flicked his wand toward instead of blowing against the whole cloth.

How do they get the wind to stop blowing? They continued to practice on the piece of cloth. Barmor pointed his wand at the cloth and with a simple flick said, "Ventus finis." The wind stopped. One problem solved. They needed the wind to stop when they collapsed the sails of the ship so that it would remain stationary when they did not want to move but resume when the sails were stretched out so they would be able to move forward when needed.

Barmor copied Zeke's oval, reverse circle, and flick movement, along with the "ventus sempiternus" incantation. When he performed the flick, he pointed at the upper right corner of the piece of cloth and followed the edge of the cloth down the right side, left across the bottom, up the left side, and right across the top. The wind and purple smoke continued while he traced the piece of cloth. The never-ending wind was blowing against the whole piece of cloth. When they folded the cloth, the wind still had not stopped. With the cloth folded he used "ventus finis" and the wind stopped. Now they unfolded the cloth. When it fully unfolded and tight, then wind was now blowing against the whole cloth. They folded it again and the wind stopped.

With the problems now solved it was time to get some sails made for the ship, install, and enchant them. There was sail maker in the city, Lapis Mitigo, just inside the gate coming from the port. Barmor went to purchase some sails, while Zeke tried to work out how to add a pattern to their sails, every ship in the port had some sort of design or crest on their main sail.

It was not very long before Barmor returned with a cart full of folded sails and rope. They made their way down his private dock, toward the large ship he had made a few days ago, they had named it Cherry of the Sky. With their wands in their hands, they made quick work of hanging the sails. They could design a crest later; it was time to take the ship on a test flight.

With the sails hung tight, Zeke lifted the ship until it was several hundred feet off the water. He repeated the oval, reverse circle, flick movements, and traced the outline of the main sail and said, "Ventus sempiternus."

After he finished the outline of the sail, it filled with a wind out of nowhere, and the ship lurched forward. Zeke grabbed the helm. He then turned the wheel to the right, the bow of the ship slowly turned to the right. When he turned the wheel to the left the bow slowly turned left. Zeke, satisfied that the ship would fly and was steerable, wanted to see if it would slow and stop. He dropped the main sail. As soon as it began to drop the ship began to slow down, and eventually stopped. He raised the main sail again, as Barmor enchanted the fore and aft sails.

With all three sails full of a strong, steady, gale force wind. the Cherry of the Sky streaked through the sky. The turning speed was about the same as when they were only using one sail. With the air being a thinner medium than water, the ship flew faster with all three sails full of wind than Longtail could fly. Even at the altitude they were flying at it was not long before they could no longer see the tower of Landis Mitigo.

Zeke made a large circle to the left until they were heading back toward the city. As got close to Landis Mitigo, Zeke began descending slowly and gently with "demitto". They dropped back into the water about a mile offshore, then timed it so that when they dropped the three sails, they would coast to a stop right next to the dock. The first flight was an absolute success.

As they drifted into the dock, they threw the mooring line out and got tied off to the dock. As they deboarded the ship and walked back up the dock Longtail came to greet them. When they reached the hut and sat down on their stools, they began to discuss the next steps of their plan.

"What do you think about a griffin and sabretooth for a crest?" Zeke asked. "We need some sort of crest for our mainsail, everyone else has one."

"Absolutely." Barmor replied ecstatically. "That would be great."

"We could figure out how to stitch it in with magic." Zeke said.

"The word for thread is filum, grypus is griffin, and rumpheum dentatis cattus is saber toothed cat." Barmor explained.

"Awesome." Zeke said enthusiastically. "That is what we will work on tomorrow. After the progress of the last few days, especially today, I think it is time to celebrate."

"I have just the thing to quench your thirst." Barmor said with a chuckle, and he stood and disappeared into the hut. He returned a couple of minutes later with two glass bottles with a dark brown liquid in them, and two bone cups. The bottles contained apple cinnamon rum. Barmor poured each of them a cup of rum. They each took a cup and continued to discuss their next steps.

One of the things that they knew for sure was that when they did leave and arrived at a new place, Cortis Mundi, or otherwise, they would practice discretion. The culture around Landis Mitigo was really relaxed. The general rule here was, if you got it, flaunt it. Magicians could practice whatever ability they had here as long as they did not hurt anyone else. Other places may not feel the same. So, when they arrived at a new destination, they needed to learn the local customs first.

They also wanted a different word to call themselves. A magician was one who had one or a few abilities but was happy at that level and did not feel the need or have a want to learn more. Zeke and Barmor were different, they wanted to learn as much as possible. Before they began to teach others, first they needed to know for certain whether anyone could learn the skills or if only certain people had the ability to perform magic. They decided on the words witch and wizard. A wizard was a male that wanted to learn, and could learn everything about magic, while a witch was a woman.

Eventually conversation turned to the what ifs. While most people were good and wanted the world to succeed. There were bad people, what if one of them had magical abilities, and used their power for bad. Used it to do harm to, or control others. That would not be good. One of the things that they would need to learn would have to be how to defend themselves. Or maybe there already were evil wizards, the voyage they were about to embark on would give them more information.

It was early morning when they finally went to bed. It was late morning when they got up. One of the things that they had discussed the night before was checking out the Landis Mitigo library. Although it was only a small port city, they were curious if the library contained any more information about magicians or magic.

After spending the rest of the day looking through old scrolls and tomes in the library, they found a few interesting things. Most mentions of magic were just about those that had built the large, impressive monuments and cities around the world. There were also a few other people that had demonstrated different powers other than being able to lift large, heavy objects. There were those that had powers involving fire, horticulture, healing, or an affinity for wood like Barmor had. However, there were a couple pages taken from captain's log that mention of a man that seemed to do many strange and evil things to anyone he felt inferior to himself. The man also had a large following of people who all seemed to have magic abilities as well. According to the pages, the man traveled all over the world, getting stronger, and looking for more followers. They also found a map of the world.

The map was a composite of many different source maps. The map contained accurate shorelines and was to scale. The map also contained detailed topographic information as well. It showed cities with approximate populations, lakes, rivers, and mountains. It turned out the world was much larger than anyone had imagined, and according to the information on the map, a population in the several millions.

Satisfied that they had learned most of what the small library had to offer, and now a little concerned about this strange wizard that sounded like someone that needed to be feared, they returned to their hut to finish getting ready for their voyage.

When they returned to the hut there were dozens of people standing around waiting for them. Even though most people in Landis Mitigo were accustomed to seeing people using magic, seeing two men lift a ship three hundred feet out of the water and fly away raised some questions. After Zeke and Barmor explained that they were convinced that most magicians had the ability to learn more about magic than the one or two gifts that they knew about, and that they themselves were teaching themselves to use more and greater powers, most of the spectators were intrigued. A few also had the same belief. Most magicians had more power than they were aware but did not try to learn more. There were a couple onlookers that had been let down that they did not possess magic abilities.

Zeke and Barmor gave a short demonstration of what they could do. After the display, Zeke asked the sailors to find out all that they could during their travels. What cities allowed magic as Landis Mitigo did, what cities frowned upon its use. Having large stone structures was a pretty sure sign that someone there could use, or at least had used, magic. He asked them to ask around and find out if there were others like he and Barmor that had taken to learning as much as possible about magic. He also asked them to do that out of curiosity, Zeke and Barmor wished to keep their knowledge and investigation a secret for now. Barmor asked the locals to keep their ears open when talking to traveling merchants or other sailors that passed through the port.

After the group of curious onlookers had all left, Zeke and Barmor started packing supplies on the ship. They had a decent supply of grains, vegetables, and dried fruits. They took extra clothes, an array of other materials like cloth, rocks, dirt, wood, plants, and some different metals. They wanted different materials to learn and practice using different incantations and spells. They also took extra rope and sails.

With the ship packed and ready to fly, they were ready to go. They would leave the next day at first light. They figured it would take almost three full days to get to the eastern shores of Eastalund. It would be another four to reach the Midacundi Jungle and the city of Cortis Mundi. They would eventually go and see other regions as well, but Cortis Mundi was, by all accounts, the largest and most spectacular city and culture on the planet. If they were going to learn anything new it was going to be there.

Chapter Six

The next morning Zeke, Barmor, and Longtail got on the ship. After making sure everything was secure and that they were not forgetting anything, they lifted out of the water, raised the enchanted sails, and headed west. While Zeke set the heading, Barmor began experimenting with a piece of cloth, trying to design a crest for the Cherry of the Sky. He had decided on an image where the griffin, rearing back on its hind legs, wings spread, and slashing with its front legs, talons open. The saber tooth cat was to be crouched ready to pounce, teeth and claws bared. Both beasts would be angling towards the viewer.

It was not long before Barmor had figured out the wand movement, and proper incantation. A simple smooth swish, up and angling to the left, followed by a circle to indicate size, and the incantations, "filum grypus", and "filum rumpheum dentatis cattus", and the swatch of cloth had a griffin and saber-toothed cat teamed up, ready to fight anyone who would view it. Satisfied, Zeke watched as Barmor turned all three sails into menacing looking tapestries.

Zeke wanted to figure out how to hide the ship, and Barmor knew that having a personal mode of transportation other than walking, and smaller than a flying ship, would be great for everyone. Very few people were on a first name basis with a griffin. While the Cherry of the Sky was flying flawlessly westward, and the sun was still up, they both sat down and began working on their respective projects.

Zeke began trying different movements while using the word "tectus". After a couple hours of practice, all he was able to do was produce a light wisp of white smoke. He went to see what Barmor was working on.

He was working on a broom. The broom had a shaft made from a willow branch, and brush made from pine twigs and straw. The handle of the broom had an interesting shape. About one third of the length from the brush, the shaft had a curve in it. At the bottom of the curve, there were two branches. They stuck out perpendicular from the shaft.

"What are you doing with that broom?" Zeke asked. "We just left; the ship doesn't need to be swept yet." Zeke then said jokingly.

"I am going to see if I can make the broom fly. We can ride on them for personal transport. Not everyone can ride a griffin." Barmor answered, with a chuckle.

"That would be handy." Zeke replied. "Good idea."

Zeke went back to working on the hiding spell. After another hour and a half of trying he finally managed to find the correct wand movement. Three small counterclockwise circles, after getting back to the top after third circle, gently continue to the left edge of the box he was attempting to hide, then back to the right edge. He had to continue the left and right movement until the box disappeared entirely. Zeke inspected to see if the box was physically there. The box was there, he could feel it with his hand, but it could not be seen.

Getting the box to be visible again was easier. Three small clockwise circles then slowly raise the wand straight up, along with the word, "detego". The box reappeared. Now it was time to try it on the ship. He pointed his wand at the deck of the ship. Said "tectus" made the three small circles and began the gentle waves back and forth. The ship began to disappear from the center out. As the deck and hull vanished from sight, Barmor jumped and screamed, convinced he was going to fall. Longtail jumped up with a screech and began to fly.

It was definitely disconcerting, flying on a ship that could not be seen by the people riding it. Looking down and only seeing the ocean far below, did not give them the sense of ease. Seeing that it could be done, Zeke quickly made it visible again. Both Barmor and Longtail looked at Zeke and gave him a dirty look. Zeke just laughed. Watching them panic when the floating ship disappeared before their eyes was hilarious. After their panic had ebbed Zeke went to see Barmor's progress with the flying broom.

Barmor had managed to get the broom to hover when he sat it on it but had no movement. He was currently trying to get wand movement figured out while using the word "obtempero". Shortly after Zeke walked up, yellow lightning zapped the broom. Barmor swung his leg over the broom. When he pushed off with his feet, he and the broom lifted off the deck of the ship. He made the broom go forward, backward, yaw left and right, and turn circles in both directions. He also raised up over Zeke's head the back down and landed on the deck.

Zeke turned and pointed his wand at the three sails in turn making them loosen and collapse in on themselves. As the ship slowed to a stop, he turned to Barmor and asked, "How about a race?"

Barmor said, "Yeah, that sounds great."

Hearing this, Longtail came trotting over, and bowed his front end so Zeke could get on. When both men were on their mounts, they both took off into the air above the ship. Barmor took a few minutes getting the feeling for the flying broom he had created. He swerved left and right, climbed and dove, did a loop the loop, and a couple barrel rolls. He was able to lean forward to gain speed and lean back to slow down. While he was practicing his maneuvers, Zeke followed along on Longtail.

Zeke was able to keep up with Barmor, however the broom was nimbler than the griffin. Longtail was able to get to top speed quicker than the broom, and could go faster as well, but would tire while flying at his top speed and broom not being a living thing would not. In a short race with several tight turns and quick maneuvers the broom would beat the half eagle, half lion creature. In a longer, straighter race, the griffin would win. As far as being used as personal transport, the broom would work very well. They headed back to the Cherry of the Sky. After they landed back on the main deck, Zeke opened the sails, and they continued toward their destination again.

When they were underway again, they discussed how the first flight on the broom went. Zeke was impressed at how maneuverable it was. Barmor was ecstatic that it was as fast as it was and elated that it worked at all. While it was a perfect first flight and worked great as a prototype, they both knew with more knowledge about broom flight and different woods and designs, it could get even better. Happy with how the prototype had turned out, conversation turned to trying to find out what else they would be able to learn.

"Learning to protect ourselves would be a good thing." Zeke said.

"Agreed, but, sometimes, defense is not enough. We will need to learn some offense as well." Barmor responded.

"Yes, eventually we will meet someone who will be bound and determined to kill us or others. We will need to have a way of stopping them." Zeke agreed.

They started by learning how to shield themselves against harmful spells. After attempting several different words. The only word that they were able to get any response from their wands was "contego", with that they only got a simple flash of gold. It took them another hour practicing, to find out that they could cast a shield at a target by making two large clockwise circles with their wand arm, followed by making a cross with the wand, then flicking towards the target.

They then added the word "sui" to "contego". They started with "contego sui" and tried several different wand movements but did not get any effects out of their wands. They eventually tried "sui contego", which produced a silver smoke. After another hour they figured out that making a circle around their head with the wand pointing at themselves, the circle started in the front and then went to the left and around.

Zeke was now enveloped in a nearly invisible shield. While in the shield, everything had a slight shimmer, like looking through a mirage. When the shield was impacted by a magic spell a small ripple appeared at the point of contact. The shield could not be seen from the outside.

The shield would protect against magic but would not protect from physical attacks. While Zeke was using a shield, Barmor could not penetrate with any spell or anything sent toward him with magic, however if Barmor walked up and tried to punch Zeke, the shield was ineffective. Eventually the shield would diminish and disappear. Magic hits would shorten the life of the shield. The shield would still allow Zeke's spells out.

They spent the rest of the day practicing other spells. By the time the sun went down in the west they had learned several new pieces of magic. They learned that using the word "obfendo" with a simple small v motion knocked a target back with a shock. "Religo" and whipping the wand in an s shape would bind the targets hands and feet together. To quickly block an incoming attack, the word "oppilo", while whipping the wand from the shoulder of the wand arm toward the target worked well. To trip an opponent and make them fall they used the word "lapsum" while using a downward slash followed by a horizontal slash forming a backward L.

When the sun had set it was time to relax. They chatted about the things they had learned. They would be very useful. They agreed that they should try practicing attacking each other, so that they could get a feel for what it would be like in a real fight situation. They would start dueling the next day. Just as they were about to go to bed the lights of a small coastal city came into view below. That meant that they were about halfway to Cortis Mundi.

The next day they began dueling with each other using the magic they had learned. The aspect of being attacked while trying to use magic added a new challenge trying to concentrate on what spell to use and remember the wand movement. After they had gotten the hang of trying to attack each other, while defending themselves, dueling was a good way to learn and try new magic.

One of the things they figured out was that simply slashing the wand toward their target without saying any incantations would send a green spark. The green spark did not cause any harm or leave any marks. It would simply hit the opponent. Getting hit by the green spark could throw off one's aim, interrupt the opponent's wand movement, or make the opponent say what spell they were trying to use wrong. They could use the simple hit to buy them some time to use a stronger spell, or it could be used to string together spells in different combinations. While dueling, Barmor tried "elido" while making and x with his wand to break Zeke's shield. A successful hit would shatter a shield.

After dueling for almost an hour, they both started getting very tired. Fighting took a lot of stamina, both mentally and physically. When they began getting tired, spells were not as strong as when they were fresh, and shields dissolved faster. When they began to get tired, they decided to take a break and rest. Their afternoon dueling session lasted longer before they started getting tired.

Over the next couple of days, their stamina and strength had increased, and the dueling sessions were lasting longer and longer. The more they practiced, the stronger their spells and shields got. They felt they had become quite formidable. Even if they came across someone who had discovered as much about magic as they had, and wished to do them harm, Zeke and Barmor felt confident that they could defend themselves.

Three and a half days after passing the coastal city, they saw the very impressive city of Cortis Mundi. Cortis Mundi meant The Heart of the World. It was surrounded by a large, beautiful jungle. The jungle stretched beyond the horizon in all directions from the city except north. The jungle only continued north for a couple miles before giving way to massive sea. Standing in the middle of the city were three large golden stone pyramids. There were two massive lions carved out of stone standing watch over the city and pyramids. Peeking through the canopy of the jungle, they could see the tops of other smaller pyramids and other large, beautiful monuments. There was definitely magic being used there. There was a large river traveling south from the sea, between the stone lions and pyramids, and disappearing into the jungle.

The pyramids stood tall and proud. They were so bright white in color that in the afternoon light, they were as bright as the sun. Their top stone was bright gold colored. The light reflecting of the sun seemed to illuminate the jungle for miles.

Before they arrived, Zeke made the ship invisible, and brought the ship down to the sea. When they were back in the water and were sure that no one would see a ship appear out of nowhere, they made the ship visible again. They sailed into the port and moored at dock by themselves. They spent the rest of the evening discussing how they would proceed.

The next day they would talk to travelers and the citizens of the city and find out about who built the massive pyramids and lion sculptures. They knew that the structures were built by magic, and they wanted to learn more about the magic that Cortis Mundi used. They were also hoping that the city would have a library that could do their own research. They wanted to learn as much as possible before continuing west on their journey.

Chapter Seven

The next morning, before daylight, Longtail took off to go hunt and probably hide from all the people. It was mid-morning when Zeke and Barmor left the Cherry of the Sky to go check out the markets. They talked with local market vendors, and merchant sailors, each selling their own unique goods. Most of the streets were made of cobblestone. The three enormous pyramids stood at the heart of the city. The streets leading to and around the pyramids were carved from large pieces of granite.

At the base of the pyramids there were several smaller stone buildings, and a single larger two-story stone structure with battlements, and towers, with a wall surrounding it. This large fortress was also gilded like the tops of the pyramids. Zeke and Barmor were sure that the rulers lived in the fortress, and stone buildings around it were probably annex buildings used for different purposes. One would probably be the library they were seeking. All of the private dwellings were made of wood and were very simple huts.

As they walked around and talked to vendors and other shoppers, their suspicions were confirmed. The Superi, or Gods, lived in the fortress and their servants lived in some of the smaller stone structures. The pyramids were used for performing very powerful magic. Magic was a sign of the Superi, and strictly forbidden to anyone except the Superi, the royal guard, and the servants of the Superi. If any low born person was to learn or try magic, they would be killed by the Superi or their servants. The Superi knew when magic had been cast and could track down those who had attempted it.

They learned that there were three ruling Superi, King Sol, Queen Lunam, and their son, Prince Ostello. King Sol was several hundred years old, so was Queen Lunam, no one really knew for sure. All they knew was that magic kept them young. Prince Ostello was at least a hundred years old. Most of the Royal Guard, and the servants could also perform some magic as well. King Sol had built the pyramids over three hundred years ago when he started the civilization of Cortis Mundi. It took him and his servants six days to build the three pyramids. Queen Lunam carved the two lion statues in a week.

They were carved to honor the Lion of the Stars. Lion of the Stars was a creature formed in the sky by the stars. When the Lion of the Stars returned to the night sky it marked the beginning of the growing season. By carving the lion statues in honor of the Lion of the Stars, they believed they would have a long and prosperous growing season, therefore a fruitful harvest.

One thing Zeke and Barmor were very intrigued to learn was that Prince Ostello was not around any longer. For one, he did not like to stay put for very long, he preferred to travel as much as he could. For two, he did not like his father's mandate that only Superi and high born were allowed to do magic. In his time, he had seen many low born peasants, either accidentally or on purpose, perform very powerful forms of magic. Ostello believed that those peasants could be used as servants or emissaries. Used to do their bidding, then discarded like refuse. Sacrificing the low born that could use magic meant that they would not have to sacrifice the stronger magic users like the Royal Guard, and the servants.

King Sol forbade anyone other than high born to use or learn magic. It had been prophesized that a single, low born magic user would bring an end to the Superi. Ostello did not believe in prophecies, there was no possibility of a low born citizen anywhere in the world that would be stronger than himself, let alone King Sol. Ostello believed that the only reason that his father would make up the prophesy was to keep magic sacred. If everyone feared magic and no one except the Superi could use it, the people would be too afraid to revolt. One magic user could not stop the Superi, but tens of thousands of could.

To prove to his father that low born magic users were a commodity to be used, controlled, and sacrificed, Ostello took a handful of Royal Guards and servants to gather his own followers. He would start his own city with his own people. He would use those people to do his bidding and create a larger and richer city for himself. Leaving Cortis Mundi specifically to disobey his father's orders, King Sol permanently banished Prince Ostello from the entire region.

"Excuse me. Travelers." A voice said behind them after a local vendor had finished telling them the story about Ostello. "That was twenty years ago. King Sol banished Ostello twenty years ago. Prince Ostello has a new desire now. Well two, more knowledge, therefore more power. His other desire is removing his father from the throne. Ostello has been traveling the entire world since. Gathering followers and any knowledge that would lead to more powerful magic. He intends retake Cortis Mundi for himself."

"We were not sure it was him or not but," Zeke said, "we had heard from another sailor, there was a guy up north doing just that, gathering followers and seeking power, but sounds similar."

"That is him, but he is no longer up north though." The merchant sailor responded. The sailor was probably about forty years old, wore black cloth pants, and a white shirt. His blue hair was tied back in a ponytail that went to his shoulder blades. He was a little shorter than Zeke and Barmor and was very muscular and tanned brown. He obviously had been a sailor his whole life. "He has gone to the west. There is a large forest there. He has taken his following there to train and eventually plans to wage war on Cortis Mundi and his father. When he attacks, any who will not bow to him will be killed or slaved. Those that join him will learn the magic that he and his followers have spent twenty years learning, those that choose not to follow him will be slaves and forced to do his bidding."

Barmor said sarcastically. "He sounds like a wonderful person."

"Does he stand a chance against King Sol?" Zeke asked.

"Oh, without a doubt." The sailor replied. "He could have removed his father years ago. I've seen it with my own eyes. I once watched him kill a man from across a courtyard with the wave of his hand, all because Prince Ostello thought he was ugly."

"You know him?" Zeke asked.

"I was once fooled by his suave, silver tongue, and promises of riches and power." The sailor answered. "I deserted him when I saw how cruel and evil he had become."

"Do you have magic abilities as well.?" Barmor asked. "Can you perform some sort of magic?"

"I can." He answered. "Everyone can learn how to do magic, with the proper training, and attitude. The common misconception is that only certain people are capable of magic, but in truth everyone can, some are just more naturally gifted than others. However, there are certain traits that not everyone has. I for one, have the ability to sense magical power, and usage. That is how I know that the two of you are both very naturally gifted in magic and are both self-taught."

"That's impressive." Zeke said. "Does he plan to stop with his father, or does he intend on total power?"

"Total power." The sailor answered. "Only thing those with power want is more power. Once he has taken care of his father, he will spread his evil over the whole world."

"I suppose," Zeke started, "You want us to help you stop him."

"From the sounds of it, we are nowhere near strong enough to stop him." Barmor chimed in.

"You aren't." The sailor answered. "Not yet at least. Right now, you need to prepare. The archive here has an abundance of knowledge about magic, but only high born are allowed to access. Thankfully, I am one. I was a high-born servant to Prince Ostello before he was banished, and I left with him. I hope to gain an audience with King Sol and warn him what is happening. Maybe, after I tell him all that I know, he will allow the two of you to access the archive. He may even change his mind on low borns and start teaching them magic. Shall we go meet the king?"

"Why not? Let's go see the king that will probably kill us for using magic." Zeke and Barmor said in unison.

"He won't kill you," The sailor said. "As you are not from here, how are you to know his rules. The worst he would do is banish you from the realm."

The short muscular sailor led them through the city streets to the gates of the golden fifteen-foot-tall walls surrounding the golden fortress. As they reached the gates, two tall men in golden armor approached them and spoke. "Halt. What is your business at the Royal Palace?"

"My name is Mahdrin. I once belonged to the Royal Servants. I left with Prince Ostello when he fled. After witnessing for myself the evil in his heart,

I deserted him. I did not return until now for fear I would be killed on site for desertion. I am returning now because I have vital information for King Sol and Queen Lunam regarding Prince Ostello. These travelers I have met also have information."

"Wait here." One of the guards said, then turned and looked at the golden palace.

They did not have to wait long. King Sol appeared in front of them from out of nowhere with a faint pop. King Sol was over six feet tall. He had red hair and a beard that he kept both trimmed and neat. He was of average build with a bit of a gut. His golden crown was small and simple, not over imposing.

"You have news regarding Ostello." King Sol said plainly after speaking to the guard.

"We do." Mahdrin replied.

"Follow me"

Zeke, Barmor, and Mahdrin followed King Sol. He led them across the Palace courtyard, to a private gazebo. The Queen was already sitting there. She was also tall, just under six feet tall. She had golden blonde hair, tied in a braided ponytail down to her waste. She was slim and gorgeous, with piercing blue eyes, and her small tiara was sitting perfectly on her head.

When they arrived at the gazebo, Mahdrin started, and retold the story he had already told Zeke and Barmor. Then Zeke and Barmor told their story about how they had been teaching themselves magic. King Sol and Queen Lunam were actually very impressed with how much they were able to teach themselves with no formal training.

King Sol, however, was still apprehensive of allowing Zeke and Barmor into the magic archives to learn all their magic secrets. He was afraid if he allowed them into the archives, his demise would come from their hands. They assured him that they only wanted to learn all that they could and would defend against evil, and eventually after learning all they could, they wanted to teach others to defend themselves against evil. The very evil their son was looking to spread.

Zeke stood up, pulled his wand from inside his robe and said, "I will show you some of the things we can do." Zeke gave them a demonstration of a few of the things they could do. The King and Queen were very impressed, the wand he had made directed the magic better, and allowed for quicker transitions between spells. After the demonstration the King was less resistant to allowing them into the archives.

King Sol stood and started talking. "I will allow you access the city archives. Then I will allow you to leave my realm. If anyone wants to follow you to learn magic, I will allow them to go with you, but they may never return to the realm. When my son attacks, you and those that follow you will not intervene. What happens between me, and my son will be our destiny. If my son defeats me, then that is how it was supposed to happen, he will be your problem then. I shall hope that he is convinced to stop rather than killed, but if so, that is also his destiny. As for the two of you, learn what my archives can teach you, then go and share your knowledge, outside of my realm, as long as it is mine, you may never return. Mahdrin, you may either chose exile, in which case if you ever return to the realm, you will be killed on sight. Or you may choose to rejoin my ranks and obey every order. Your first and final order will be to spy on Ostello, by any means necessary and report back to me. What do you choose?"

"I will spy on Prince Ostello for you, Sir." Mahdrin answered quickly.

"The two of you will now be escorted to the archives." King Sol spoke again. "You may stay there as long as you wish. Learn whatever you can, when you leave the archives, you will be escorted by Royal Guards to your ship. Then you and those that wish to follow you will leave and never come back. I will make an announcement, letting the people know of their choice."

Five Royal Guards approached from the rear. "Come with us."

Zeke and Barmor stood and followed the guards. The guards led them back across the courtyard, to the back gate of the fortress. From there, the guards led them to a large stone building at the base of the pyramids. Once they reached the entrance of the archive, the guards told them to follow the stairs down into the building and take a left at the bottom.

Zeke and Barmor continued down the stairs. When they reached the bottom of the stairs, they were directly underneath the largest center pyramid. They took the left and entered a room that was about two thousand square feet of shelves full of books and scrolls. The shelves were more than twice as tall as Zeke was and had sliding ladders that slid the length of the shelves.

"We are going to be here a while." Zeke said.

"Yes, we are." Barmor replied with awe.

"Let's divide and conquer." Suggested Zeke.

Zeke went to the left and Barmor went to the right. They started by meticulously examining every tome and scroll. Most of the information was repetitive, and a lot of the information did not pertain to wand usage. It seemed, even in the largest city on the planet that was several hundred years old, not very many people had thought of using a wand to channel the magic. However, they did find a few journals referencing wands, they made sure to pay close attention to those writings. Most of it was about wand care and creating wands, some of the best woods and cores to use. The archive did not contain just magic. It contained information about arts, animals, engineering, and sciences. There was also a lot about history.

They did learn some new spells to be used with a wand. Some were offensive attacks, while others were used for defense. The most important thing they learned about was the art of "iter statum", the ability to disappear and instantly reappear wherever they wanted.

There were even highly technical rituals that could be performed to create very powerful magic. Another thing that was very interesting to them was the art of making special serums. These serums could be used for a variety of applications, from healing wounds to making the drinker forget who they were, even having the ability to look like someone else.

One of the journals that they found had a description of how to record writing. The writings could be stored in other objects to be recalled later. They recorded everything in the archive, and stored it on their wands. That way, when they had their school and their own library, they could reproduce King Sol's massive archive.

Chapter Eight

It took them almost three days to get through the entire archive. When they left the archive, there were three guards waiting for them. The guards escorted them through the city along the cobblestone streets towards the city gate leading to the port. When they reached the port, King Sol appeared in front of them, again out of thin air.

"When you think you are ready to start teaching others, send word." King Sol said. "When I hear from you, I will announce to my people that they are free to join you to learn your skills if they wish."

With that, King Sol disappeared into thin air. The guards directed them to their ship. They continued toward their ship, the guards told them to leave first thing in the morning. The guards turned and returned to the city.

They discussed where they would go from there.

"I think we don't have a lot of time." Said Zeke. "We need to find a place to practice full time. We have a lot to learn before we try to go up against Ostello. If Mahdrin was right, it won't be long before Ostello attacks King Sol."

"I think you are right." Agreed Barmor. "Maybe we can learn enough to stop Ostello before he moves on King Sol."

"No." Argued Zeke. "King Sol made it clear. We are not to intervene before Prince Ostello attacks. If Ostello attacks and kills King Sol, that was his destiny. We are not to mess with their destiny. We are better off having Ostello, who does not know that we exist as an enemy, rather than King Sol, who knows who we are and what we can do."

"That is true." Barmor said in agreement. "I think it is time to find a place to start building this school you keep talking about. Some place where we can practice and learn as much as we can. Where do you think would be a good place to start this school you are thinking about?"

"I think somewhere that is fairly easily accessible." Zeke replied. "Somewhere that prospective students can find easily. Or somewhere that is hard to find and start our own means of transportation."

"We already have our own means of transportation." Barmor stated, tapping his toe, and looking down. "The ship."

"That is true." Zeke nodded in agreement. "We could have them go to where the ship is moored, and the ship will could fly them to us. So maybe somewhere in the mountains."

Barmor's map told of a land locked mountain range that was probably a day flight with the Cherry of the Sky. It may make a good spot. They decided that they would check out the mountain range first. In the morning, they would sail north around the city of Cortis Mundi, then when out of sight of the city and other ships, they would disappear and lift off.

The next morning, after they lifted the invisible ship out of the water they headed northeast. When they were high enough in the clouds to not be seen, they made the ship visible again. While they were traveling towards the mountain range, they relaxed and talked about the school they were going to start. They knew that they should be practicing, preparing for Ostello, but they also knew that they would not be able to defeat him alone. They would need the school, and their future pupils to defeat him and his armies. So, for the time being it was about their school, not only learning the magic, but also learning how to teach others.

They would find a place that, if, in the future, the school could not handle its occupants, it could be added onto. A place that was relatively protected. A place where people would want to come to learn. They hoped this school would be around for generations to come and would teach the magical arts to many students.

Once they had their school built, the students would come to learn. The students that were particularly interested in or good at certain aspects of magic could help teach others while still learning themselves. Zeke felt everyone could always learn something from others. Just because he knew how to do something, did not mean someone else did not know how to do it better or easier. There was always something to learn.

It was midday the next day when they saw the mountain range. They brought the ship lower so they could get a better look. They decided to use the broom and Longtail to investigate the mountains for the right location. They took off, cruising through canyons and along cliffs. It took them nearly the rest of the day looking for the perfect spot. It was just about dark when they saw it.

Both Barmor and Zeke had found the same canyon from two different sides at the same time. The canyon was very deep, broad, and secluded, with tall cliffs on all sides. From north to south the canyon was about two miles long, and from east to west it was five miles wide. On the south side, the canyon narrowed to a small stream, that wound itself down through the mountains. The north side of the canyon was crescent shaped, with near vertical cliffs reaching above the clouds. From the air, the canyon resembled a large eye. In the bottom was a large, beautiful lake that took up about one third of the valley floor, the rest was covered in lush forest. There were only two ways into the canyon, traverse the narrow winding stream, or from above, over the top of the rugged mountains.

They flew down and landed on the northern shore of the lake. Even though it was late fall, and they were high in the mountains, the valley floor was pleasantly warm. They slowly turned all the way around, staring at the magnificently beautiful granite and limestone canyon walls.

"It's perfect." They both exclaimed at the same time. They got back on their mounts and flew to the north end of the canyon, to get a better look at the north face. That was the perfect location for a large castle to be carved into the canyon wall. The castle could be raised above the valley floor, so the southern end, where the stream exited, could be seen over the treetops. After they marveled for a while, Barmor flew back to the ship on his broom.

Barmor brought the ship down and landed it in the lake. He found a piece of driftwood on the shore and constructed a large dock and moored the ship. When he returned to the north wall, Zeke had used his wand to draw a three-dimensional design of his idea for what the castle they would create as the school, should look like. The blueprint was floating in the air. From Zeke's perspective, the floating lines corresponded to actual size on the canyon wall. They could walk around the wireframe design and modify it as they wanted. The floating blueprint was enchanted, the lines started as red, when a wall or section of castle was complete, the corresponding lines would turn green.

The castle design consisted of east and west wings, along with a north and south annex. Both wings and annexes would all have two tall towers with bells in each. The towers and castle sections would all have interconnecting halls at different levels, creating many different routes from one place to another within the castle. There would be caves, tunnels, stairways, even hidden passageways. Of course, there would be classrooms, dormitories, library, dining, and medical facilities as well.

Barmor pulled out his wand and turned a stump into a stack of books. Using the freshly formed books, Zeke used his wand to recreate the books about engineering and carving stone, he had copied from King Sol's archive. They worked late into the night studying the reprinted books and making minor adjustments to the floating blueprint. They practiced manipulating stone, using large rocks they found on the valley floor. They knew it was going to be a daunting task carving a castle out of a cliff face.

The next day they started carving. Using the word "deleo" and small right-handed circles they began to carve away and erase unwanted stone. It was going better than they had anticipated, but still slow. By the end of the first day, they had the entrance hall and a few corridors leading from it done. It took them ten days to carve the entire castle.

When they had finished making the castle, they needed to find out where the closest ocean access would be, sailing was currently the most common means of transportation. Using the map they had found at Lapis Mitigo, and flying there on the broom and Longtail, they found a large bay that connected to the ocean. They made a dock to load and unload ships. They returned to their newly made castle and wrote a note to King Sol describing how to get to the bay and to let them know how many people they should expect, and when they should expect them to get to the bay. The note also asked for any information regarding Ostello. They gave the note to Longtail and had him deliver it.

While Longtail was gone, they began reproducing the rest of the books they had copied from King Sol's archive. With the word "liber" and a left-handed square movement of their wands, they were able to transform wood pieces into books. They began filling the books with the writings from

Cortis Mundi's archive. When they had reprinted all their saved writings, they moved the books into the large cavern they had designated as the library. As learning was the center of knowledge, the library sat in the center of the castle. The east and west wings had classrooms and dormitories. The north annex would be faculty housing and offices. The south annex held the entrance hall, dining, and medical facilities. The library sat in the middle of both wings and annexes.

They had decided to create clans within the school. The clans would be chosen by the students themselves, instead of the school placing them in the clans. While each clan will learn any and all aspects of magic, the clans will be divided into what the students want to achieve in life and while at school. Those that wanted to specialize in health and healing would join the clan of the Phoenix. Those that wanted to grow their knowledge of crafting, architecture, and engineering could choose the Centaurs. Those who yearned for the cunning arts of serums, misdirection, and stealth, would fit right in with the Yeti. The ones who always want to be the very best, and most well-known, Dragon would be their best bet. Those that want to achieve a general mastery of all magical arts, should seek the Griffins. The ones that see magic as the path to better all mankind, and further the world as a whole would want to choose the Unicorn. The clans will be like a family. There will be a yearlong competition between the clans, earning points for achievements. The competition will be geared toward mastering different magical arts. Dueling, making serums, and creating new forms of magic will all be parts of the competition.

The first generation of students will be any and all that want to join and learn. After a few years it will be limited to children and young adults. After that, adults can follow the path in life that they choose to follow. After the school had been established for a few years, kids will start school at the age of ten. Schooling would last ten years, with each year learning more advanced forms of magic. Each year will be broken down into three separate blocks, each block will be three months long, with a month off in between. At the end of the third block, the clan points for the year will be totaled up, and the winning clan will be awarded a special wand statue to be displayed the next year.

It took three days for Longtail to return from Cortis Mundi. He returned with King Sol's reply that said:

There is a ship with sixty-five people wanting to learn more about magic from you. I apologize that there is not more, but I think my stance on low born magic has a lot of people afraid of repercussions, even though I assured them there would be none. Others, I believe, are happy with their current existence. That being said, there are fifty low born and fifteen royal servants that have a wide variety of powers, including serums, architecture, magic sensing, defense and attack, to include a few. They will arrive at the bay you described in six days. Mahdrin has arrived back with Ostello. He seems preoccupied with growing his ranks and training his army in his brutal and evil ways. If I hear more, I will send word.

"We have three days." Zeke said after reading the note from King Sol.

"Sixty-five is better than none." Barmor responded.

"Yeah. I am guessing that when Ostello attacks, if there is anyone left alive, we will gain some, if they are able to escape." Zeke answered.

Two days after Longtail returned, they boarded the Cherry of the Sky, and headed to the bay. They arrived that evening. The students would arrive sometime the next day. They wanted to be there waiting for their new students when they arrived.

Chapter Nine

It was mid-morning the next day when Zeke saw them sailing into the bay. "Look. There." Zeke exclaimed. "Here they come."

The ship sailed up to the dock, when the crew tied the ship off and the passengers filed onto the dock, Zeke introduced himself, Barmor, and Longtail.

"Hello." He spoke. "I am Zekious Starbo. This is Barmor Woodheart. Who is ready to leave their old life behind, and start a new one?"

There was a murmur of general excitement among the new students. Zeke thanked the crew of King Sol's ship for bringing the students.

"So!" Barmor followed up. "Let's go see the castle we have built and learn some magic. And most importantly, have some fun."

The murmur of excitement got louder. Zeke motioned toward Cherry of the Sky. The were some words of disgust and general dissention amongst them as they realized they were getting on another ship. Once they were all boarded, Barmor took out his wand, pointed it at the deck, and raised the ship out of the water, then elevated it to flying level. When it was high enough. Zeke pointed his wand at the sails and made them stretch out, and the ship took off to northeast.

Gasps of awe exploded when the ship lurched forward in the air. As the ship was flying toward the hidden canyon, Zeke and Barmor took turns talking about their time together and teaching themselves how to perform magic. They told the new students about how they practiced by trial and error. They explained how they eventually taught themselves enough to impress even King Sol. He allowed them to access his archives and the information they had gathered there.

They purposely did not tell them where they were going, Zeke and Barmor wanted the students to not know what they were expecting and see the valley and castle for the first time with no preconceived notions. Just before they got to the valley, Zeke made the ship invisible.

The entire group of students jumped and screamed in horror. The screams quickly turned to absolute amazement when they saw the valley. They were totally speechless when Zeke took the ship around the whole valley then took the ship down and landed in the lake.

After they landed Zeke and Barmor lead them to the castle. As the castle first came into view through the trees, all of the students froze. Then one by one they eventually regained the use of their bodies, and slowly started approaching the castle. Zeke and Barmor gave them a tour and described what they intended to do with every room and section of the castle. When the tour had was finished, they let the students explore the canyon and castle on their own.

They had planned an extravagant dinner for that night in the dining hall. When it was time for dinner, Zeke made all the bells in the towers ring at the same time. When the bells started ringing all the students started gathering in the entrance hall. When all the students had arrived, Zeke led them to the dining hall, where Barmor had prepared a fantastic meal, from foods gathered from the valley. When everyone had more than they could eat, and the tables had been cleaned up, Zeke stood up and gave a speech.

"Welcome the first class of Occulta Vallem Magia, The Eye of the Magic Valley, the first school to train witches and wizards. This is going to be a learning experience for everyone involved. You are here because you want to learn how to do magic. We are here because we want to teach magic. Starting this school will take learning, patience, and growth from all of us. You will learn how to craft your own wands by finding the wood you are drawn to and collecting something from an animal that is special to you. You will make your own broom to fly on, and many other things that are necessary for your future. You will choose a clan. That clan will be like your family. You and your clan will succeed together and fail together. Points will be awarded for your successes and taken away for your wrong doings."

"The Pheonix clan wants to pursue the medical arts of health and healing. The Centaurs seek the crafting arts of engineering and architecture.

The Yeti are those that will specialize in stealth, serums, and misdirection. Dragons want the title of being the very best. The Griffin seeks to learn everything from magic there is to learn. The Unicorn is selfless and seeks to learn magic to better all of mankind and to help the world move forward."

"While the clans are aimed at certain aspects of magic, you are encouraged to learn all that you can. Mastering new techniques will earn you more points toward the Clan Champion and the Wand of Knowledge statue, to be awarded at the end of the year."

"Tomorrow everyone will go out to the forest and find the kind of wood that calls to you, then we will help you start crafting your wands. However, wands are not just wood, they will have a core as well. That core will probably be something from an animal that you are also drawn to or connected to in some way. For example, my core is griffin wing feather, given to me by Longtail, after I rescued him from a hunter, Barmor's core is the tooth from a saber-toothed cat he killed after it killed his grandfather and father. Spend the evening thinking about what wood and creature you might be connected to. Who is ready for clan choosing."

The students lined up and chose their clans. Of the sixty-five students, nine chose the Pheonix, and nine more wanted to master the crafting arts of the Centaurs. Ten of them preferred the silent arts of the Yeti. Eleven felt more drawn to the Griffins as they wanted to learn everything that they could. The Unicorn clan gained its first eleven members that wanted to learn magic to advance mankind. Fifteen felt that they wanted to be the best, and most famous witches and wizards so they joined the Dragons.

After everyone had chosen the clan that they wanted to be a part of, Zeke explained that the Pheonix dormitory was located in the east wing east tower. The east wing west tower would be the dormitory for the Griffins, and the east wing basement would be the Centaurs dormitory. The west wing west tower would house the Unicorns, while the west wing east tower was the home of the Dragons. The Yeti would call the west wing basement home. Zeke had chosen the east tower of the north annex as his office, and living quarters, while Barmor took the north annex west tower.

"There is one more matter that needs to be talked about." Zeke said after describing where the dormitories would be. "I am not sure how many of you are familiar with Prince Ostello. He is King Sol's son. He was banished from

Cortis Mundi over twenty years ago for wanting to teach magic and use low born citizens as a form of magical slaves. We have learned that, in the last twenty years, he has become increasingly evil. He now plans to attack Cortis Mundi and kill King Sol. He hates his father for not agreeing with him and for banishing him. King Sol will not allow us to help. He said it is between him and his son. We may only face Prince Ostello if he attacks and kills King Sol. So, for now he is not a threat, but some day it may become more."

The next morning, after everyone had eaten a great breakfast, Zeke and Barmor headed outside. The students began wandering through the forest seeking the wood that they would use for their wands.

"You may feel drawn to a certain type of wood." Barmor explained. "When you find a type of wood you like, try a few different pieces. When you find the right piece, when you hold it in your hand you will feel the energy. You will feel like you were meant to have that piece of wood."

"Now your wand will need a core." Zeke told them when all the students had returned. "

All of the students who had decided to come learn from Zeke and Barmor had agreed to being banished from Cortis Mundi, so they had brought all of their belongings. It turned out that nearly all of them had brought something that was animal related that they were attached to. There were only a few that needed a core.

There was a fifteen-year-old boy named Dalvo that had always been intrigued by trolls. Zeke sent him down the stream to the south to see if he could find a troll. There was woman, Chiana, in her late thirties that had always felt connected to mermaids. Barmor loaned her his broom to fly to the ocean to try to find a mermaid. Ridmeus was in his late twenties and needed to collect something from a dragon. Zeke explained how to fly the Cherry of the Sky and told him that when they were looking for the valley where they had built the castle, he thought he had seen a dragon layer about a hundred miles to the north.

The rest of the students all had something to use for a core. Zeke and Barmor showed them how to turn the wood they selected into a thin sheet.

"Hold the stick in your hand and use the word "tenuis"." Barmor directed. "While you do it, picture in your head the wood turning into thin sheet like a parchment."

Out of the sixty-two students still there, most were able to quickly turn their wood into thin sheets. The two students that had the most difficulty, were both young kids, one was five, and the other was seven years old. After they had gotten help from older students sitting near them, they both were able to transform their sticks into sheets.

"Place your core in the sheet of wood," Zeke instructed them. "Then hold the sheet in your hand and use the word "circumligo" to wrap the wood around your core. While you do that, think about the shape you want your wand to take. Whether you want it smooth, knobby, twisted, or whatever you think fits your personality."

There was a series of "pops" as the students formed their wands. Again, the two young kids had more trouble than the older students. That was completely understandable. Being so young, not only did they have a limited understanding of the instructions, but less time for their magical powers to develop. With help from the others though, they were both able to produce their wands and more quickly than they had accomplished making their sheets.

"How do they feel?" Zeke asked when everyone had got their wands made.

There was an air of excitement and awe as everyone held their newly formed wands. Everyone, even the kids, could feel that their wands were complete. They all felt the energy flowing through them and knew that they had made wands correctly. Zeke gave them a few simple incantations and movements to use to go wonder around and practice. They would wait until the other three had returned to continue with lessons.

Dalvo got back the next morning with a lock of green hair. Dalvo had a slender build, but even at the age of fifteen, was still about the same height as Zeke at just over six feet tall and had yellow hair. Also, like Zeke, his parents had died when he was young, except his had died from disease. He had grown up fending for himself on the streets of Cortis Mundi.

"What did you get?" Zeke asked Dalvo when he got back. "Is that a ponytail?"

"It is." Dalvo replied. "I saw him yesterday afternoon and tracked him back to his horde. I waited until he fell asleep and snuck in and cut off his ponytail. Growing up taking care of myself on the streets, I learned really quick, how to be sneaky and unseen. That is why I chose to be in the Yeti."

"That is perfect." Zeke congratulated him. "That should work great for you."

Zeke showed him how to make his wood sheet and then wrap the hair with the sheet. Then when his wand was finished, Dalvo tried it out. He was elated, his wand was fantastic. The wood he had chosen was a piece of aspen. When he had formed it into the final product it came out to eight inches long and very narrow and bendy. It had knots on it and was very natural looking. Zeke then had him go practice a few simple spells. Now they only had to wait for Chiana and Ridmeus to return.

Late that evening, after dinner, Chiana got back with a section of mermaid dorsal fin. Chiana was slightly pudgy, was about a foot shorter than Zeke, and sported raven black hair that she kept in a bun. When she arrived, she landed the broom at bottom of the stairs leading to the castle, where Zeke was waiting. She showed him the piece of dorsal fin she had wrapped in a piece of cloth.

Zeke explained how she could turn the elm branch she had found into a thin film. She then laid the fin in the elm swatch and held it in her hand transformed into her wand. When she was finished, she showed it to Zeke, it was twelve inches long, had a nice taper to it, was brown and black with one full revolution of twist.

"Very well done, Chiana." Zeke complimented her. "How does it feel?"

"It feels like it a part of me." She replied. "It feels like if I ever put it down, it would be as bad as cutting off my hand, I can't explain why."

"That means you have chosen correctly." He answered. "That means you, the wood, and the core you have chosen, along with the style you have created, are one."

He gave her the same simple spells to practice as he had everyone else. He told her to continue practicing and try other things if she wished, to improve her skills, if she could. They would resume lessons when Ridmeus had gotten back from his quest for a core. Zeke and Barmor wanted to be able to teach everyone at the same time to begin with so that they got a good comparison of all of their skill levels.

Over the next two days, while they were waiting for Ridmeus to return, most of the students found themselves in the library browsing through the books Zeke and Barmor had copied from King Sol's archive, teaching themselves new spells. Zeke and Barmor were very impressed with everyone's initiative, learning on their own, as that was how they had made it as far as they had.

When Ridmeus had returned, he had his own wand already finished. Ridmeus was shorter than average, at just over five feet tall. He was very stout, had white hair and looked young for his age. The wood he had chosen was birch, eleven inches long, and contained dragon scales for a core, and included white and black indicative of birch bark. When he found the dragon lair, he used his wand, unformed and with no core, to freeze the legs, wings, and upper body of dragon. He explained to Zeke and Barmor that he guessed, and got lucky, with the word "refrigero" and a left-handed triangle followed by small right-handed circles to throw ice at the beast.

While the dragon was frozen, he scraped some scales from her tail. Then as he was riding on the ship with nothing to do, he was messing around with word combinations, and was accidentally able to blend the birch and scales into the wand design he had desired.

Zeke knew that Ridmeus was going to be a powerful wizard. Like himself, Ridmeus had figured out how to craft his own wand and used an incomplete wand to collect his dragon scales. Zeke expected big things from Ridmeus.

Chapter Ten

The next day actual instruction began. Zeke and Barmor were correct, everyone had the capability to learn magic, even the young kids were able to learn the simple spells, however there were some that were definitely more naturally skilled than others. Their first lesson was brooms. Barmor showed everyone how to make their first broom. By the end of the day everyone was flying around the valley with their own brooms.

Zeke and Barmor were also learning as they were teaching. They would use the books as instructional aid and teach from them. There were even times when the students would get the day's lesson figured out before Zeke or Barmor would. When it came to teaching the subjects that the students who were former Royal Guards or servants were already familiar with, they would be the ones to teach those lessons.

After the students had begun really getting a grasp on the use of magic Zeke started a dueling competition, a magical understanding competition, a serum competition, and a stealth competition. Barmor had been working on a couple of magical games the students could play as well.

The dueling competition would consist of one student dueling another from a different clan. The winning student would earn five points for their clan. The duels could be set up by Zeke and Barmor pitting students or clans against one another. The duels could also be one student or clan challenging a different student or clan. They could also be used to settle disputes between students.

The magical understanding competitions would be a series of magical challenges that the clans would face as a team. Each challenge would require the entire clan to use their understanding of magic to find the solution.

The challenges would be timed, the clan that completed the challenge the quickest and used to most ingenuity would be awarded fifty points. There would be several challenges throughout the year.

The serum competitions would test the students' ability to identify serums and ingredients, create known ingredients, or develop new serums. The student or clan that won the serum competition would earn five points for their clan.

The stealth competitions would be a cross between hide and seek and capture the flag. Each clan would be given objective to guard while also trying to gain control of the other clans' objectives. Only stealth, misdirection, concealment, and discovery could be used. There would be no attacking allowed. If a student used an outright attack or was caught or seen by a rival clan, they would be eliminated. The first clan to collect all of the objectives or the last clan with any active members would win. The winning clan would gain another fifty points.

The first sport that Barmor created was called lapidem. He also built a set of raised seats around an area that would be designated as the lapidem field. The lapidem games and other competitions would be held in the lapidem field. The game of lapidem would consist of two teams, each consisting of five players on the field. Substitutions could be made by either team at any time as long as the exiting player was off the field before the new player came on. There were four stones, a black, a blue, a green, and a red stone. A stone would randomly appear on the ground somewhere in the field. Each time a stone appeared it would be a random size and color and only one stone would appear at a time. The black stone would be worth five points and would appear most frequently. The second most common stone would be the blue stone and it would be worth ten points. The green stone would rarely appear and be worth fifty points. The red stone would only appear once and would mark the last stone of the game, it was worth one hundred fifty points.

Each team had a basket that they had to protect, and the baskets would appear at random places around a two-acre field. The two teams would be on brooms, and a stone would appear somewhere on the field. The players could either physically grab, hold, or throw the stone, or could use controlling magic to get the stone into the other team's basket. When a team got a stone in the other team's basket, they would score the points of that stone. When the red stone was made into a basket the game would be over and the team with the most points would win. In the case of a tie, one final, random stone would appear after the red stone. Magic was not allowed except to move the stone.

The lapidem championship would be separate from the clan championship and have its own trophy. Each clan would play against all of the other clans, the two teams with the best record would face each other in the championship game. Lapidem would take a lot of teamwork, skill on a broom, and precise wand work to move the stones into the baskets. The first game would be after the third week of lessons, and the clans were encouraged to start practicing when they could.

Rosten was one of the students who was a master at serums for the Royal Guard. He was a few inches taller than Zeke, had a scary thin frame, short dark green hair, and black eyes. He always wore several large rings on his fingers, and the talons of a harpy eagle on a necklace. He started teaching serum lessons. He was in his late fifties and had always had a knowledge of ingredients. The first serum lesson he taught them about several ingredients, and how to identify them. Then he had them go and find those ingredients in the valley or take their brooms and find them in other nearby valleys if they needed to. After the students, along with Zeke and Barmor had gathered the ingredients, Rosten taught them how to make a draught that would allow the drinker to have magnified vision.

They also learned how they could test certain ingredients to see what kind of serum they could be useful in. Rosten showed them that if a certain leaf could be used as a pain reducer, or antiseptic, it could be used in a healing serum. He explained that it was not the ingredients alone that made a serum, but the order that the ingredients were added, along the proper temperature and correct blending process.

Wimber was a Royal Servant before leaving Cortis Mundi. She was in her mid-forties with an average build, five and half feet tall. She had long flowing red-blonde hair, and a dark complexion. She was a master of "iter statum", the art of disappearing from your current location and instantly appearing at another.

She explained how one should visualize where they want to be, then imagine a rope connecting where you want to go to where you are. While you were thinking about the rope connecting the two locations, one simply needed to relax their body and imagine your body is the rope. She had everyone line up and try it one at a time and transport to a circle she had drawn on the ground.

Wimber then demonstrated what it would be like. She disappeared from where she was with a tshup sound. Then she reappeared inside the circle pwisht sound. Then it was Zeke's turn, he did as she had instructed. He pictured a rope tethering him to the circle. Then he imagined himself as the rope, then relaxed his body. As soon as he started relaxing his body, he found himself spiraling headfirst through space. Then everything stopped.

When he opened his eyes, he was standing in the circle. He lost his balance, fell to one knee, and threw up. He stood up and thought that was the weirdest and most unnatural feeling he had ever had. But it was amazing. He could instantly be anywhere that he wanted to be.

"How far can you insta-fly?" He asked Wimber as he left the circle.

"As far as you want as long as you can picture yourself there." She answered. "Insta-fly, I like that."

Barmor did not get it figured out on the first try like Zeke. Insta-flight was a very complex form of magic, and not everyone was able to get it the first try. By the end of the first lesson, only half of the students were able to get it figured out.

The first week of lessons also included a more in-depth look at attack and defense spells used in dueling. Combat skills were taught by Mevlar, another former Royal Servant. He was in his late fifties, right at five foot tall, and was slightly overweight. He had red hair, with a mustache and goatee. Mevlar's left arm was a few inches shorter than his right.

Mevlar taught them to stun, block and use combinations to eliminate attackers. Even though none of the spells could actually kill an opponent, magic was funny. Sometimes a simple block and reflecting a spell back at one's opponent could take them out of a fight. Defeating an opponent did not mean you had to kill them.

"The first duel will be at the end of next week." Zeke explained at the end of their first lesson. "It will be between the Yeti and Centaurs. The Dragons will face off against the Griffins. The Pheonix and Unicorn would also duel."

The first week of lessons flew by. All the students were really taking to learning magic. Zeke and Barmor's teaching structure seemed to be working well. The day's lesson would take place in the morning after a good breakfast. After lunch they would break into groups, whether it was groups of friends or among clans. The groups would go to practice by themselves with the ones that understood the lesson helping the those that did not. The rest of the afternoon would be spent practicing amongst themselves or leisure time. Most students usually spent their leisure time trying to gain more knowledge in the library or working on what they had already learned.

In the second week of school, they began learning about magic sensing. The art of magic sensing was thought to be a rare form of magic. It was the ability to sense someone's magical power and how much power they had. After the first lesson there were only a few that were able to ascertain how much magical power someone had. Zeke was not able to sense anyone's power, however Barmor was, that explained how he was able to know that Zeke had powers when they first met. So, Zeke realized, there were some forms of magic not everyone had the ability to perform, or had a harder time learning them.

The second week also consisted of transformation. The art of transformation was the class of magic that was used to change one thing into another. Transformation would be very useful in battle, also in society. Anything or anyone could be transformed into anything else. If a person was transformed into something, it would not kill them. The transformed person would just have to wait until someone else came along and transformed them back. "Muto silex" was Zeke's favorite transformation spell, it could change someone into a rock.

Everyday magic was full of other useful magic to be used in everyday life. Making ships fly, creating brooms, and carving castles from stone cliffs was just a taste of some of the things that were taught in that class. Zeke would teach them to how to pick things up and move them. They would learn how to make carts pull themselves from city to city to transport goods. They would learn how to enchant items, like torches so that they would light when someone walked into a room, or garbage cans to make anything put in them disappear.

In magical creatures, taught by Zeke and Barmor, they would learn about vampires, werewolves, dragons, unicorns, and other creatures there were created by or could use some sort of magic. Their first lesson taught them about gnomes. There were several different species of gnome, some loved human interaction and could be very helpful, but some could be very mischievous. Gnomes lived in different kinds of soils and could insta-fly and were adept at manipulating natural items and turning them into foods. As it turned out, the cliff where Zeke and Barmor had built the castle was home to a large tribe of cliff gnomes.

Those cliff gnomes took it upon themselves to move into the castle shortly after the students had arrived. The gnomes started taking care of the castle and valley. Without being asked by anyone they had started preparing the food for the meals at the castle. They made gardens and planted flowers and vegetables. They became housekeepers, groundskeepers, and cooks all on their own.

The fourth day of the second week was kept open for studying, practicing, or relaxing. The first dueling challenge would be the next day. Having a day to either relax or train would be good for all the students. They had a big dinner the night before the first dueling competition.

The next morning the gnomes served up a great breakfast. There were pancakes, omelets, bacon, biscuits with gravy, with sausage, cornbread and toast. There was fresh orange juice, coffee, milk, and tea. Everyone ate their fill and got ready for the duels to start in the early afternoon.

Chapter Eleven

Everyone went to the lapidem field and sat down in the seats Barmor had created. They waited in anticipation for the dueling competition to start. They were all very curious how they were doing to compared to the other clans.

"First up will be the Centaurs and the Yeti" Zeke announced when it was time for the dueling to begin. "The clans will fight as teams. The last clan with one person still standing and able to fight will win. Centaurs will start on the north side and Yeti will start on south side." He said as he pointed toward the far side and close side of the lapidem field.

The field had been converted to battlefield. It had walls, rocks, tunnels, and bunkers to provide cover for the duels. The nine Centaurs headed to the north end of the field, and the ten Yeti went and lined up on the south side of the field. The remaining students went in the elevated seating outside the field to watch the match and await their turn at battle.

"GET READY." Zeke shouted. "BEGIN!"

When the battle began, one of the Yeti formed a dense cloud of fog that settled down on the arena. The spectators in the stands could still see well enough, but Zeke was sure those that were engaged in battle would have a hard time seeing. It did not take long for the spectators to see sparks and streams of lights of all different colors traveling this way and that across the battlefield.

"The Centaurs draw first blood," Zeke announced. "As Theoga turns Damgar into an oak tree. Then Theoga gets taken out by a jelly leg charm from Marvdon."

Another Centaur got tied in a knot by the knotted-up charm, "nodum". Then Marvdon got stunned. Then a third Yeti got locked inside a stone wall. A fourth Yeti had her unmovable spell blocked and sent back to her. The battle continued until Dalvo was the last Yeti, and there were three Centaurs left.

Dalvo took out another Centaur by hitting him with "excors" taking away all his senses, making him deaf and blind. The next Centaur hit the ground with the stiffening charm "rigesco", stiffening his whole body. One left from each clan. Dalvo was the last Yeti, and Markar was the last Centaur.

Markar was in mid-twenties, with short white hair, clean faced with radiating green eyes. Markar was almost six feet tall, and athletically built. Markar and Dalvo were very closely matched. Both young men had natural talent and picked up magic easily. They both also had quick reflexes and had spent a lot of time in the library and practicing. In fact, although they were from different clans, they were actually friends and spent a lot of time together and helping each other out.

Dalvo favored using "rigesco", While Markar liked to use "furatelum" to take away someone's wand. In the last moments of the duel, both fighters used their favored spells simultaneously. Dalvo missed, Markar did not. Everyone thought the fight was over. Everyone, except Dalvo.

"Trudo." Dalvo shouted, thrusting his hand instinctively forward towards Markar. "Sublego." He did not know if it would work without a wand, but it was worth a try.

It worked. Markar fell backwards and did not catch Dalvo's wand. The wand flew back to Dalvo's hand. Markar rolled to his feet. He knew as soon as Dalvo had his wand back he would attack again.

"Rigesco." Said Dalvo as soon as he had caught his wand.

"Averto." Said Markar. "Furatelum."

The disarming spell was not needed. There was Dalvo, lying on the ground, his body as stiff as stone. Markar's block had sent Dalvo's stiffening charm back at him. Markar had won the first school duel for the Centaurs.

Zeke and the rest of the school were very happy with the first clan duel. All of the spells got reversed and the students from both clans stood and congratulated each other on an amazing first duel.

"What a well fought duel from both sides." Zeke announced. "Congratulations to both clans. Rosten and the other eight Phoenix will face Mevlar and the ten other Unicorns. The Unicorns will start on the north end, the Phoenix will start on the south end."

Zeke was hoping for another great duel. These duels would be a great evaluation of how the students are doing. Although the nine Phoenix were outnumbered by two, Zeke was still expecting it to be a good match. The Phoenix headed for the south end of the lapidem field while the Unicorn headed north.

"Everyone, get ready" Zeke announced. "FIGHT!"

When the second clan duel started, both clans started taking cover behind the stone walls trying to sneak up on the other clan to get the upper hand. Mevlar was the first to eliminate a Phoenix, by turning her into a hedge. Rosten reversed the hedging spell. Another Unicorn got the drop on another Phoenix, turning a young man into a kitten, but the Unicorn was quickly hit by stiffening charm.

The Phoenix continued to stay together and anytime one went down the rest of the clan would attack back, then tend to the injured team member. One by one they eliminated the Unicorns. As the Centaurs and Yeti watched, they were a little sad that they did not study more healing magic and had used the Phoenix' tactics of healing their injured teammates. They all understood there would definitely be more practice in the healing arts.

The Phoenix easily won. They had all eight members still fighting, when the last Unicorn got frozen with "refrigero".

"Good way to work as a team, Phoenix." Zeke announced as the two clans left the field and walked back to stands where the rest of the students were sitting. "Congratulations to both clans. The teamwork, healing as the battle goes on, will be exactly what we will need to do if we end up having to go up against Prince Ostello. Well done."

Zeke announced the Dragons and the Griffins. The fifteen Dragons headed for the south end of the field, while the eleven Griffins headed to the north. When Zeke announced the beginning of the duel, the two clans stayed together as teams, similar to the strategy used by the Phoenix. The match lasted much longer than the first two.

Working as a team and healing their injured teammates kept both clans at full force. When a person fell, they were brought right back into the game. They were going to have to get creative. They started trying to eliminate the other clan all at once. Large scale attacks only need to be blocked or dodged by one or two team members. The remaining fighters would just release the rest of their team from whatever trap that they were being held by.

There would be no time out or pausing the match, so the teams had to develop a strategy while fighting. Ridmeus had an idea for the Griffins to win. They would have to try spells and charms that were harder to reverse. They were also going to try to disarm the fighters. It was his hope that, without wands, they would begin to tire more quickly and not be able to recover from attacks as fast. Only problem, the Dragons had started to try the same strategy. Also, most of the Dragons and Griffins had been practicing without wands as well. While using a wand was not required, it made it easier to focus spells and took less energy from the witch or wizard.

Both teams retreated to their respective ends of the field. Ridmeus explained a new plan. He had his doubts that shields would last very long in with the caliber of magic they were dealing with, but they might buy them a little more time. With shields up they did not have to block the first wave of incoming attacks.

When the next wave of attacks began the Griffins insta-flew behind the Dragons. As soon as they acquired their feet, all of the Griffins used "sui contego" to get personal shields. Then, having caught the Dragons by surprise, the Griffins disarmed as many of them as they could. The ones that got disarmed were turned to stone. They were able to disarm ten of the Dragons, of that, eight were turned to stone.

Now that there were now more active Griffins than Dragons. The Griffins did not let up on the remaining seven Dragons. Three started using "tonitrum" to produce loud claps of thunder. Three more started sending flashes of light with "fulminis". Three more of the Griffins were wildly disarming anything that moved. The two remaining Griffins were throwing all sorts of attacks at anyone still standing.

The Dragons did not have time to try to help the ones turned to stone when the attack first started. Being so caught off guard from the initial attack and with the sound and flashing lights, the Dragons all became disorientated.

When the final blitz attack was done, two Dragons had been hit with the jelly limb charm "gelata", two more had been hit with the stiffening charm, the remaining three had been tied in knots.

All the spectators stood and started cheering for the amazing battle they had just witnessed. The Dragons got released from their magical traps, and they all shook hands and hugged the Griffins. After the celebration on the field had ended, the two clans walked toward the stands. When they reached the stands the rest of the students all ran to congratulate them. Zeke stood and walked to the bottom of the stands.

When everyone had settled down Zeke began to speak. "What a marvelous display of the knowledge you have gained in the last two weeks. All three fights were spectacular to watch. I am guessing that the Centaurs and the Yeti did not know that they were allowed to heal or save their clanmates as the battle was going on. That is absolutely fine. It was great to watch the individual battles as well. When we go up against Prince Ostello, it will more than likely be very fast paced and confusing like that last blitz attack from the Griffins. There may be some one-on-one battles, but teamwork will be our key to our survival, and we will need to be able save our injured and trapped to succeed. Our next dueling competition will be set for two weeks. We will make it a larger single battle. We will split all the students into two groups of three clans each. It will be the Yeti, Unicorns, and Griffins on the red team. That will make the Centaurs, Pheonix, and the Dragons the blue team. Next week will be our first lapidem game. The Centaurs will take on the Dragons. Keep practicing and keep learning in your free time. We will take the next couple days off to relax. Great work today, everyone."

The students all slowly started getting up and heading back to the castle. When they arrived at the dining hall, the gnomes had set a massive dinner full of everything one could imagine. There were also wines, ales, and rums. Everyone ate and drank more than they should physically be able to. The drinking and debauchery lasted until the early hours of the morning.

Chapter Twelve

When the students woke up late the next morning, most went to the library. They all knew and understood that if they were to face Prince Ostello and his army now, they would not stand a chance. They had sixty-seven with Zeke, and Barmor, Ostello had several hundred. While everyone else was studying, the Centaurs and Dragons went back to the lapidem field with their brooms to get ready for the first lapidem game.

The first class the next week involved learning how to break spells and charms put on others, some of the students had already been learning this on their own. They also learned about healing physical injuries as well. Being able to break spells and attacks put on allies will be important in all future battles. Even when not in battle, knowing how to break spells and heal injuries will be a great asset to have.

Spell breaking was taught by a former Royal Guard healer by the name of Tundia. She was short, and very frail looking, and in her early fifties. Although she looked very small and frail, no one was worried about her. She was actually quite limber and strong; she could pick up a man Zeke's size without even a grunt. She had long green hair that she kept in a ponytail wrapped in bun on the right side of her head.

The next day, another former Royal Guard, Roych, began teaching battle strategy. He was in his early forties, but looked as though he was in his late sixties. When he served in King Sol's Royal Guard, he was one of King Sol's most trusted battle commanders. Roych had brown hair and big bushy eyebrows. His large nose hooked slightly to the left because it had been broken so many times. His bright yellow eyes were deep and set far apart. His face and arms were covered in scars from years of fighting.

The third day that week the students got a more in-depth look at griffins. Griffins were very strong and could fly long distances. Griffins also had the ability to form strong mental bonds with people or other creatures. Zeke called Longtail and a few moments later the large brown and black griffin came flying over the cliffs, coming from the north. He landed with a soft thud next to Zeke in front of the rest of the school.

Zeke told them about how he had rescued the large eagle headed lion from the hunter's net. That was how Zeke was able to have such a bond with Longtail. Longtail was able to read Zeke's mind and Zeke was learning how to understand Longtail. Zeke told them how after the rescue, when he was still holding his wand and felt it needed something else. When he touched Longtail for the first time, the wand felt complete. Longtail gave him a feather from his wing. Zeke used that feather for the core of his wand.

Longtail gave a screech. Zeke explained that griffins are very fierce in battle and are very protective of those that they are bonded with or who they consider family. One of the students asked if anyone could form a bond with any griffin. Longtail screeched and flapped his wings. Zeke told them what Longtail was trying to say.

"Yes. If that griffin is not already bonded to something, or someone else. However, if a griffin is bonded, it may still develop familial feelings to those who are close to the bond. For instance, while he is bonded with me, he considers you all family. He will still fight to protect all of you, but I am the only one that can understand him, and he always knows where I am."

"Is it common for griffins to bond with people?" One student asked.

"Are there other animals that can form that kind of bond with people?" Asked another student.

The students were all very interested in magical creatures. Some students were visibly jealous that Zeke had such a fantastic bond with such an awesome creature. Zeke told them that in his studies he had found that many other creatures could develop some sort of special bond with people. Strong bonds like he and Longtail had were rare and were usually dependent on circumstance. He had even read about some people being able to turn into animals.

"Werewolves for example," Zeke explained, "are people who get bitten by another werewolf and turn into a werewolf on the full moon. I have read that some werewolves, with practice, are able to transform when they want to. I have also read about a very difficult and lengthy magical process that one can perform to turn into an animal at will. I am trying to learn more about it."

An older student stood up and said, "My name is Pormin. I have found all of the steps for the process. It is very hard to perfect and disastrous if not done precisely. While King Sol banned the use and learning of magic, he did not ban reading. There were still those that tried to learn magic, and I have done a lot of research on the topic. I have always wished that I could turn into an animal."

Pormin was in his late sixties. He had light, red, shoulder length hair that was starting to turn white. He had small orange eyes, and a small nose. Other than the white hair, and short stature, Pormin looked very healthy for his age. As he finished telling his story, the man's form melted away. In his place stood a large eagle.

The eagle stood about five feet tall. Its talons were about three inches long, and beak was almost five inches. Its feathers started at bright yellow around the neck and faded to dark brown at the tail. The Eagle had a ruffle of longer feathers around the neck that looked like a lion's mane, and a row of feathers that stood straight up on its head like a mohawk.

The Eagle flapped its eight-foot wings, squawked, then melted away. Then Pormin was standing in its place again. Everyone cheered with excitement. They all started asking all sorts of questions. They all wanted to be able to turn into animals. They all had the same few questions, could they pick the animal they turned into? Was it the same animal every time he transformed? Did it hurt? Could he still do other magic while in eagle form?

Pormin told them you do not get to choose then animal, he had wanted to be a dire wolf. Now that the process was complete, he always turned into the same eagle. The first transformation was very uncomfortable, it did not hurt but was not a normal feeling. Once the transformation was complete, the discomfort went away. He still got the feeling every time he transformed, but he had gotten used to it.

He went on to tell them that the process required repeating a magical ceremony at precisely the same time every day for a month. During his research, he had learned that not doing the ceremony exactly the same way every time could result in a partial transformation, a permanent change, or even death. The ceremony had an incantation phrase and over fifty different movements with all different parts of the body.

After Zeke and the others heard about the complexities and hazards of the ceremony, they knew it would be a while before they were ready to try it. Zeke told them he would review the ceremony with Pormin and look through his research. With the dangers involved, he may want to put an age requirement on the transformation. He was afraid the younger students may not have the precision that was needed for the ceremony.

The next day, the day before the first lapidem game, they had another session with Mevlar. He helped them put together combinations. By stringing together blocks, attacks, and using insta-fly at the right time would make them unpredictable. As the next dueling competition was going to be three clans on each team, the teams were encouraged to work together to design a battle plan that would utilize the strengths of the clans. That afternoon they were free to do as they wanted. While the Centaurs and Dragons prepared for their game the next day the rest of the students either broke into small groups to practice their magic or went the library.

The next day everyone had a good breakfast and headed to the lapidem field for the first game. The Centaurs spread out with their brooms on the north end of the field, and the Dragons to the south end.

"Dragons, are you ready?" Zeke shouted. They all yelled and waved their brooms in the air.

"Centaurs are you ready?" Zeke shouted again, followed by cheers and waves.

"Begin!"

As he shouted a black stone appeared in the center of the field, both teams mounted their brooms, and five players from each side took to the air. A gold-colored basket appeared thirty feet off the ground above the Dragons and a silver one appeared above the Centaurs. There were shouts of "sublego" from both sides as they raced towards the black stone.

The stone had been hit by the pulling spell from both sides so it levitated and would move a little south, then a little north then back again. The spells had lost their potency, and the stone began to fall back to the ground. By that time, two Dragons had reached the stone on their brooms. They both leant over to scoop up the stone with their hands in an act of misdirection.

The Centaurs could not be sure which one had the stone, so they went after both. The two Dragons split up and took separate paths towards the silver basket. The feint worked, as the Centaurs were busy focusing on those two, a third Dragon flew straight to the basket. When she arrived, she turned, pointed her wand at the stone, still laying on the ground, and used the pulling spell. The stone was never actually picked up. It flew directly to her hand. She caught it and dropped it in the basket.

"Dragons draw first blood." Barmor shouted.

The baskets disappeared. The gold basket reappeared on the west side of the field, fifty feet off the ground. The silver one on the east side of the field, sitting on the ground. Everyone started looking for the next stone.

Centaurs were the first to see it on the south end of the field. Green this time, and half the size of an eagle's egg. Three Centaurs sped off toward it, the other two started running interference. One of the three picked up the small green stone, and all three started flying west, weaving in and out of each other. Passing, or at least pretending to pass the stone from one to the other.

The three Centaurs were able to easily score. The third stone was another green one, this time it was the size of a man's head, on the east side of the field. This time the baskets were moving erratically around the field. The Dragons were the first to pickup the large green stone. They started flying toward where the silver basket was. When they were about fifteen feet from the basket, it flew to the opposite end of the field, and gained twenty feet in altitude.

The Dragons turned around and headed to silver basket's new location. As they were flying toward the basket, they were passing the large green stone back and forth. They were just about to basket again when the stone carrier was cut off by three Centaurs and was forced to pass it off. As the stone was in the air one of the Centaurs used "sublego" pulling the stone to her. She caught it and zipped off toward the gold basket.

Just as she reached the basket and dropped the stone into the basket, the basket moved, and the stone fell toward the ground. The Dragons were quick to react, using "sublego" to gain control of the green stone once again. When the Dragon caught the stone, the silver basket appeared right next to her. She turned and dropped the stone into the basket.

The silver basket disappeared as quickly as it had appeared. The green stone fell toward the ground again. Before anyone could react, the gold basket appeared on the ground directly below the stone. The green stone landed in the basket. Another score for the Centaurs. There was a sound of disappointment among the Dragons. The score was now one hundred to five.

The fourth stone appeared at the north end of the lapidem field. Another green stone, this time the size of a pebble. Everyone was surprised to have three green stones in a row, as they were supposed to be very rare. Three players from each team all tried to use "sublego", but as they were all flying on brooms and the stone was so small and far away, no one was able to hit it with the pulling spell. The Dragons were the first ones there to pick up the small green pebble.

The Dragons were desperate to score, being so far behind the Centaurs. Both baskets were flying in overlapping figure eight patterns at the south end of the field. While the Dragons got in a tight phalanx formation and flew toward the baskets, the Centaurs made a wall blocking the baskets.

As the Dragons approached the wall of Centaurs, three Centaurs charged the incoming Dragons, hoping to break apart the phalanx. No one was going to give in. The three Centaurs crashed into the Dragon in the front position of the phalanx, knocking him and the stone carrier in the center of the phalanx off their brooms. The two Dragons and one of the Centaurs fell to the ground and were not moving.

The players from both teams sitting on the sidelines reacted quickly, using "sublego" to pull their injured players to sidelines so they could send in their substitutions. During the crash, the stone carrier dropped the green pebble. By the time the substitutions were on their brooms and heading for the action at the south end of the field, the Centaurs had taken control of the stone and scored again.

Those still on the sidelines tended to their injured teammates. No one was severely hurt. The Dragon that was at the front of the phalanx had a concussion. The other Dragon and the Centaur just had gotten the wind knocked out of them. After they were sure their teammates were okay, they looked back at the action.

The baskets were floating side by side near the north end of the lapidem field. They were going from ground level to forty feet in the air, in spiral motions. There was a red stone the size of a man's fist on the ground just north of the baskets. All the players on the field were racing towards the red stone. The Centaurs had one hundred and fifty points; the Dragons had five. The red stone was worth one hundred fifty points, the Dragons could still win.

The new Centaur and the two new Dragons were the closest to the stone. All three were neck and neck racing towards the red stone. The three players were fifteen feet away from the red stone, the Centaur was in between the two Dragons. Another Dragon from farther back was able to land a pulling spell on the stone. The stone flew towards her hand, almost hitting the new Centaur in the face.

Just before the Dragon was able catch the stone, a different Centaur intercepted it with their own pulling spell. That Centaur got run into by another Dragon. The stone went flying over the Centaur's head and was caught by a Dragon. The two nearest Dragons joined him. The three began weaving in and out of the nearby Centaurs, making their way to their silver basket.

When the three were about twenty feet from the baskets, the baskets were just beginning to lift back off the ground. The stone carrier threw the red stone toward the baskets. His aim was a little off. With the speed of the basket's ascent and rate of spiral, the stone was going land directly in the gold basket, scoring for the Centaurs.

On of the new Dragons was still near the baskets and was able to see the trajectory of the stone.

"Sublego." The Dragon said. The stone flew to his hand, just in time. He caught the stone and flew unhindered to baskets. When he arrived at the top of baskets path, he waited until the baskets reached their highest altitude. He deposited the stone into the silver basket, just before they started to go back down, making sure it would score for the Dragons.

The Dragons won one hundred fifty-five points to one hundred fifty. The player that won the first ever match of lapidem for the Dragons was a young man by the name of Giarmo. He was twenty-two years old, had orange hair. He resembled Zeke in build, being six foot two inches tall, was very muscular. Giarmo ran away from his farmer parents when he was twelve. He grew up on the streets of Cortis Mundi, running a crew of misfits, orphans, and runaways. They would use sweet talking, trickery, and hustling, to get citizens to part with money or food.

"What an amazing first match of lapidem." Zeke announced as all the players arrived back at the seats where the rest of the school was watching. "It definitely adds an element of difficulty, when the baskets move, and not knowing where the stone or baskets will appear. Barmor sure outdid himself enchanting the stones and baskets to be so random. I am very pleased how it turned out, and I am sure this game will be enjoyed for generations to come."

Zeke went on to say that the next lapidem game would be in three weeks, between the Yeti and the Griffins. The next week would be the three-on-three dueling competition. The week after that would be the first magical skills competition, and Zeke and Barmor were working on a good challenge for everyone.

"Now let's all make our way back to the dining hall and celebrate the successful first game of lapidem. I bet the gnomes have some great food prepared for us." Zeke announced.

When they arrived at the dining hall the tables were piled high with food and drink. Everyone seemed to be enjoying the scholastic schedule that Zeke and Barmor had devised. Four days of hard work learning and practicing, a day fun for the whole school. A night of celebration, and two days relaxation and freedom to do as they pleased. Zeke and Barmor were very pleased at how fast everyone was picking up magic and how far they had come in a few short weeks.

Chapter Thirteen

Although Zeke was happy with how the students were progressing, he still had his doubts that they would have enough people. The threat of Prince Ostello and his army kept everyone focused. Zeke knew they could have forgone any of the fun competitions and made the students work every day, but he also knew that pushing that hard would make everyone tired. No one is at their best when they get tired and run down. Zeke also understood if you can make learning fun, people learn better. As far as Zeke was aware, they still had anonymity, therefore time on their side. It could still be years before Prince Ostello decided to attack King Sol. Or it could be tomorrow. Zeke was nervous that if it was sooner rather than later, they would not be strong enough.

Zeke wrote a letter to King Sol requesting information regarding Prince Ostello. He asked if the king had received any recent news from Mahdrin, or if the king had heard of any other magic users elsewhere in the world that Prince Ostello had not yet recruited. Zeke sent Longtail to Cortis Mundi with the letter.

He asked Barmor to insta-fly to Landis Mitigo to find out if they had heard of any other magic users from travelers coming to the port. Barmor was to spread the word that they had started a school teaching magic to anyone that wanted to learn. He would let them know that while they had already started instruction, if they knew of anyone that wanted to learn, they were encouraged to join. If they got any new students, even though they would be behind, Zeke and Barmor felt that, with this current group of students, they would catch up quickly.

Over the next week, lessons intensified. Instead of one class in the morning and practice in the afternoon, they would start having several classes each day. During their combat skills class they worked on more combinations. Instead of just one on one, they worked on engaging multiple adversaries at once, so the students could get a better understanding of being attacked from multiple places at the same time. Mevlar also pushed them harder and longer to test their stamina. Everyone did very well, even the younger kids. Not only were they doing longer attack and defense combinations at multiple targets, but they also had to integrate spell breaking to assist allies.

During their spell breaking class, they had to learn to identify different spells and charms quickly without losing focus on everything else that was going on around them. Being able to quickly identify a certain spell so they could remove that spell from an ally, while still being able to fight could save a lot of time in battle. Tundia also taught them to use magic to stitch bleeding wounds, and mend broken bones.

During that week's serums lesson, Rosten taught them to brew a pain reducing serum used to eliminate pain from a wound. He showed them how to make antibiotics to fight infection from wounds. He also taught them very complex adrenaline serum that would heighten the user's senses. Using the adrenaline serum, one's adrenaline would be increased, allowing the user to focus better, see and hear better, and have quicker reflexes. Even though serums were not allowed in the dueling competitions, it would be very useful when it came time to face Prince Ostello.

Roych, Tundia, Wimber, and Mevlar had a joint session incorporating battle strategy, attacks and defenses, and spell breaking all together with insta-flight. Being able to move and attack quickly makes them a harder target to hit. A big part of battle strategy was knowing when to be in big groups, and when to be spread apart. Another strategy Roych showed them was having certain fighters attacking while others are helping. Having the awareness to switch from attacker to healer depending on position on the field was going to play an important part in both the dueling competitions and the forthcoming battle with Ostello.

Roych showed them how to build walls and other means of cover during battle. In a true life or death situation cover could mean the difference between seeing the next sunrise or seeing the ever after. Everyone that knew how the field would be set up for the next dueling competition was keeping the secret, but this knowledge would be very important for battles to come.

Even though they had all gotten very used to using wands, and magic was easier to do with one, being able to perform magic without a wand without one would be very useful. As Dalvo had demonstrated in the first dueling competition, being disarmed, or even breaking your wand during battle was a definite possibility. Having the ability to perform magic without a wand was also going to be very useful. Another very useful talent is to do magic without actually vocalizing the words. Silent magic means you can perform spells without the enemy hearing what you said or taking the time to say it. This skill would give them a slight advantage.

The first three days of the week were very busy, with a lot of new material to focus on. The fourth day that week they had an easy magical creature lesson learning about jackelopes. Jackelopes were large hares that grew horns like deer. They stood about three and a half feet tall at the top of their heads. The horns gave them another foot. They had immense speed, almost invisible. It was said that if you were able to actually see one long enough to count the number of points on its horns, you would have great luck for the rest of your life. People often carried the foot of a jackelope for good luck. The horn of a jackelope also had special powers, one bite would ebb hunger and keep you fed for days if you were starving.

After they had finished their lesson about jackelopes in the late morning they had the rest of the day off to do whatever they pleased. Everyone decided to split into their teams for the next day's duel. The Yeti, Unicorns, and Griffins met up in the Griffins dormitory, while the Centaurs, Pheonix and Dragons occupied the Dragon's dormitory to begin discussing battle plans.

The Yeti, being led by stealth and misdirection would use their special knowledge to create distractions during the battle. They would take turns creating sound and light distractions, as well keeping the battle layered in smoke or fog so the others would have a hard time seeing. If they were not manipulating the ambiance, they would be healing or fighting as needed.

The Unicorns, being persuaded by advancing the word, would start as healers, and try to create structural cover for their allies. Fighting would come second for them. If they were not actively building structures or healing the defeated, they would fight as much as they could. Trying to distract the enemy would be as needed for the Unicorns.

The Griffins, choosing to be the most well rounded, would lead the fight. Fight, heal, fight, heal, distract. As long as the Griffins could keep the other team occupied defending themselves, the Yeti and Unicorns could keep healing, and distracting. If they started falling behind on the healing, distraction, or creating cover, the Griffins would pick up the slack with the healing and keeping the others distracted with lights and sounds.

The Centaurs, Pheonix, and Dragons had a similar plan. They would use each of the clan's strong suits. They would stay together in a group and work as a team. Their main focus was going to be defense. They would block and defend what they could and heal or break the spells on the ones that got hit with inhibiting spells.

The Centaurs, with their affinity for engineering, would form structures to use as cover to defend their position. They could set up bottle necks and pinch points to limit the number of attackers. Using walls and other structures, the Centaurs were sure they could lure the opposing team into a crossfire.

The Pheonix, being the healers, naturally would oversee triage. They would try to hang back and stay out of the fray, so they were available to heal when needed. If they could not manage taking care of the injured teammates, the Centaurs would fall back to assist.

The Dragons would be the front line. They would block spells and defend the rest of the team. They would not attack unless they saw an opening for an attack to be effective. When they did attack, they would concentrate their spells in one small group, in hopes of taking out as many at once as they could.

That night, Barmor returned from Landis Mitigo with some disturbing news. Prince Ostello had been sending out emissaries all around the world to recruit for his cause. His numbers would now be nearly a thousand strong. He was also making alliances with magical creatures as well. He had an army of centaurs that would fight for him.

Centaurs had the same intelligence as humans and could use magic as well. They were much larger, faster, and stronger than people. They could easily defeat people in physical combat. While magic would still work against centaurs, magic from humans was less effective against centaurs. Magic produced by centaurs was also stronger and more effective against humans.

"The centaurs must be getting something in return." Zeke responded when Barmor returned and told him his findings. "Centaurs despise humans. They see humans as inferior beings, like most people see them. I highly doubt that they would get involved in a human conflict."

"I completely agree." Barmor said. "Ostello must have something to offer them. I'm afraid it gets worse. Ostello knows, like we do, that anyone is capable of magic. He has also learned that people's magical power is not restricted to just one form. Just like we have learned and are teaching others to perform all sorts of magic, he is doing the exact same thing. I am afraid he also learned that using a wand makes magic easier and takes less energy. I heard merchants talking that he and his followers all carry some sort of small stick."

"Uh oh." Zeke replied after a long pause. "King Sol will not stand a chance. Nor will we for that matter. Prince Ostello is not afraid to kill those that get in his way."

"You're absolutely right", Barmor added. "He has no qualms about killing. From what I have heard, after his exile, he wants King Sol dead. Ultimately, he wants to worldwide domination."

"I hope we are able to stop him." Zeke said. "We definitely have our work cut out for us. We cannot allow him to get world domination. He will destroy mankind."

"And we lost our element of surprise." Barmor told him sadly. "I saw Mahdrin in Landis Mitigo. He was recruiting. I am sure he has told Ostello about us."

"Maybe he is just doing what he needs to do to keep Ostello's trust?" Zeke suggested.

"I do not think so." Barmor replied. "I think he was actually spying on King Sol when we saw him at Cortis Mundi. When he saw me at Landis he immediately turned and left the area, I kept seeing him lurking, trying to hide. My assumption is that he is actually one of Ostello's top hands and was sent to see what King Sol knew. We were there when he got his exile and took his assignment to spy on Ostello. If he was truly helping King Sol, I do not think that he would hide from me, he would have come and talked to me."

"That could be." Zeke said. "We will see what King Sol says. I sent Longtail to Cortis requesting an update from him. If he does not give us the same report about Ostello, then we will know Mahdrin is actually a double agent."

The more Zeke thought about it, Barmor had a point. Thinking back to when they first met Mahdrin, he was too eager to give them information about Prince Ostello. When King Sol banished him from the region and forced him to work as a spy for him, he did not think about his choice for very long, he made his decision really fast. While exile gave him the freedom to live his life as long as he never returned to Cortis Mundi. If he got caught spying on the prince, he would surely be killed. Prince Ostello was not the kind to put up with getting stabbed in the back.

If Mahdrin really was working for Prince Ostello, then maybe everything he told them was a lie. What they did know was that he was obsessed with learning more magic. He was investigating everything he could get his hands on about magic. He had learned how to use wands. And he was gathering followers, teaching them all that he had learned about magic use. What they did not know was if he was actually going to attack his father and seek world domination, but it was highly likely.

Something Zeke knew for sure was that if push came to shove, and they had to go up against Prince Ostello and his army of witches and wizards, they were greatly outnumbered. The next day's dueling competition would be a good test to see how the students have progressed. Although it would not be on the scale as an all-out battle against Ostello, it would still give him an insight into their strengths and weaknesses.

Chapter Fourteen

The next morning Longtail returned with a letter from King Sol. The letter gave further confirmation that Mahdrin was giving the king false information. The letter stated that Prince Ostello was staying in the large jungle civilization to the west and training those people how to use magic. He and his followers were staying in the largest city in the heart of the jungle, of Superbia Saltu. The letter went on to state that Ostello had not made any significant advances in his magical abilities.

Zeke wrote a rebuttal to the king. He informed him that Barmor had just returned from a trip to Landis Mitigo. Zeke told the king about the information that Barmor had learned while he was there, about how the prince was sending out recruiters. He also told him how, it was their understanding, that Ostello had figured out how to use wands as Zeke, Barmor, and their students have. Zeke implored the king to not give Mahdrin any more vital information, as he was most certainly not being truthful with King Sol.

Zeke gave the letter back to Longtail. "Can you please take this back this back to King Sol? I am sorry making you leave so soon again."

Longtail nodded his head and flapped his wings. Zeke got the feeling Longtail was saying that he was happy to help. The griffin took the letter, and jumped into the air and took off to the south again.

Zeke went down to the dining hall, where everyone was eating. The air in the dining hall was filled with excitement. Zeke could overhear students making predictions about that afternoon's duel as he walked past the tables to the front table where Barmor was already seated.

When everyone was done eating Zeke stood to address the students.

"Good morning, everyone." He started. "We have had some disturbing news last night and earlier this morning. Mahdrin, the man that King Sol had sent to spy on Prince Ostello, has been working for the prince all along. Barmor went to Landis Mitigo, to see if the island port had heard anything new. Mahdrin was there recruiting followers for Ostello. According to what vendors and sailors told him, the prince has been sending emissaries all over the world, recruiting. I had also sent Longtail to Cortis Mundi, requesting information. King Sol told us that all Mahdrin's reports told him only that Ostello is hiding in Superbia Saltu, quietly gathering followers. Merchant sailors told Barmor, he has taken over Superbia, and forced its citizens to fight for him or be his slaves. One merchant sailor told Barmor that they are practicing new magic on the slaves. Very violent and disturbing magic. Magic that can torture, dismember, or even kill their opponents."

"I do not want us to sink to their level. We will beat them by taking them out of the fight in humane ways. This life is hard enough, we are all here to learn ways to make our time easier and better for everyone. We do not want to make it harder by killing those that do not see thing as we do. You have all come a very long way from where we started. Keep practicing. Keep learning on your own as well as working hard in your lessons. After today's duel I will be leaving for a time. I will be traveling to get more knowledge myself. I will see what else I can learn about magic around the world. I may also try to get a better understanding of Prince Ostello's abilities and the size of his army."

The room erupted with dissent and fear when Zeke had finished. Most of the comments were telling Zeke not to go alone. Others were troubled by the evil and violence that Ostello was capable of. Some were asking if they could go with him. There were also people that were complaining about being so outnumbered.

"I am hoping that I will be able to find more students wanting to learn magic." Zeke added. "With any luck I can recruit more students to come to Occulta Vallem Magia. I will take the Cherry of the Sky. If I am able to get any new students, I will have a way to transport them here. Good luck everyone, in today's duel. I will see you all this afternoon at the lapidem field."

Zeke left the dining hall to more murmurs of worry and angst. He did his best to hide his nervousness, but he was sure everyone could sense it. After hearing about Ostello's recruiting activities and the size of his army, Zeke was scared. Without a lot of help, Prince Ostello's army would be unstoppable. As it was, he would easily be able to cut down anyone that opposed him. The strength of his army could stop any other known standing army, and his ruthlessness knew no bounds.

Zeke got to his room in the north annex tower and contemplated where he would start his journey, while the rest of the school prepared for the duel. He knew that King Sol would not take kindly to his return to Cortis Mundi, but he felt he had no other choice. He had to convince the king that the only way to minimize casualties was to team up. It still would not be enough, but it would be a start. First, he had to be able to talk to the king without being killed on sight.

Later that morning, Barmor joined Zeke in his office in the north annex tower. He had come to discuss their future further. Barmor voiced his disapproval of Zeke going traveling alone. Zeke assured him he would be fine; he was not going to take any unnecessary risks.

"I am not afraid of you taking risks." Barmor started. "I am afraid, trouble will find you. Where will you go? You can't go to Cortis Mundi, King Sol will kill you on sight. We are to never return, remember. Do you even know where Superbia Saltu is?"

"I will start by going to Cortis Mundi." Zeke replied. "Yes, he most assuredly will try to kill me. But he doesn't know what I can do. I will convince him that we need to take this seriously and be each other's ally. The map we found in Cortis shows where Superbia Saltu is. I need to see firsthand how big Prince Ostello's army is, and what they are capable of. We need verified information, instead of this second and third hand information we have been getting."

Barmor still disagreed. He felt that Zeke should not go by himself. He wanted to go with, or at the very least send either Ridmeus, Dalvo, or Mevlar along just in case. Zeke was confident that he would be fine. He assured Barmor that he would pick up Longtail on the way to Cortis Mundi. Longtail could come for help if anything happened.

When it was almost time for the duel to start, Zeke and Barmor took off for the field. When they arrived, all the students were lined up in the field waiting. The Red team, the Yeti, Griffins, and Unicorns were on the north end of the lapidem field. The blue team consisting of the Centaurs, Pheonix and Dragons were on south end. The field was empty except for the two teams.

When Zeke shouted go, several things started happening all at once. Walls started getting erected all through the field, creating narrow passageways that opened to large rooms. A severe thunderstorm instantly broke out, with crashing thunder, sizzling lightning, along with pouring rain, and strong winds. The red team disappeared from the north end of the field. The blue team also disappeared from the south end.

The red team instantly reappeared at the south end of the field. Alone. The blue team had already insta-flown out of their starting position. The first part of the red team's strategy had failed. They were hoping to surprise the blue team by appearing right behind them at the very beginning of the match.

The blue team, wanting to catch the red team in a crossfire, had split in half. Half of the blue team insta-flew to the west side of the field and the other half insta-flew to the east side of the field.

Neither team wanted to be caught in the middle of the field. There were too many angles and places to be attacked from. The middle of the field had walls and hallways leading in all directions. It would be too easy to get caught in a crossfire. Both teams wanted to stay to the sides or ends of the field. The walls and hallways that had been conjured were narrow, with many accesses to the ends and sides of the field. The very center of the field had a large open area.

If a team was caught in the narrow halls, they would not be able to fight at full force. The narrow halls would not allow more than two or three people to stand side by side. The team that was in the open could focus all their energy on the small hallway, having the advantage of numbers.

Knowing that the current wall formation was not going to work, they were dissolved. With the storm still raging neither team was able to see the other. With the walls gone, the blue team rejoined together on the west side of the field. The red team, staying together, and wanting to find the blue team insta-flew to the east side of the field. When they arrived, they were able to see the blue team on the west side, the blue team also saw the red team now grouped together on the east side.

The blue team attempted their divide and conquer strategy again. Half went to the north end, and half went to the south. The red team, instead of attacking, decided to go on defense. They quickly conjured walls again. The walls would only allow the ends of the field to go to the center. From the center, they conjured a narrow, winding hall to the east side. If the blue team wanted to attack, they would have to do so in the narrow hall.

Seeing that the red team had put up new walls, the blue insta-flew into the center. There they made a new plan. They would send a third of the team down the hallway. When they were ready to attack, the rest of the blue team would insta-fly to the east side where the red team was waiting.

The smaller part of the blue team started down the narrow hallway. When they got to the last turn in the hall before exiting to the east side they waited. After a moment, the large group of the blue team appeared in the open area on the east side, at the same time as the small group attacked from the hall.

The red team was not there. They had insta-flew to north end again. Seeing that the red team was not there, the blue team stayed together and walked back through the hallway to the center of the field. When they reached the center of the field, the red team changed the walls again. They closed all the hallways and made the walls taller around the center of the field, essentially trapping the blue team.

The blue team, seeing the trap closing in on them, immediately insta-flew to the north end of the field, not knowing the red team was there. Both teams were caught off guard. Shields went up on both teams. Both teams started throwing attacks, but all attacks were blocked by the shields. Someone conjured a wall between the two teams. The wall was immediately taken down by someone else, but it gave both teams a chance to regroup and focus on the battle.

When the wall was shattered, both teams knew what awaited them on the other side. The teams started attacking, blocking, and parrying. The two teams were very evenly matched. If a person fell on either side, they immediately got brought back into the fight. After several minutes of fighting both teams were still fighting at full roster. The red team started to build wall after wall trying to retreat to come up with a different plan of action.

When the red team had created enough distance, they insta-flew to the south end of the field. When they got there, they all faced toward the castle, and shouted "sublego broom", when they could use their brooms, they might have the upper hand. The blue team followed them to the south end. The battle continued, both teams standing toe to toe and facing off against one another.

When the red team's brooms started showing up, they took to the air. In the first few moments that the red team had their brooms, the blue team quickly started losing teammates. The blue team was having trouble hitting the flying red team. The red team was able to dodge the incoming attacks from the blue team, while keeping them in tight group.

The blue team had to quickly retreat and got separated. The remaining fighters started insta-flying to other places around the field and calling their own brooms. The blue team had lost half of their team by the time their brooms had arrived. It looked as if the blue team would lose. The red team was still at full strength.

The blue team was spread very thin, but as the action was mostly centered in the air above the field. The red team had not seen that there were two Pheonix on the ground healing those that had been hit by the initial arial attack. In a few moments the blue team was back at full strength, and both teams had their brooms and battle was completely in the air.

Zeke and Barmor were awe struck by the ingenuity of the teams. Using the brooms to take the fight to the air was a great strategy. Now that everyone had their brooms, the battle was no longer the two teams staying in groups but had broken up into many one on one and two on two battles taking place all around the field.

The battle being so widespread, there was very little time to see who had fallen and even less to tend to them. After several fighters had fallen from both teams, it was apparent the blue team now had the upper hand. The blue team had lost only about a third of their fighters, and the red was cut to less than half. It was at this point that Ridmeus, knowing that they were probably going to lose any way, took it upon himself to go and try to help the fallen red fighters.

The blue team did not notice that one of the star red fighters was reviving the fallen red fighters. One by one the red fighters grabbed their brooms and took to the skies. By the time that the blue team had realized that someone was reviving the fallen red team it was too late. There were less than ten blue fighters when the red team was back at full force. The blue team started falling like flies on a cold day with no chance of recovery.

When the last blue fighter went rigid and fell off his broom, the severe thunderstorm instantly cleared up and the rain stopped. The red team landed and started reviving the blue team as Zeke and Barmor exited the stands to congratulate everyone on the field.

Everyone was completely exhausted and soaked to the bone. Zeke and Barmor were speechless. That was an absolutely spectacular display of the use of magic. They waited while everyone caught their breath. While they were waiting, Zeke and Barmor conjured some chairs for the students to sit, as everyone was still on the field, and it made no sense to walk back to the stands.

"Very impressive." Zeke said when they were all seated. "You have obviously been spending a lot of time in the library learning new skills. You are all very skilled and very equally matched. I guess we are going to have to start getting creative to really push your limitations. Our next dueling competition will be the Dragons and Griffins on the red team, against the rest of the school on the blue. You will have three weeks to prepare, next week we will have our magical skills competition. The following week the Griffins will take on Yeti in the next lapidem match. As I mentioned this morning I am going to travel for some time, I hope to find more students to come join the school. I would like to find out more information about Prince Ostello, and to get a firsthand accounting of his actions. I will also be searching for others to help us against Ostello for when the time comes that we must face him. Now, if you still have enough energy to walk back to the castle, shall we go see what the gnomes have prepared for us to eat."

They all stood and started trudging back to the castle. As they left the field, the chairs that had been conjured disappeared. Excited for the feast, back at the dining hall, they all headed for the castle.

Chapter Fifteen

The next morning Zeke boarded the Cherry of the Sky just after the sun rose over the canyon walls. He would first try to talk to King Sol in person again. He knew that the king would try to kill him, but he had to try convincing him not to. Hopefully he could convince him to team up when the time came. He was sure that Longtail would know where he was but by heading straight for Cortis Mundi, he would also shorten the griffin's flight back to him.

It was the middle of the afternoon when Longtail came and landed on the main deck of the flying ship. Longtail had another response from King Sol. The letter thanked Zeke for informing the king of Mahdrin's allegiance. It went on to say that he had had his fears that Mahdrin was not sending truthful information. The king had no idea that Prince Ostello was recruiting from the farthest reaches of the world. The king stated that with the new information, he was now convinced that Prince Ostello would surely take pleasure in killing the king and queen. It also mentioned that he was considering rescinding his ban on low born magic use. The letter finished with an invitation to return to Cortis Mundi so that he could learn more about Zeke's approach to magic and its instruction.

It was late that evening when he arrived at the pyramids of Cortis Mundi. As King Sol had invited him to return, Zeke did not bother with making the ship invisible. He stopped the ship over the top of the king's palace. When Zeke could see that the king and queen had come out into the courtyard. Zeke insta-flew down and landed right in front of them.

The king, queen, and all their guards jumped when Zeke appeared in front of them. The guard closest to the king and queen stepped between them and the intruder, and the others moved into attack position around Zeke. When the king saw that it was Zeke, he waved the guards off.

"You got here fast." King Sol said.

"Well, I already on my way here." Zeke said. "I left the day after I sent Longtail with the second letter, I met him this afternoon on his way back. Even before I got your invite, I felt it was necessary to try to talk to you again, even if that meant you had your guards try to kill me."

"Oh, I see." The king replied. "I know that you gave me a short demonstration last time you were here. Let's see how you do against a king."

As soon as he said that the king flicked his hand forward, knocking Zeke flying backwards. Zeke flew backwards through the air several feet and landed on his back. Zeke responded instinctively. As soon as he hit the ground, he rolled backward onto his feet, and at the same time drew his wand from his belt inside his brown cloak. When he had gotten to his feet, he immediately insta-flew behind the king.

"Rigesco." Zeke said as he appeared behind King Sol. The king went rigid and fell on his back. Zeke went over to release the king from the stiffening spell. Before Zeke could reach the king, he broke the spell himself and jumped to his feet. The king waved his hand again. This time Zeke was ready, and with a simple flick of his wand, he blocked the attack. The king kept attacking, and Zeke either blocked, or dodged all of the attacks.

The king proved to be quite knowledgeable about magic, however, Zeke was able to easily dodge or parry each attack. After several seconds, Zeke was not even parrying any more, just dodging the attacks with insta-fly, always appearing behind the king. Zeke would not even counterattack when he dodged an attack. He would simply move and wait. When the king started to tire, Zeke started to taunt the king.

"Do you want me start getting serious now?" Zeke asked after dodging another attack. The king was not only starting to get fatigued, but the comment made him angry.

"Want me turn it up a notch." Zeke taunted again after insta-flying behind the king another time. This time Zeke hit King Sol with the freezing spell, turning him to ice. Zeke immediately hit the king with a pushing spell. When he hit the ground, the ice shattered. Zeke then used the jelly limb spell. The king could not get up. Zeke approached King Sol laying on the ground.

"What?" Zeke asked Sol when he was standing over him. "You can't break yourself free of this one, are you getting too tired? Do you want me to release you?"

King Sol was completely limp. He could not even nod his head to inform Zeke that he wished to be released. Zeke removed the jelly limb spell. The king was short of breath as he stood up.

"Wow." King Sol said between gasps. "That is exactly why I have not allowed peasants to learn magic. We are not used to having to defend against it. I had no idea you were that good. You actually think that my son is capable of that?"

"Oh, for sure he is." Zeke answered. "I have sixty-five students that can do that. He has thousands of followers that can. I have only been advancing my magic for a few months. He has been learning about it for twenty years. Other than him and his followers, I am only aware of me and my school that can do it, as it is, we do not stand a chance when he actually starts his rise to power. If I do not find help before then, it will be too late. If no one else learns about magic, he and his army will kill or enslave the entire world."

"I was always afraid if the peasants learned magic and felt I was not a good leader, they would revolt." King Sol said. "Now I am certain, it will be my son that will take me out. Are you certain that everyone has the ability to learn magic?"

"Yes." Zeke answered. "There are two young children, five and seven, in my school, and are learning just as fast as the adults."

"I will start allowing my citizens to learn magic." The king said after a long pause. "Hopefully, when he realizes that my realm, with its two million citizens, are learning magic, he will decide not to attack."

"We can only hope." Zeke replied. "But I have my doubts. My guess is that when he finds out that you are now not only allowing magic, but actively teaching it, it will enrage him further. That's what led to his banishment in the first place, after all. He wanted to teach the peasants, and you forbade it. The realm of Superbia Saltu also has nearly a million people, and he has already taken control of the whole realm. He will ramp up his recruiting efforts, start teaching more of his citizen, unless he already has."

"I would like to see what his army looks like in person." King Sol stated.

"I do as well." Zeke said. "In fact, that is my next stop. After I leave here, I am going to go there. I will stay on my ship, with it hidden from sight, so I can watch without being seen. If Mahdrin is not there, I may enter the city, posing as a traveler. If Mahdrin is there I will not be able to, he knows me. Would you care to join me?"

"May I?" Sol asked. "That would be great."

"Absolutely." Zeke replied enthusiastically. "We can leave first thing in the morning."

King Sol had a guard ring the city bells, signaling the citizens to join in the city square outside of the palace walls. When the square was full, the king told his people that he had learned of further information involving Prince Ostello. He would start having his Royal Guard and Royal servants, who had magical knowledge, start teaching the magical arts. He wanted everyone prepared to stand up against Ostello and his army when they attacked. Those that wanted to learn more on their own were allowed access to the Royal archives. If there were others that wanted a more hands on, and scholarly approach were encouraged to consider going with Zeke to Occulta Vallem Magia.

The next morning, at daylight, Zeke and King Sol insta-flew to the deck of the Cherry of the Sky where Longtail was waiting. Once they landed, Zeke got the ship moving toward Superbia Saltu. Once the ship was moving in the right direction Zeke sat next to Longtail and nonchalantly stroked the griffin's neck feathers.

"What do we do now?" Sol asked.

"Now we wait." Zeke answered. "It took us four days to get here, from Landis Mitigo, I surmise it will take us the better part of six days to reach Superbia."

"How did you become so powerful?" Sol asked after a few moments of silence. "I have the power to utilize five different magical arts, you seem to have mastered them all."

Zeke thought for a few moments before answering. "I am by no means a master but, in my research, I have found that some people are naturally gifted in different arts. Some people are not naturally gifted at any. That being said, anyone can learn any magical art. My assumption is that you are a natural when it comes to your five arts. However, being the king, and whether you don't have the time or interest, and pardon my saying, your naivety of magic, never took the time to learn more."

"No offense taken." Sol replied. "When I was young, and my father was still king, I was like you, always wanting to learn more. Being the prince, I always had other things on my mind. I was never able to pick up any other art. After some time of trying my hand at other aspects of magic and not succeeding. I assumed you could only learn certain things. Then when my own son started spending every waking moment in the library, and shirking his royal responsibilities, I became annoyed. I thought he needed to focus more on his duties, like I had done. I had no idea that what he had learned down there would lead to where he is now. I will admit I did not try to gain all knowledge, just what I thought was useful or interesting."

"What all can you do?" Zeke asked.

"I can pick up anything I want and move wherever I need it to go." Sol started. "I can manipulate fire however I see fit. I can sense magic use and users. I can disappear from here and reappear wherever I want, we call it jump. I can also break any magic that is applied to me, that one is my weakest skill, I lose my skill in that when I run out of energy, as you saw yesterday. How did you learn to do all that you can do?"

"Well, it started when I was a kid." Zeke answered. "My family and I were attacked by a short-faced bear. After the bear killed my parents, it turned on me. I remember wanting to stop the bear however I could. I was so mad, and sad, I actually wished it would start on fire. And it did. I had odd things happen before that, and it was not until I was eleven that I realized that weird things happened because I was extremely emotional. Eventually, I was able to learn that a word or words describing what I wanted to do was also important. I did not really start figuring out how to do it whenever I wanted until a few years ago but it was always simple stuff like starting a fire or building a bridge. Then a few months ago, I found out using an ash stick in my hand helped a lot, that is when I met and rescued Longtail. That is also when I realized that I needed something more for my wand. After I rescued him, he gave me a wing feather that I used for a core. Since then, I have been wanting to learn all that I could. When we were in your archive, Barmor and I, actually copied all of your books. I found out how to copy the books from one of your books. When we built our school, we made books out of trees, then copied what we had saved on our wands into those books. Most of what I have learned actually came from your archives."

"So, you're telling me," Sol inquired. "You have come this far basically in a few months."

"Yes, until I got to your archives." Zeke answered. "It was mostly intuition, and a lot of trial and error."

"Would you be willing to teach me?" Sol asked. "We do have some time together."

"Yes, I can teach you." Zeke answered. "Yeah, we will be spending some time together. I only hope that when it comes time to fight, you will allow us to team up and fight together, to help ensure that Prince Ostello is stopped. We do not wish to kill anyone. It is my hope that we can talk some sense into him or build a prison to hold him and his followers."

"I like the idea of a prison." Sol replied. "I will think about teaming up. Our destiny cannot be changed has been my family's belief for generations."

"Maybe it is your destiny to be helped by a friend." Zeke retorted. With that Sol stood and nodded signifying that subject was over. Zeke also stood, "Shall we get started then?"

Zeke began teaching King Sol. Sol was curious about wands. Zeke, planning for a situation similar to this, had brought many samples of different types of wood. Zeke, having read about King Sol and his family from books in his own archive, knew that Sol always carried the horn of a unicorn on his person. The unicorn was a symbol of his family.

King Sol started trying different types of wood. When he picked up a piece of cedar, his eyes lit up. He told Zeke that it felt as though the stick was breathing. Zeke explained to him how to flatten the piece of cedar into a thin film and suggested using his unicorn horn for a core. King Sol was able to get some shavings from the unicorn horn and constructed his wand.

The finished product was an elegant looking brown wand. Sol's wand was about twelve inches long ,and had a spiral. The wand had a large grip to accommodate King Sol's big hands. He gripped his new wand and gasped.

"Now, not only is breathing, but it feels as though its breathing with me." King Sol said.

"That is awesome." Zeke congratulated the king. "Are you ready to learn more?"

Zeke started showing him how to cast different types of magic that he had learned how to do. Now that Sol had the mindset that he could learn new magic, and a good teacher, he was a natural. It did not take long for him to become proficient. The king and Zeke spent most of their time practicing and dueling. The king also taught a few things to Zeke that he had not known.

The king was able to teach Zeke how to break free from spells. By concentrating on the effects of the spell and using the word "novisa" he could break free from most spells. King Sol was getting stronger and was able to last longer each day before he started getting tired.

During the evenings when they were relaxing, Zeke would tell King Sol about the activities at the school. They talked about the game, lapidem, that Barmor had come up with. They discussed the dueling competitions and the upcoming magical skills contest. Zeke told Sol he wished he could be there to watch the first one that would take place the next day. He was curious what kind of challenges Barmor had come up with.

King Sol was also curious about the school and castle that Zeke and Barmor had designed. He suggested using insta-fly to travel back to Occulta Vallem. Zeke wondered if they could let the ship continue flying without them being on it. They were still probably two days from reaching Superbia Saltu. He was also worried about being able to land back on the ship as it was moving.

"We can stop the ship for a while." King Sol suggested. "Then we can jump to the castle, you can show me around. We can watch your contest then jump back to the ship."

"Yes. That would work." Zeke agreed. "Just one problem. You have never been to the valley. Even if I describe it to you, you will have a hard time picturing yourself there to jump."

"That's easy." King Sol said. "We jump together. You have been there. You hold onto me and picture us both being there. We do it all the time."

The next day Zeke and King Sol had a good dueling practice in the morning. When it was time to jump to Occulta Vallem Magia, Zeke waved his wand and folded the ship's sails. Zeke grabbed King Sol by the shoulder and held onto the end of Longtail's wing. He pictured the three of them standing in front of the castle, and pictured a rope connecting them to there, and closed his eyes and relaxed.

Chapter Sixteen

When he opened his eyes, all three were standing in front of the castle. King Sol was staring in amazement at the massive castle carved into the cliff side. Zeke looked at Longtail. The large brown griffin narrowed his eyes and nipped at Zeke. Telling him he did not like that feeling. Longtail launched himself into the air and flew off.

"Apparently," Zeke said, "He is not a fan of insta-flight or jumping as you call it."

"I'd say not." King Sol answered.

Students came up questioning why Zeke had returned so soon, and where the Cherry of the Sky was. Zeke explained that they were just there for the skills contest, and King Sol wanted to see the castle. After the contest they would return to the ship and continue their journey.

Zeke showed King Sol around. Sol mostly just listened to Zeke explaining how they had built the castle and followed throughout the castle and valley. When it was nearly time for the contest to start, they all made their way to the lapidem field.

Barmor had constructed a large maze in the field. The maze was filled with many traps that the students would have to avoid or get through. There were also several very complicated challenges that the clans would have to work together to get past. The clans would all go one at a time. The clan that completed the course with the least casualties, and in the shortest time would win. There were multiple ways to get from one big puzzle to the next. Those that were not competing could see down into the maze from the stands around the field.

The Yeti went first. They started down a passage on the left from the starting point. As they got a short way down the passage, the entire passage was enveloped in a thick darkness. The students all held up their wands that were now each emitting a bright light. They came to a tee in the maze and could either go left or right. The hall to left went a short distance then turned right. The hall on their right went to an intersection which they could not see past.

The Yeti decided to go left. After they made the right at the end of the hall, the next hall was bathed in a blindingly bright light. Everyone had to close their eyes. Some one used a spell to fill the hallway with fog. The fog blocked enough of the light they could see the end of the hall made another right turn. When they turned right the hall went through another intersection and with another right at the end.

The left side of the intersection was blocked by a large stone door. As soon as the Yeti clan arrived at the stone door a black cloud formed above the maze, so the spectators could not see what was happening. The door had a large circle carved into it that was divided into ten pie slices. The Yeti tried several different spells to move the rock. They all worked together to try to lift it, push it, pull it, and slide it left or right. They tried to carve it away, they tried to reduce it to rubble. They tried to get it to swing open. There was nothing that they tried that had any effect on the stone.

After several minutes, one of the students saw that each of the ten pieces of the circle had a line pointing to the center of the circle. Originally, they had all thought the lines were just marks on the stone. The students all took out their wands and put them on the lines, pointing toward the center of the circle. When the last wand was placed on a line, the stone slowly sank into the ground.

As the stone slid into the ground, the black cloud disappeared, and the spectators could see what was happening again. In front of the Yeti clan stood six hallways. Again, they chose the hallway on the left. As they entered the hall a strong wind was blowing down the hall from the far end. They could not enter the hall without being blown backwards. They conjured a large flat stone and used the pushing spell, "trudo" against the stone. They were able to block the wind with the stone and push it. They then could follow the stone to the other end of the hall. When they reached the end of the hall, they turned right into another hall that connected the six halls. When they stepped out of the windy hall, it collapsed and disappeared, leaving only the other five remaining.

There was a single hall going forward off of the connecting hall. It was blocked by another stone. Again, as they approached the stone a dark cloud blocked the viewers from witnessing how to get past the stone door. As the dark cloud settled in, a table appeared with ten different serums on it. Ten different shelves appeared on the stone door, with a different symbol above each shelf.

The symbols were stick drawings of people. One of the stick drawings was laughing. One with x's over eyes. Another one with large eyes. One of the drawings appeared to have a wound with an x on it. Still another one had the same wound with a thick circle around it with an x. One of the stick drawings had big arms and legs, one had appeared to have eyes on the back of its head. There was one that appeared to be running fast. One of the pictures depicted a person walking silently. The last one had a person with an x through the whole person.

They first had to decipher what the picture drawings meant. There were some that seemed quite straightforward. There were other drawings that were harder to figure out. The drawing of the person laughing was pretty obvious, one of the serums had to be a laughing serum. The x's for eyes also did not take much figuring out, a blinding serum. The large eyes, the yeti were sure was sight enhancing serum. The wound with the x could be pain, while the wound with the circle could mean an infection. The drawing depicting the large arms and legs could be describing a strengthening serum. The students were confused by the illustration of eyes on the back of the head, possibly an adrenaline serum. The next two were also quite obvious, a speed serum and silencing serum. The last was also obvious, a death serum.

They had to identify which of the serums matched the correct shelf. They knew the healing serum and antibiotic serum were both clear. The laughing serum, blinding serum, and dragon vision were green. Strength, speed, and the adrenaline serums were all blue. They were sure the person with the x was meant to depict the killing serum, which none of them had studied yet, nor had they learned about silencing serum.

Three of the serums on the table were clear, three green serums, three blue ones, and a black one. The three green and blue serums they could sample to see what they were. Two of the clear serums would be healing and antibiotics. The remaining clear serum could be silencing, or it could kill you. The black serum looked scary, but it would make sense that a killing serum would be clear to hide it in someone's drink.

By conjuring a flower, they were able figure out which one of the clear serums was the death serum. After that the rest of the serums were easy to figure out. When the last serum was placed on its proper shelf, the table disappeared, and the stone slid to the left.

Beyond the stone was a raging river, and no bridge. They instinctively conjured a bridge. As soon as they attempted to make a bridge, the river swelled and washed away the bridge. Then one of them used insta-fly to get across the river and landed in the same spot that they had just left. Nothing they tried worked, they could not get across the river. When they tried to turn it to ice and walk across, the ice would just float away. If they tried to touch the water and swim across it would turn to a wall of fire.

They were so busy trying to get across they had not noticed that the stone had slid back blocking the entrance. When they turned around and saw the stone, it had the circle divided into ten pieces, like the first one. Each of the pieces was numbered and had a different set of lines in each piece. After some speculation they realized that the lines resembled different wand movements for spells. They all picked a piece of the circle and performed the corresponding spell at the same time.

They noticed that the numbers in the pieces of the circle were not in order. They tried performing the spells in order one after another. Still nothing happened. Then they tried following the circle in both directions, again the stone did not move. They also tried casting in order again, this time the youngest member started and as the numbers went up so did the age of the caster. The stone slid to the left again. They were on the other side of the river and there was a single hallway leading forward, out of the maze. Expecting more surprises, they slowly followed the hall. As they exited the stone doorway and started down the hallway, the dark cloud disappeared again.

There were no more surprises to exit the maze. As they exited everyone watching started cheering. As they got back to the stands everyone was asking about what was going on when the dark cloud blocked the maze. Barmor told them not to answer, they are not supposed to know until they get there. The Yeti clan completed the tasks in thirty-six minutes. Next to tackle the contest was the Centaurs.

The Centaurs chose the middle hallway to start. Halfway down that hallway they were surrounded by fire. The fire was quickly put out with water from several of the wands. They continued straight through the intersection at the end of the hall and started down the next hall. They could see the first stone door ahead of them. They started going a little faster when all of a sudden, the dirt and stone started swirling in a massive tornado. The dirt and stone started settling on the ground, piling up around the Centaurs. Several of them cast the stopping spell, "subsisto", to stop the dirt and stone from swirling around. They all scrambled out of the hall, and stopped in front of the first stone door, as the dark cloud settled in.

The Centaurs figured out the secret to placing their wands on the stone to open the first stone door. Now, they faced the five halls that all met at the second door. The Centaurs chose the middle hall again. When they started down the hall everything went dark and there was an invisible force stopping them from going more than a few feet into the hall. Looking around the saw a light coming out of the darkness about twenty feet off the ground.

They conjured stone steps up to the light. The light was a small narrow tunnel. As they started through the tunnel, it started closing in behind them. They were almost running through the tunnel when the floor suddenly gave way to a slide. They all fell down the slide and crashed into a pile in front of the second door.

The door where they had to identify the serums stumped the Centaurs for a while. When they did finally get past the serums and got to the river, like the Yeti, they did not hear the stone close again behind them. When they did finally see the door behind them and realize that they were not to actually cross the river. It also took them several tries to figure out the age correlation for the numbers on the third door.

They exited and walked to the stands. The Centaurs completed the tasks in thirty-two minutes, just a little faster than the Yeti. The Pheonix went third. The first two hazard hallways, the Pheonix took both right-side halls. The first hall confounded them and made them sleepy. When they entered the hall, they lost all sense of direction, or what they were even supposed to be doing. All they wanted to do was lay down and take a nap. Luckily there were two older students that were less affected than the others and were able to keep them motivated to continue.

The second hazard hall contained two giant scorpions. The scorpions were twenty feet long, had three-foot-long stingers, and spat acid. By the time the Pheonix were able to get their shields up, two of the students had been stabbed with stingers, and one younger kid had been hit by acid. The same two students quickly turned the two scorpions to stone. They grabbed their injured and ran past the scorpions and out of the hall. When they got out of danger, they healed their injured.

At the first door, the Pheonix quickly figured out how to place their wands on the stone to get the door to open. They arrived at the four remaining long halls. They chose the hall that was just to left of the closed hall that the Centaurs had taken. When they entered the hall, they were taken over by pleasure. They did not want to leave the hall. They all sat down enjoying the feeling, after a few minutes the walls of the hall started closing in on them. One of the students that was not affected by the euphoria hall was the only one to realize they were stuck in a trap and was able to shake off the pleasurable feeling. He was able to get everyone to reluctantly keep moving. When they exited the hall and faced the second door, and feeling of euphoria left them.

They were able to quickly get past the serum door. They had spent a lot of time studying serums on their own. They were able to pick the serums by using appearance and smell. They were held up at the river for quite a long time. When they had realized that the door had closed behind them, they really got puzzled. It was a long time before they figured out the spells had to be cast youngest to oldest. They exited and returned to the stands. Their delays had cost them a lot of time. They accomplished the tasks in thirty-two minutes plus three minutes of penalty for suffering injuries, for a total of thirty-five minutes.

The Unicorns were the next clan to tackle the tasks. After watching those that had already gone, they knew what hazards awaited them on the first two halls. They chose to follow the same path that the Yeti had taken. Going through the darkness, then blinding light seemed the quickest and safest.

They blazed right through the first two halls, and in just a few minutes were at the first door. They quickly figured out that they needed to place their wands on the stone to get it to sink open. They took the last remaining hall on the left after the first door.

When they got to the hall a torrential flood came, boiling down the hall and washing them out of the hall. They conjured steppingstones that were not washing away. They traversed to the far end of the hall. The Unicorns had a hard time figuring out the pictures describing the serums. They also had a hard time identifying the serums. They lost most of the lead that they had gained in the first sections trying to get through the serum door.

When they had reached the river, it did not take them long to figure out that they were not to cross the river. So, they turned around and saw the door had closed behind them. The age aspect of the door caught them off guard for a few minutes. Ultimately, they made their way back through the third door quicker than the previous three teams. When they returned to the stands, Zeke announced that they had completed the tasks in twenty-one minutes, and they currently had the lead.

Griffins were next to prove themselves. They also stayed to the left for the first two halls. They ran through the darkness, and blinding light. They easily knew what the circle and lines meant, getting through the first door quicker than anyone before. There were two remaining long halls leading to the second door, the Griffins chose the farthest door on the right. When they got a short distance into the hall, the floor disappeared beneath them. They fell into a deep, steep, and dark ravine. As they all began picking themselves up off the bottom of the ravine, the walls started closing in on them. If they did not react fast, they would be swallowed up. They quickly conjured a stairway that wound its way up the far wall.

They reached the top of the stairs and the second door just as the hall was completely sealed off. They identified the serums by smell and color. As they approached the river, one student was looking back when the door closed them. They immediately studied the door. They deciphered the wand movements right away; however, it was several minutes before they thought to go by age.

They got back to the stands and Zeke and Barmor congratulated them on the record time so far of eighteen minutes. The Dragons went and prepared for their turn. As soon as Zeke shouted begin, the Dragons jumped to the first door, bypassing the first two halls. The rest of the students all murmured to themselves about not thinking about that. When the Dragons reached the first door the dark cloud did not appear over the field. Since everyone else had already gone, there was no reason to cover what the task was.

The Dragons tried every form of magic that they could think of to destroy or move the stone door. It was a long time before they realized that they simply had to put all of their wands in the circle. They also had a hard time getting all of their members squeezed in next to the door because there were so many of them.

When they made it through the door, they jumped to the next door again. The serums were a breeze. When they got through the door and were attempting to get across the river. They had tried everything they could do to try to get across, to no avail. They attempted to get across for a long time when someone noticed that the door had the same circle as the first did on it. It was only a matter of minutes before they tried casting the different spells ascending in age.

They returned to the stands cheering and smiling knowing that they had the fastest time. When they got back and sat down. Zeke stood and began to congratulate them.

"Great job everyone." Zeke said enthusiastically. "I commend you all for your use of magic and knowledge and courage in changing situations. The Dragons had the fastest time of nine minutes, however they are penalized five minutes for each time they jumped to next door, for a total of nineteen minutes. You acted creatively by using insta-fly but you missed the opportunity to gain more practice and grow your skills. Making the Griffins the winner with eighteen minutes and are awarded the fifty points for being the fastest."

"Thank you, Barmor, for designing the first skills contest. King Sol and I will be leaving again shortly. We are going to Superbia Saltu to get some more information about Prince Ostello. We are getting different reports, and we could all benefit from having some facts set straight. Again, great job, everyone. Keep up the good work."

King Sol felt the need to stand and tell everyone good job as well. He was excited to see how far everyone had come and told them that he had dropped his law regarding low born magic use and would start teaching his citizens. He told them that when they had finished school, they would be allowed to return to Cortis Mundi. He and Zeke gave their farewells and left back toward the castle. Zeke gave King Sol a quick tour of the castle. When they finished and exited the castle, Longtail met them at the bottom of the steps to the castle.

"I am sorry that I did not warn you that it feels weird." Zeke told the griffin apologetically. "Are you ready to go again?"

Longtail gave a chirp and shook his head. Which meant, no he was not ready, but get it over with. Zeke grabbed King Sol and Longtail and jumped back to Cherry of the Sky.

Chapter Seventeen

They all arrived back at the floating ship, Longtail threw his head again and stormed off towards the bow. Zeke opened the sails, and they got underway heading to the west once more. With any luck by, tomorrow night they would be in Superbia.

"You and Longtail have a very special bond." King Sol commented. "I have not known many people to tame such an exotic animal."

"Oh, he is not tamed," Zeke answered. "but I thank you. I rescued him from a hunter's net about a month before we first came to Cortis. Yes, it is a special bond, I believe it is called imprinting. Some creatures can imprint on you if they feel particularly connected to you."

"Yes, I have seen it before, but not very often." Sol added. "Imprinting is very rare. It could have been a different person, a different griffin, or even have both of you and even just one detail changed, and it may not have happened. It is slightly more common in canine and equine species, but neither felines, nor raptors are very inclined to imprinting. I have never heard of anyone imprinting a griffin. He seems to understand you."

"Yeah, he can understand me." Zeke answered. "I am learning to understand him. Now that he has imprinted on me, those close to me will also be like family to him. I do not know if he would allow any of my students to ride on him, but he will allow me to ride. He may possibly allow Barmor to get on, but I think it would depend on the situation."

There was a screech from the bow. "Let me rephrase that." Zeke corrected. "He would allow Barmor to ride. If I told him that a student needed to ride, he would do it but under protest."

"You got all of that from a little screech?" Sol asked.

"I hear, or feel maybe, what he says in my head or in my soul." Zeke answered. "I am not really sure how it works."

With that Longtail came over, laid down next to Zeke and rested his head on Zeke's leg. Zeke nonchalantly began petting him, while continuing his life story with Sol. Zeke went on to tell Sol how he had flown Longtail to Landis Mitigo, where he met Barmor, and about their early days together, that were filled with a lot of trial and error. They also learned a lot about magic, with no formal training or manuals. They were completely self-taught, until they started reading from Sol's archives.

After it started to get dark, conversation slowed down, as they began to stare at the stars. With the ship being so high in the air, the stars looked close enough that they could reach out and touch them. Although Zeke had spent several days on the ship, he had not noticed how big and bright the stars appeared, because he had usually gone to sleep around dark. The stars and moon were so bright that they could see the deck of the ship perfectly without candles or lights from their wands.

They finally turned in for bed late that night after marveling at the stars. There was even a very active meteor shower, that they got to watch for several hours. The next day they continued their dueling practice. King Sol was proving himself a quick learner and formidable opponent. The morning after that, when they woke up, they were able to see a land mass in the distance.

Around midday they were over the land, and they could see a large jungle. Down in the jungle below them, they could see many small villages, there was even a road system. By the end of the day, they were able to see the large city of Superbia Saltu, and its massive step pyramid. Zeke turned the ship invisible, so that no one saw the flying ship. They arrived at the city just a little after dark. Zeke brought the ship to a halt above the center of the city close to the pyramid.

The next morning, Superbia started their day by half of the citizens gathering in a large city square, where Ostello and his Royal Guard led a large magic lesson. The citizens broke off into many smaller groups. Each of the small groups started in a different area of the square learning magical concepts that were taught by a few of the guards. Each group would practice what they learned on slaves. After some practice the groups would rotate to the next set of guards.

The magic that Ostello and his guards were teaching was all violent and dark. The citizens were taught to maim and torture. They were learning how to cause extreme pain, mental anguish, and even how to control the victim. They were learning how to make their opponent do whatever the caster wanted. They were even taught how to kill their opponent. At midday the gathering broke off and the citizens went back to their daily duties.

After a short break, Ostello and his guards gathered back in the square with the other half of citizens from the city. That afternoon, Mahdrin returned from his scouting journey. He reported to Prince Ostello, probably telling him about seeing Barmor in Landis Mitigo.

When he saw Mahdrin, King Sol wanted to attack him from the ship. Zeke had to convince him that that would be a bad idea. If he did, the prince and his followers would know Zeke and King Sol were there, and they would probably not be able to escape in time. This was a fact-finding mission. Reluctantly, the king agreed.

That night, Prince Ostello used magic to make his voice travel through the whole city. He stood on the steps that led to the entrance of the pyramid and addressed the citizens. His voice carried in every direction, reaching deep into the jungle. Zeke and King Sol were able to hear ever word, as if Prince Ostello was standing right in front of them.

"We need to start working harder. We need to continue recruiting wherever we can. I have learned my father has started allowing peasants to learn and practice magic at some school somewhere. That school is still small, but they are learning a wide range of magic, and spend a lot of time playing games. I am not too worried about them; we have the numbers to easily take them out. When the time is right, we will attack them first. Then their survivors will join our ranks. Then we will move to attacking my father, after he is taken care of the rest of the world will bow to us. I do not know where the school is, but we have scouts searching for it. By the time the scouts find it, we will be ready to begin our attack. We think that his school way north by the ice wall somewhere. Now get to bed. We will continue working tomorrow. You are still under curfew."

"Wow." Zeke said to King Sol when Prince Ostello had finished his speech. "He truly does want world domination."

"That is not my son." The king answered sharply. "He has been corrupted by his lust for power and knowledge. Yes, it does appear he is seeking world domination. His ruling style, ruling by fear will not last. It will cause dissent in his peasants. I may be the King. In my time, and watching my father, I have learned if your people are not happy, they will not respect you. When enough of them are not happy they will start to revolt. I am guessing there are thousands of people in this city who only do what Ostello says out of fear, especially because he has recently taken over. Now that they are learning magic, their confidence and numbers will grow. He will have a revolution. And I just want to add, he is no prince!"

"Do you think his people are not happy?" Zeke asked. "They all seemed happy to be learning magic. He may have just recently taken over the region, and he rules by fear, however, he is teaching them magic and promises them more knowledge and power. I do see you point though, it may not happen soon, but at some point, maybe after he has complete control, there will be a revolution."

"They are happy to learn magic." Sol replied. "Only so that they can use it against him in the future. I would be willing to bet there are people talking about fighting back against him at this very moment."

As he said that, Zeke looked at Longtail and nodded. The large griffin jumped up and launched himself off of the invisible floating ship.

"What is his doing?" Sol asked.

"He is going to go make a few passes over the city." Zeke answered. "If you are right, he might be able to hear the people talking about it, griffins have excellent hearing. If they are not happy, maybe they can join, you or us. Maybe they would be willing to by our spies."

"Oh, okay. That is a good idea." King Sol agreed. "I cannot go down there, if Ostello or any of my former Royal Guards see me they will instantly recognize me. You could have a look around though."

"I am sure Mahdrin told them all about me." Zeke said. "I am an outsider. I am sure they will recognize me as not part of the city as well."

They watched the sun go down and the moon come up as they were waiting for Longtail to return. It was a couple hours after dark when he had returned. When Longtail returned, he landed on the invisible deck with a screech.

Longtail walked over to Zeke and flapped his wings with a click of beak and tapped his talons on the deck. Zeke told King Sol that there were small groups that seemed to be talking about leaving Superbia, but the chatter all seemed to be distant, like they were underground. Zeke wondered aloud if maybe the citizens had made underground tunnels to meet in secret.

"We have to find those underground tunnels." King Sol said. "If we can find those, we can get more information, or maybe get them to leave with us. We could jump down there and try to find those meetings."

"No, I think using insta-fly would be a mistake." Zeke replied. "I am sure the prince has spotters that are magic sensors all over the city to pick up on anyone using magic, or breaking curfew. I have a better idea. We will land downstream on that large river and sail up the river tomorrow into the city. If we are just travelers, we can chat up the citizens and maybe find out where these meetings are. If you lose the royal threads and the crown, change your hair, and shave the beard off, you would not be as recognizable."

"The clothes, crown, and hair won't be a problem." King Sol said. "We are not touching the beard."

Zeke conjured some basic brown pants and a white shirt. He then waived his wand and King Sol's red hair and beard turned black. The king changed out of his royal robes and took his crown off. Zeke steered the ship out of the city and headed for an uninhabited section of the river.

When he set the ship down on the river, he made the ship visible again. They waited until the next morning before sailing up the river to Superbia Saltu. When they arrived at the city port around midmorning they were welcomed as simple travelers traveling upriver to see what goods they could trade for.

As they wandered through the market, Zeke and King Sol chatted with the local venders. They tried to keep their inquisitions as general as they could, asking about the city and its culture. They asked how the citizens felt about Prince Ostello. Most people seemed to like him, but there were some that acted like they liked the prince; however, Zeke could tell that they really did not care for him or his style of ruling but were too afraid to talk about it. It took them most of the morning to finally find someone willing to openly express their distaste for Prince Ostello.

The vender told Zeke and Sol that while he liked to learn magic, he knew that the prince was a very evil person that would not hesitate to do horrible things to get complete power of the world. When Zeke asked if there were any others that felt the same, the vender said that there were several.

They called themselves the Guardians. They liked to think they guarded the city and mankind against those that wanted to destroy their peace and freedom. The Guardians had underground tunnels where they would gather in small groups, planning to overthrow the prince. Their tunnels also led deep into the jungle where the Guardians could go and practice and learn more about magic on their own.

With the vendor being so open about the Guardians and their distaste for Ostello, Zeke felt a little more comfortable telling him who he was. "Do you know much about that school up north?" Zeke asked the vender.

"Only what Ostello has told us." The vender answered. "That they want to stop Ostello from taking over the world and take it over for themselves. Apparently, they are weak, and have very few numbers. Their form of magic is simple theater tricks compared to what we can do. Just a bunch of kids with no real direction. What do you know?"

"I hope Ostello keeps telling you that we are a bunch of weak kids." Zeke chuckled in response. "It will make him, and his followers underestimate us. I am the one who started the school. While, yes, we have some young kids. We also have several of King Sol's former Royal Guards. My students are very skilled and powerful. We do not aim to kill, nor do we want to take over the world. We want to learn all aspects of magic. Our goal is stop evil and help all of mankind progress in peace."

"If you think you are so good, you should come to our meeting tonight we will see how you fair against us." The vender told Zeke. The vender told Zeke and King Sol how to get to where the meeting would be, after dark that night. Zeke said they would be there.

Zeke and King Sol returned to the ship and sailed further upriver closer to where the vender had told them the meeting would be. When night fell, they left the ship and walked through the jungle to where the vendor told them they would find the Guardians.

As they walked through the jungle, they could hear voices. They followed the voices, after a few minutes they were able to see lights emanating from a clearing further ahead. When they reached the clearing, there were two hundred people there practicing different magic. Some one on one, some in small groups.

Zeke and King Sol entered the clearing and all activity stopped. All two hundred people turned and faced them, ready to attack the newcomers. Zeke and Sol drew their wands, and so did the two hundred others. Zeke's suspicions had been confirmed, Prince Ostello had learned, and was teaching how to use wands as well. The vender pushed his way through the crowd to the front.

"Wait. Wait, I told them to come." The vender spoke and pointed to Zeke. "He is the one that started the school up north."

Everyone relaxed. The vender continued, and pointed at King Sol, "That is King Sol from Cortis Mundi. Some of you do not know who I am. My name is Grambine, I was once a high council to the former Dux Saltu before Prince Ostello came in and killed him."

"What makes you think that he is King Sol?" Zeke asked.

"Grambine chuckled. "You can change the clothes and the hair, but that face definitely belongs to man that Ostello loathes so absolutely. The only man that is known to command an army large enough to possibly stop Ostello's tyranny."

Zeke and Sol smiled, Grambine was good. He was obviously very smart. He used to serve the former leader of the jungle region. He knew that the man standing in front of him was King Sol. Zeke was trusting this man more and more. As Grambine was talking everyone relaxed more and began putting their wands away.

"I invited them here to show us what they can actually do." Grambine added. "According to Ostello, Zekious and his school of young soft kids is nothing to be feared. I believe that we can learn a lot from them, and we will need to work together to stop the evils that are coming."

When he finished talking, he suddenly attacked Zeke with a wave of his wand and a painful looking spell. Zeke was lucky that he was paying attention and was able to jump out of the way using insta-fly. Zeke landed behind Grambine, and used the disarming spell, "furatelum". Grambine's wand flew out of his hand and was caught by Zeke.

"Hahaha." Grambine laughed. "You think I actually need my wand to do magic. You are sorely mistaken."

Grambine thrust his hand out and closed his fist. Whatever attack he was trying to use on Zeke was blocked and deflected upward and out of the clearing. Zeke instantly started stringing spells together in rapid succession, as he walked forward. He kept Grambine focusing on blocking the attack and moving backward. King Sol was cheering on Zeke, telling him to keep toying with Grambine until he got tired.

Zeke jumped behind Grambine again, when Grambine finally realized where Zeke had disappeared to, he turned toward him. Zeke disappeared again. Zeke kept jumping behind Grambine until he was starting to get angry and tired. After several seconds, Zeke decided to start attacking and hit his adversary with "gelata", turning his limbs into jelly.

"It's easy to not get hit by attacks if you are always behind your opponent." Grambine said when Zeke released the spell helped Grambine up.

"Okay, you are not satisfied with my skills," Zeke taunted, "we can have rematch, and I will stay in front of you."

Zeke handed Grambine back his wand. Grambine took his wand and was the first to attack again. Zeke put up his shield, and stood motionless for the first few attacks, until his shield weakened and broke apart. Then Zeke began blocking and parrying the attacks. He again hit Grambine with the disarming spell, taking his wand a second time. Furious and humiliated, Grambine continued attacking Zeke with just his hand. Zeke did not move his feet, and continued to block and counter Grambine's assault, eventually hitting him "rigesco", making him go stiff.

"Okay I admit you are pretty good." Grambine admitted when Zeke let him stand back up. Zeke explained that all of his students could do that. He told them about the dueling competitions that they have and magical skills contest that they had, and about lapidem. The Guardians wanted to know more about the school and to see it as well.

Zeke was a little apprehensive to show them the school. If Prince Ostello knew about the Guardians, he may have had people embedded in the group. If they were permitted to see the school, and leave, they could report back to him. He also wanted people, there in Superbia, that could undermine

Ostello from the inside, and report to Zeke and King Sol about the Prince's activities.

On the other hand, having more students for the school would be a bonus. He could possibly bring some new students back with him. He was still worried that some of those new students may not be trustworthy.

"Your hesitation tells me that you are still afraid that you may not be able to trust all of us." Grambine said as if reading Zeke's mind. "I have a solution, I think. Some of us will join King Sol, and some of us will join Zeke at his school, and the rest of us will stay here to gather more Guardians. Those of us who go with Zeke, will stay at the school. Those that want to go with King Sol will stay in Cortis Mundi. The rest of us will try to bring Ostello down from the inside. I can assure you that everyone here wants to see Ostello stopped for good."

Chapter Eighteen

Zeke and King Sol agreed to those terms. A hundred of the Guardians would leave the next day with Zeke and King Sol, fifty for each. Grambine would stay behind and act as a spy for Zeke and King Sol, reporting back news on Prince Ostello. They would leave on the Cherry of the Sky the next morning.

After everyone had boarded the ship, Zeke lifted it out of the water and unfurled the sails. After they had left the jungle and were flying back towards Cortis Mundi, Zeke was wondering if he could speed up the journey any. He instructed all of the new recruits and King Sol to hold on tight to something on the ship. Zeke took hold of the center mast of the ship.

He imagined the ship, and all of its occupants at the city of Cortis Mundi. He imagined the ship being tethered to the spot he was picturing at Cortis Mundi, closed his eyes and relaxed. When he opened his eyes, it had worked. The ship and all of its riders were in front of three massive pyramids, indicating they were at Cortis Mundi.

Zeke and King Sol said their goodbyes and promised to keep in contact with each other. Zeke set the ship down in the port and King Sol and his new followers left the ship. When they had all gotten off, Zeke told the others to hold on to the ship again. This time he pictured the ship and all of the riders on the lake in the valley where Occulta Vallem Magia was located.

When they arrived at the valley, Barmor and students were having a transformation lesson. Zeke and the recruits joined the lesson. The new students had enough magical understanding to fall right into place. After the transformation lesson, they had a serums lesson to finish off the morning.

In the afternoon they attended a battle strategy lesson, followed by spell breaking.

After watching the new students in the day's lessons, Zeke realized that something was off with the new students and their wands. Prince Ostello had not figured out the correlation of the core for the wands, it appeared. Nor had he realized that certain wands were better for some people. Zeke began talking to new students about their wands. None of them had cores in their wands, and they were using whatever Ostello had told them to use.

Zeke tasked the new students with trying different types of wood, either from the forest in the valley or other samples Zeke and Barmor had gathered in their travels, for their new and improved wands. If they did not have what they needed for a core, Zeke could take to find the cores they needed. Zeke still did not trust them enough to let them leave unattended.

That night at dinner, Zeke had the recruits choose their clans. The clans all gained eight new members except the Griffins and the Dragons, who each got nine. There were still two more days before the next lapidem match between the Yeti and Griffins. There was not a lot of time to get the new students up to speed for the game. The new students would have to do their best if they had to get in the game. After the new students chose their clans. Zeke stood up and told everyone what he had seen.

"King Sol and I went to Superbia Saltu. We witnessed Prince Ostello and his army. We saw their violence and depravity. It is true, they practice by torturing and killing slaves. He has scouts everywhere trying to find our school. They feel that we are not a threat. They think that we are nothing except a bunch of young kids with no skill and no proper training. That being said, when they find the school, they will attack us before they move on to King Sol. They know that right now they have a lot more fighters than we do. When they have killed or captured all of us, they will then attack the king."

"Their practice centers around attacking. From what we saw, and what some of the citizens told us, they do not learn much in the ways of defense. Even though Prince Ostello's army is roughly the same size as King Sol's, they also think that Cortis Mundi will be an easy fight. Not only because they intend on killing everyone, and they do not think the king will use lethal action. They also have been learning magic for a couple of years, and King

Sol is only now starting to learn and teach magic. Prince Ostello has more experience."

"What the prince does not know is, there are those that are preparing to stand up to him. They call themselves the Guardians. They want to protect and better mankind. They want a life of peace and are willing to fight to get it. Some of those Guardians have joined King Sol, and some have joined us. Those that just chose their clans. The Guardians that have stayed in Superbia will gather more information and try to defeat Prince Ostello from the inside. They will also be in contact with us and King Sol to keep us informed of the prince's activities."

"Tomorrow, I will try to find some more protection for the castle. If we can make the school invisible from above, that will help us remain hidden. I will also find a way to make sure that no one uninvited can just jump into the valley. After the upcoming lapidem match I will be leaving again. I still want to visit the south lands to see if the 0people there know magic or want to learn."

The next day Zeke went to the library to find links for ways to protect the school from attack. He should have thought sooner, but until recently he had felt that Prince Ostello would not even consider a school of sixty-five people a threat so therefore would not even think to attack them.

While he was in the library Barmor came to help him look for ideas to help protect the valley and castle. They eventually found clues for a couple enchantments. One was a concealment spell that would mask anything that did not appear to be natural. They could cast that on the valley, and anyone or anything that was seeing the valley from above would only see a gorgeous mountain valley, with trees, cliffs, and a lake. The students and the castle would not be seen. Only those that knew the caster personally and did not wish them harm could see into the valley from above and actually proceeded to the valley floor. It would be a great level of concealment. He would also perform the same charm from the stream on the south end of valley.

They also found clues for an enchantment that would block all sound. If someone was above the valley, even though they would not be to see the castle and students, they may be able to hear sounds emanating from the valley. With the sound blocking enchantment, they would not be able to hear the sounds either. If someone were to be above the valley, they would not see or hear anything going on down there. It took Zeke and Barmor several hours of practice and tweaking to get the enchantments to work.

After they figured out the protection enchantments, they went and joined the day's lessons. First was attacks and defense, followed by creatures. In attacks they learned how to defend against some of the violent forms of magic that Prince Ostello was teaching. In order to learn how to defend against them, they had to learn how to carry out those attacks.

Learning how to do those violent spells was taught by some of the new students that had just returned with Zeke from Superbia Saltu. The nature of the dark magic made learning them very difficult. Some of more evil spells would only work if the user was targeting actual living beings. Others, the magic castor had to truly want to cause harm. As Zeke and his students were not going to start torturing or killing classmates to learn some magic, they were only able to learn the words, and wand movements.

After lunch, they began one of their non magic classes, sciences. They were introduced to mathematics and astronomy. Even though they were not magic, the sciences would be very important for everyone's future.

There were no lessons the next day so everyone could relax and enjoy the lapidem match. After lunch, everyone went to the field for the game. The Yeti took their starting spot on the north end of the field, and the Griffins lined up on the south end. Zeke, Barmor and the rest of the school sat in the stands to watch. King Sol and Queen Lunam also jumped to the valley to come watch as well.

When everyone was seated and both teams were ready, Zeke announced the beginning of the game by shouting, "Begin!"

With that, a large black stone appeared in the center of the field. The Griffins would be protecting the gold basket, which appeared on the east side of the field, thirty feet off the ground. The Yeti's silver basket was right next to it. All ten the players quickly got on their brooms and began racing towards the black stone on the ground. Some of the players from both sides were trying to use "sublego" or other controlling magic to gain control of the stone.

A Griffin was finally able to pull the stone towards him, and it was caught by Ridmeus. Ridmeus was able to fight through the Yeti to the baskets. Just as he was about to throw the stone into the silver basket, the baskets moved. The silver one was now on the ground at the north end of the field.

As Ridmeus turned to go north, a Yeti hit him, knocking him off his broom, and he dropped the stone. A second Yeti was able to pick up the stone and began heading south, towards the gold basket. She had the stone stollen from her by a Griffin, just as the baskets both moved to the west side of the field, forty feet above the ground.

The Griffin moved to the west toward the baskets. He was about to be hit by three incoming Yeti and threw the stone to another teammate. The teammate caught the stone and flew straight to the baskets. He was about to drop the stone just as the baskets moved again.

The silver basket was on the east side of the field, now sitting on the ground. As the Griffin turned around to go east, he was hit by two incoming Yeti. Again, the stone was dropped, but was picked by Ridmeus for the Griffins.

Ridmeus took off speeding toward the silver basket, that was still on the east side of the field. He managed to get to the basket before it moved and dropped the stone in the basket, scoring five points for the Griffins.

A small blue stone was the next to appear, at the north end of the field. Both baskets were then moving up and down, side by side, above the stone. The Yeti were the first to pick up the stone. The baskets being so close to the stone, the Yeti were easily able to score ten points.

Another small black stone appeared at the south end of the field. Three Griffins stepped off the field allowing three substitutions to come on from the south end of the field right next to the stone. The silver basket was making large circles thirty feet in the air about the center of the field. The gold basket was halfway between the center and the north end of the field. A Griffin grabbed the stone and flew toward the silver basket.

Before the Griffin flyer could make it to the silver basket, the baskets changed places. The Griffin player kept flying towards the basket's new location. The Griffin was about to be hit by three Yeti flying right at him. She threw the stone to another teammate, but the stone was hit, midflight, by a "sublego" from a Yeti player. The Yeti caught the stone and proceeded to the gold basket, which was making circles in the middle of the field.

When the Yeti defender dropped the stone into the basket, the baskets both changed location again, and the stone fell to the ground. The silver basket was in the northeast corner of the field, on the ground. The gold basket was in the northwest corner of the field. Before the Yeti player could dive to pick up the stone, it had been retrieved by Ridmeus, and the griffins once more.

He was able to dodge all incoming Yeti players and had a clear flight to the silver basket. He dove to deposit the stone in the basket and scored another five points for the Griffins. Tying the score. The next stone to appear was green and the size of a man's head, in the southwest corner of the field.

Seeing that Ridmeus was about to score, the rest of the Griffins had begun to spread out to edges of the field. If Ridmeus were able to score they would, hopefully, be close to where the next stone would be. If the baskets moved, they would be closer to where the silver basket would reappear. When Ridmeus scored, and the green stone showed up. The Griffin player that was closest to the south end of the field quickly swooped in to grab it.

She picked up the large green stone, with some difficulty, and sped off towards the baskets. The baskets were just east of the center of the field making figure eights. The silver basket was traveling horizontally, and the gold basket was traveling vertically. The baskets' paths overlapped in the middle.

When she reached the baskets, all the other nine players on the field were there. Before the Griffin stone handler had a chance to drop the green stone into the silver basket, a Yeti stole it from her by hand. When the Yeti player got a hold of the green stone, she was able to pass it to the top of the scrummage of players to another Yeti. The receiving Yeti player was quickly able to deposit the large green stone in the gold basket. The Yeti were then leading sixty points to ten.

King Sol and Queen Lunam were on the edges of their seats. They had never seen anything like this before. They kept asking about the details of the game. What was the difference between each stone, why the baskets kept moving, and how they had come up with the game. Barmor explained that he had enchanted the baskets to randomly change location at random intervals, and how he enchanted a stone to take a random size and color and new location after each time it was dropped into a basket.

"You learned how to do that all from the books in my library?" King Sol asked.

"Some of it I put together from the books, but the rest was several days of trial and error." Barmor answered.

Another green stone showed up on the north end of the field, tiny this time. The baskets both moved to the south end of the field. They were making large, fast ovals, taking up the whole end of the field. The baskets were traveling in opposite directions, going from ground level to forty feet in the air.

The Yeti were the first to retrieve the stone on the ground. The stone carrier took off to the south, followed by the rest of the players on the field. When they all reached the south end, there was a large collision between all the participants. Three players from each team got knocked off their brooms and fell to the ground.

Both teams retrieved their injured players and sent in substitutions. In the ensuing chaos the stone had been dropped. Ridmeus was able to recover the small green stone, and quickly threw it to another Griffin who was waiting along the path of the silver basket. The tiny green stone was intercepted by a Yeti that had just arrived at the south end of the field.

The Yeti player rose to the top of the gold basket's arc. He arrived there at the same time as the basket. However, just before he could drop the stone into the basket, he was hit from beneath by a pursuing Griffin, dropping the stone again. By the time anyone had gained control of the stone, the baskets moved once again.

This time, the baskets were now sitting idle one hundred feet in the air above the center of the field. The Griffins were now in control of the tiny green stone. They were in a tight group passing the stone amongst each other, keeping it away from the encroaching Yeti. All ten players on the field were climbing fast towards the high stationary baskets.

The group made it to the baskets that were sitting side by side. Ridmeus now had control of the stone. When he reached out over the silver basket and dropped the stone, they moved away from each other. The stone fell rapidly towards the ground. He used "sublego" to pull the stone back to his hand. Before it made it back to his hand, it was grabbed by a Yeti flyer.

The Yeti player moved up toward the gold basket. When she got ready to drop the stone, the baskets moved back together. There were three Griffins charging at her. She threw the stone towards the gold basket. The stone was again intercepted, this time by Ridmeus. He quickly spun around and dunked it into the silver basket. The game was tied once again at sixty points.

As the baskets disappeared, everyone dove for the ground and began scanning the field for the next stone. They were rapidly approaching the ground, and scanning the length of the field, desperately seeking the next stone. They all saw it at the same time. There, sitting on the southwest corner of the field was the glint of a tiny stone. A red stone.

"What is the red stone?" Queen Lunam asked without looking away, not wanting to miss any of the action.

"The red one is the last stone of the game." Barmor answered. "It's worth one hundred fifty points."

A small Yeti girl was able to get to the stone first. She picked up the stone and took off to the northeast corner of the field where the baskets were waiting. Following the strategy of the Griffins in the last play. The Yeti huddled in a tight group passing the stone between each other. The baskets were zig zagging back and forth going from ground level to forty feet off the ground.

The Griffins circled around the baskets and charged head on back toward the Yeti. The two groups clashed together again with several thuds and grunts from the players. The stone carrier was able to break free from the crash and sped for the baskets. Two Griffins broke free and followed the Yeti player.

With a well-timed "sublego", Ridmeus was able to steal the stone just as the Yeti dropped the stone into the basket. Instead of the stone falling into the basket, the stone flew to Ridmeus' hand

\. The second Griffin flew straight at the Yeti that had just dropped the stone. He blocked her from getting in Ridmeus' way. Ridmeus was now clear to score. He flew to the path of the baskets and dropped the red stone into the silver basket as it passed by.

The crowd erupted in cheers, and everyone was on their feet as the stone fell into the basket. The players from both teams on and off the field flew over and landed next to the stands. King Sol and Queen Lunam were speechless at the amazing display of flight and skill on the field.

"That was awesome." King Sol said as he walked to the entrance to the stands and began shaking hands with and congratulating all the players as they entered. Zeke and Barmor were also congratulating the players.

"King Sol is right." Zeke started. "That was an amazing game of lapidem. The skill at which you must play is one thing, but having the luck of the stones and timing the baskets is a completely different thing. At least the baskets didn't cheat you by changing positions at the last moment, making you drop the stone in the wrong basket like it did during the last game. This was the first game that you got to play with all four stones. Our next lapidem match will be in three weeks. Next week will be our next dueling competition. The dueling competition will be the Dragons and the Centaurs against everyone else. Yes, you heard that right it will be two clans against four. You have all been pretty closely matched. When we face Prince Ostello, we will be greatly outnumbered. The following week be our first stealth competition. Just a reminder, I will be leaving again to go to the southlands to see what they know about magic, or if anyone would be willing to join us when the time comes. Now shall we go see what the gnomes have prepared for us?"

"Gnomes?" King Sol and Queen Lunam asked at the same time.

"Yes. Gnomes." Barmor answered as everyone left the stands and began making their way back to the castle. "Gnomes make the food here and take care of the castle."

Chapter Nineteen

King Sol and Queen Lunam jumped back to Cortis Mundi after dinner. Early the next morning Zeke and Longtail boarded the Cherry of the Sky. Zeke pointed the bow of the ship towards the southeast and prepared for his longest journey aboard the flying ship yet. He did some experimenting and was able to add more winds to the sails, allowing the ship to fly even faster. Now it would only take a couple days to get to the south lands.

When Zeke saw the shoreline, he followed it until he saw the city of Miror Austri. The city was nowhere near as big as any of the other cities Zeke had seen, the city had a population of maybe ten thousand. The people of Miror Austri lived very simply. Everyone lived in small huts, and they had no massive stone monuments. They were farmers, fishers, and raised livestock.

Zeke had already made the ship invisible before reaching the city. He sat over the city and watched the people go about their daily business. He wanted to know more about these people before he made his presence known. He wanted to know what kind of culture they had. What kind of language did they have? Was it their own dialect or did they speak the common language? Did they know anything about magic? Maybe magic was forbidden like when he had first met King Sol. He was also concerned about how they might react to his ship appear out of nowhere, floating in the sky.

After watching them for a while, Zeke could tell that they had their own local dialect, but also spoke the common language. The city did not have a large port like any of the other cities Zeke had seen. Zeke had the feeling that they did not do much trading with the rest of the world. Traveling this far south over so much open water was a very long and treacherous journey. The port they did have was merely for small fishing vessels.

That night, after the sun had disappeared into the waters to the west, the people of Miror Austri gathered on the beach and watched the stars and moon. Zeke listened as they discussed different star patterns. An elder stood and recited a story about two holies coming from the stars a long time ago and teaching them how to fish and farm. The elder carried a tall staff that he used as walking stick. When he was done telling the story, the elder raised the staff into the air, then stabbed it into the sand of the beach.

When he did this, hundreds of small campfires ignited all along the beach. Zeke knew at that moment that they did know at least a little about magic. Even if that was the only magic that they knew, at least it was a start. The next day he would make himself known and go and talk with the people and hopefully he would be able to talk with the elder the told the story. The next morning, Zeke removed the invisibility spell from the ship, while he was still in the air. He knew that it would get their attention.

When everyone started staring, he set the ship down in the water at the end of their dock. By the time the ship was in the water, and he had folded the sails, nearly everyone was on the beach staring in wonder. Zeke exited the ship and began walking up the dock toward the waiting crowd.

When he reached the crowd, the elder that spoke the night before came forward and introduced himself. "I am Forvy. Who, may I ask, are you?"

Forvy was a tall, thin, dark-skinned man. He was in his late sixties, and several large hoop earrings in both ears. He also had two large hoops through his nose, and his left eyebrow.

"My name is Zekious." Zeke replied. "I am pleased to meet you. May I ask how you were able to start all of those fires last night on the beach?"

"Pleased to meet you as well, Zekious." Forvy said. "I had help from the ancients. Some of us are lucky enough to get control over the earthly elements from our ancient ancestors. How did you know about the fires? How did you get the ship to do what it just did?"

"Well, the I know about the fires because I arrived yesterday, my ship was invisible, it could not be seen." Zeke answered. "I can use all sorts of magic, not just the earthly elements. What if I were to tell you that everyone here can do it too, with the proper training?"

"No, not everyone can play with powers." Forvy said sharply. "We are selected by the ancients, and those few selected can only manipulate the element that was given to them."

"I have seen two million other people that used to think exactly like that." Zeke replied softly. "Now those two million people can all do things like this."

When he finished talking, Zeke took out his wand, and pulled a stone from the sand to his hand. Then sent it back it away. He then turned the stone to ice, then caught it on fire. Forvy and everyone else jumped. Some jumped from fear, others jumped because a rock flying back and forth then catching on fire scared them. They had never seen anything like that before.

"You know of two million people that can do stuff like that?" Forvy asked excitedly.

"No. I know of two million other people that can do far more than that." Zeke answered. "That was just a taste. That leads me to why I am here. Those two million people are a part of an army. The army is led by a man that wants to enslave the world. A man that if you do not do as he says, he will torture and kill you. If he thinks you are ugly, he will kill you. That man's father is the leader of another two million people, people that will be learning to do that and more. The father is a just man who only wants the best for his people."

"The son wants two things in life. Firstly, he wants to kill his father. Secondly, he wants complete world dominance. He wants to control everyone in this world, the way that he rules his people now. If you disagree with him, he kills you. I have a small school where I teach students magic. The son, Prince Ostello, is going to attack my school when he finds it. Then he will attack his father, King Sol. If he is not stopped, after that he will be unstoppable. Eventually he will find you here. I have come here in hopes of finding more students that would like to join my school. More students that would like to come learn magic. Learn magic and defend the world. Then, when this is behind us, help move the world forward."

"That does not sound good." Forvy said when Zeke was done telling his story. "I am not sure that we can be of any help though. There is only a couple of us each generation that is gifted the use of powers."

"I know you believe that magic is very selective." Zeke replied. "I assure you that those that appear to be given a special power can do so much more.

It only takes concentration, the right frame of mind, and the willingness to be taught. To prove this, I ask for five volunteers that do not seem to have the gift. I will teach them a few things here and now."

At the sound of being able to learn magic, there were several people that stepped forward that wanted to learn. Zeke informed them that anyone could do it, he was just asking for five so everyone could see that it could be done by anyone. Zeke lined five stones on the beach, while five of them lined up beside him. He showed them how to do the calling spell, "sublego" without a wand. He explained how to use the phrase, the hand movement that they needed, and told them to picture the stone moving to their hands.

All five of the volunteers easily called the stones to their hands on the first try. Everyone else was very impressed that anyone could perform magic. Some of them even took what Zeke just showed the five volunteers and started practicing the calling spell all by themselves. Several people came rushing over to Zeke asking him a myriad of questions. One of the most common questions was about his wand. Zeke explained how he made it, and the advantages of using it over not having one.

Others were already volunteering to come with him back Occulta Vallem Magia. Everyone wanted to learn magic for a multitude of different reasons, but most did not want to leave their home. Forvy said that those that wanted to join Zeke's school were encouraged to do so. He then asked if it was possible for a few people to travel to Zeke's school to learn what they could and come back and start their own school back in Miror Austri.

"That absolutely would be possible." Zeke announced happily. "Having many schools around the world would be great for all of us. Those that do not want to stay at our school can learn the basics and copy the tomes from our library then return here and learn and teach as they gain the knowledge from them. That is how we got started, we copied King Sol's library and made our own books. Now we study those books and learn from them. This form of magic is new, so it does still take a lot of trial and error finding the correct words and movements. We have also started creating our own volumes with what we have learned."

Zeke also asked if he could copy their writings. Forvy informed him that they did not have any tomes or scrolls, their knowledge was all passed on by the elders repeating their people's stories. He also told Zeke that were very few people there who could read or write. Zeke told him, those that came to Occulta Vallem would be taught how to read and write as well.

Everyone was very excited for the opportunity to learn magic. Zeke spent the rest of the day teaching the Mirori more basic magic. Zeke wanted to leave the next day, to go back to the castle. He had gained another sixty students that would be joining his school. There would be an additional fifteen people flying back to the hidden valley with him. They would learn to read and write and get the basics of magic. They would be able to copy the writings in the library. When they were ready, they would return to Miror Austri, bringing their knowledge back with them.

They could then bring the information back and continue learning while teaching the citizens of Miror Austri. It was everyone's hope that they would be able to help when it came time. No one liked the idea of being ruled by a maniac with a power complex. They all understood that a person like Prince Ostello would not be good for anyone.

That night Forvy and the others had planned a huge bonfire and magnificent banquet, in Zeke's honor. Before the bonfire, they all gathered on the beach, and watched the stars, while Forvy told a story, passed down from their ancestors. The story told of a time before the ice and cold.

The world was a different place. The north was not frozen, and the seas were higher. The people were in small, nomadic warring tribes. There were no cities like there was then. Most of those people died when the ice and snow started. After the freeze, people began living close together and relying on each other for survival, giving rise to the cities the world had now.

After the story, Forvy raised his staff that he used as a walking stick in the air and stabbed into the sand again, lighting the large bonfire. There were tables all along the beach piled high with food. After everyone had eaten their fill, the tables were removed. The people continued to party around the bonfire, singing, dancing, and storytelling. The next day Zeke decided to stay another night. He continued teaching some of the people from Miror Austri more basic magic. He began showing them how to find and build their wands.

Zeke also began teaching them to read and write before he left. If they were to make any sense of the writings that will be brought back, they would need to be able to read it. He started by teaching them the alphabet and the sounds the letters made. By the end of the day, most of the people he was helping were reading small words and were able to stumble through sounding out larger words.

Zeke, his sixty new students, and the fifteen additional travelers would be leaving the next day. Zeke felt very successful with his time in Miror Austri. He had been able to gain recruits for his school. He had convinced the rest of the people that everyone could perform magic, and they were very excited about the opportunity. As long as everyone had time to prepare before Prince Ostello started his march of terror, and everyone was able to stay in contact and could work together, they might have the numbers to bring Prince Ostello to a stop. Zeke finally felt that they might stand a chance.

The next day Zeke and the travelers boarded the Cherry of the Sky. Zeke demonstrated how the ship flew, and how it was controlled. When the ship was traveling northwest toward the castle, Zeke wrote a letter to King Sol. The letter thanked him for coming to last week's lapidem game, it also informed the King that he had gotten sixty new recruits. He let King Sol know that the fifteen people of Miror Austri would be learning the basics of magic from Zeke and the school. They would gather all the information that they could from the school's library. With the basic knowledge, and recorded writings gathered from the school's library, they would return to Miror Austri. There, the Mirori, would be teaching themselves magic.

Zeke knew that Longtail did not like the feeling of jumping. He sent the griffin to Cortis Mundi, to deliver the letter to King Sol. After Longtail had taken the letter, and launched himself into the air, flying to Cortis, Zeke explained to everyone what he was about to do. He told them, because he knew where the valley was and what it looked like so he could get them there instantly. All they needed to do was hold on tight to something on the ship. He would jump them all, along with the ship back to Occulta Vallem Magia.

Zeke explained that jumping was a weird sensation, especially for someone who had never done it. He told them that the feeling only lasted for a fraction of a second but may have lingering effects after the process was over. When he was finished telling them about what he was going to do, Zeke grabbed hold of the side rail of the ship, focused on the ship, with everyone on it, being back at the valley. He closed his eyes and relaxed his whole body.

Chapter Twenty

Zeke opened his eyes, he, the ship, and all seventy-five riders were back in the beautiful, hidden valley. Several of the people who were on the ship ran to the railing of the ship, and stuck their heads over the railing and began to throw up. Zeke knew exactly why they had to throw up. He still felt as though he might every time he jumped.

When everyone had regained their senses, they were totally speechless. They were taken back by the views of the valley and the castle. No one said a word as Zeke set the ship back down into the water of the lake in the valley. Everyone was too busy staring in amazement.

As Zeke and the others walked up the valley floor toward where the students were beginning their battle strategy class, Barmor came walking up nervously. He had letter in hand. He told Zeke it was a letter from Grambine.

"I am sorry, it is not good news." Barmor said sadly as he handed the letter to Zeke. "Prince Ostello has narrowed his search for the school. He knows that we somewhere north of Cortis Mundi, but south of the ice wall."

"You're right." Zeke replied. "That is not very good news. I have some good news though. The people of Miror Austri have been shown what is accomplishable with magic and have agreed to help when the time comes. I also got sixty new students for the school. Fifteen more people traveled here with me. We will teach them to read and write, and the basics of magic. They will copy down what they want from our library, then return home. There, those fifteen will start their own school, in Miror Austri. They will use the knowledge from our library to teach the people there, in their own way."

Zeke's confidence that the upcoming battle would be winnable, now began to wane. Knowing that Prince Ostello's scouts were closing in, he was now afraid that they did not have much time left before he attacked. The other thing that they did not have much time before was winter. All the mountaintops around the valley were already covered in snow. Even though it was getting cold, and winter was rapidly approaching, the valley floor was still decently warm. If Prince Ostello was to attack during winter, it would end very badly for everyone. If the battle persisted very long, more people would die from the cold.

There was another thing that was beginning to worry Zeke. If this upcoming battle went into a full force battle between the two largest armies in the world, and all the people that were willing to help, it could decimate the entire population of the world. King Sol had about two million people in the city of Cortis Mundi. Prince Ostello also had about two million people, in Superbia Saltu. There were another million people in smaller cities and living by themselves out in the wilds of the world in small warring tribes.

Both the King and the Prince were both talking to shipping merchants that came to their cities, spreading the word about magic and the upcoming battle. The two leaders also had their own emissaries traveling the world, trying to recruit. This war would be talked about for ages, regardless of the outcome. Even the people that were not directly involved with the war would still be affected.

Zeke was hoping that he could find a way to stop Prince Ostello and the war. He hoped it could be done without having two armies that each have two million people face off against one another. With his thoughts wandering, Zeke was not able to follow that day's battle strategy lesson very well. The serums lesson was not any better.

After lunch, Zeke was a little better focused during attack and defense, and spell breaking classes. After the day's lessons were finished, Zeke and Barmor gave the new students and the visitors from Miror Austri a tour of the castle. The tour finished with the library. The new students and the visitors were taken aback at the size of the library.

With the number of tomes and scrolls in the library, suddenly the visitors felt that reading and remembering all of the information in that room was going to be a daunting task. They all felt that it would take a lifetime to read all the books. Barmor and Zeke assured them that it would not take that long. They told the visitors that they have only been reading a little bit each day for a couple of months and are almost halfway through the library.

That night at dinner, after the tour, the sixty new students all got to pick their clans. All six clans had gotten ten new members. The next morning the sixty students, and the fifteen visitors, would be making their wands. The next morning's lessons would be postponed so the new students would not get any farther behind. Zeke knew they were at a disadvantage, but getting more people at the school would be worth the late start.

Nearly all of the people from Miror Austri wore some sort of jewelry made from different parts of different animals. After selecting the wood that they needed, finding some sort of animal to be part of their wands would be the easy part for them. After a large healthy breakfast, they went out to find the wood they would use for their wands.

By lunch all of the new students and the visitors all had their wands made. The new students would not be competing in the duel. Zeke and Barmor knew that with their lack of any experience, they would not be any help and would be a liability. The new students were more than happy to just sit and watch the competition, wanting to see what the other students could do. King Sol and Queen Lunam would be attending the match, as well. The dueling competition would be their first demonstration of such a wide range of magical capabilities.

When everyone got to the field, the Dragons and Centaurs took their starting position on the north end of the field. The other competitors took the south end of the field. The new students and visitors were excited to get a demonstration of what they would be learning. King Sol and Queen Lunam, along with Zeke and Barmor also took their seats in the stands and got ready for what they expected to be an exciting duel.

After the events of the last dueling competition, everyone just started on their brooms instead of having to call them to the field during the battle. There was yet to be any rule about using the brooms in the dueling competition. The players felt that winning by any means necessary and demonstrating the full range of their abilities was exactly what Zeke and Barmor were looking for. They were not wrong. Zeke and Barmor wanted to push the students to their extremes. As long as every competitor was able to be righted at the end of the match and no one died, they were doing their jobs of preparing their students for what was to come. Not only the eventual war, but life in general.

When the fight began, everyone took off on their broom. No one bothered to create any walls, cover, or any kind of subterfuge. The Centaurs and the Dragons stayed in a group. They stayed close enough to be able to mass attack other small groups, but far enough apart that they were not susceptible to a mass attack themselves. Being the smaller team, they would inevitably be facing attackers on all sides. If they were bunched together tight, they would be easier to hit. If they got too spread out, single fighters would be susceptible to getting surrounded to easily.

The other team made up of the rest of the competitors, broke off into several small groups. Three of those groups took to the air, while the other three groups stayed on the ground. Their hope was to divide and conquer. They would try to catch the Centaurs and Dragons in many crossfire situations while surrounding their opponents. The larger team had enough fighters to have a few of them hang back, out of the fight, assisting those that had got taken out.

The Dragons and Centaurs began by attacking the groups on the ground. The attack started by separating the three ground groups from everyone else by encircling each of them with fire. The fires were tall, and the tops of the flames came together. The fire created domes around the groups of blue fighters on the ground. As the blue groups were trying to extinguish the fires surrounding them, they could not see out to attack the fighters on the red team. The red team would fly in circles around the domes, with each pass, they would pick off a few blue fighters that were caught in the domes of fire by sending spells through the fire. The fire domes were small enough to force the blue fighters into tight groups, even though the reds could not see the blues they were still sure to land attacks on someone. They would also relight the fires where the blue team had managed to put them out.

The flying blue groups caught onto what the red team was up to. One of them started to try to help one of the stranded groups. They began trying to help put the fires out and attempting to heal their injured. They landed next to a dome of fire. The red team, on their next attacking run, they added another circle of raging fire around those trying to help, making concentric circles and stranding the saviors as well. The other two groups of the blue flyers tried to flank the red team on their attacking run, by following the red team. One blue group was behind on the left, the other was behind on the right.

Just as the red team was able to eliminate one of the stranded blue teams, another was able to break free from the inner circle of encroaching flames. The red team increased the size and heat of the wall of fire around the blue group that they had just eliminated, making it harder for the rest of the blues to come to the rescue. With the two groups chasing them, the red team had to break off from attacking the blue groups on the ground. The group of blues that had just broke free from the fire were trying to rescue their stranded teammates. The Dragons and Centaurs set more fire around the rescuing blue group.

The red team was trying to create blockades behind them to slow down the blue groups that were chasing them, by using fire and stones. The red flyers at the back of the group were doing a good job of blocking incoming attacks from blue chasers. They were succeeding in keeping them slowed down. After they were able to gain some more distance from the blue chasers, the red team was able to return to attacking the blue fighters on the ground.

There were now two sets of two concentric circles of fire. There was a group of blue competitors trapped behind each wall of fire. With each pass, some of the red team would light the fires again where the blue team had been able to put the fires out. Other red players would attack those trapped by the fires. Their strategy seemed to be working.

The blue fighters on the ground were kept busy dealing with the fires and trying rescue their teammates. The two sets of concentric circles were close enough together, and the red team was spread out far enough, that some of the red team was always attacking a group of blue fighters trapped by fire. While the red fighters in the back were keeping the blue chasers blocked and slowed down. No one on the blue team was able to do anything except defend themselves. The red team was slowly picking the blue players off one by one.

After several passes, another group of blue fighters trapped by a wall fire was eliminated. The small groups of blue fighters on the ground did not even have time to try to get on their brooms and fly out of the fires. All they could do was try to slow the fires and block the unrelenting attacks. The fire walls were proving very hard to extinguish, and they naturally tried to reconnect with themselves when a portion had been extinguished. A member of the Dragon clan had developed this, almost sentient, fire when studying real dragons and the fire they breathed.

Even though the red team seemed to be the obvious victor, they were not perfect. The blue groups that were following the red team had managed to hit a couple red fighters with attacks, causing them to fall to the ground. The red team took their path of attack lower and managed to break the spells that had taken out their teammates.

Instead of rejoining the other Dragons and Centaurs on their path of destruction, the two red fighters that had been brought back, decided on a different route. They opted to fall in behind the two small groups of blue followers, flanking them. They started picking them off, one by one from the rear. They would attack the blue chaser that was farthest behind the group, so rest of the group would not know they were being attacked from the rear.

The tides began to turn about the time half of the blue team had been taken out of commission. Two of the small, stranded, blue groups were able to extinguish the fire between them. Now the two groups had a lot more room to maneuver, and one less fire to contend with. They quickly started attacking the outer ring of fire that was still trapping them. Even though the ring of fire was larger, the top was still coming together, making a large dome. Th could have simply flew up out of the fire, however, they would still have to fly directly through it.

The red team quickly saw what was happening. On their next pass, they made another circle of fire surrounding the group of blues. This time, the circle was off center, sharing a portion of the wall from the larger ring of fire. The new circle of fire was much smaller than the first circle that the blues had just taken down. That forced the group of blue fighters to focus on the fire again.

The red team used dragon's breath to continue trapping the, now three, stranded blue groups into smaller areas, making it harder for them to fight back. They also used it to try to slow down the two blue groups that were flying behind the red team. The fire would slow the flying blue fighters a little, but not stop them. The two red players were still behind the blue groups, attacking those lagging behind.

The red team continued attacking the blue groups that were trapped by the fires. When they finally eliminated all of the blue defenders that were trapped in the fires, all they had left to contend with was two groups that were chasing them on brooms. At that point, instead of running from the blue chasers, the red team turned and attacked them head on. By attacking the remaining blue fighters head on, they would not be able send anyone to assist the blues that had already been eliminated. The remainder of the battle stayed in the air. Anytime a blue player tried to leave the scramble to go revive their fallen comrades, they were quickly taken out by the red team.

The head on battle was not fairing very well for the red team either. Both teams were losing players rapidly. The blue team still had more fighters than the red team. Eventually both teams' numbers were in the single digits. There were eight blue players, and four red fighters left. With so few numbers, the fight left the air and continued on the ground. It appeared that all of the effort the red team put in to keeping the blue team held off was not going to be enough. Everyone watching felt that the red team may actually lose. They were still outnumbered two to one.

The fire had worked for them for the majority of the match, so in a final desperate attempt, two red fighters used the dragon's breath spell, "draco anima", again, catching the remaining blue players in a small fire circle that was tall and hot. The red fighters got back on their brooms and continued attacking the blue fighters now trapped by the fire. From the air, while the blue fighters were trapped in the fire, the red team was able to eliminate the remaining blue fighters. The epic battle was finally over. The Dragons and the Centaurs had come out victorious.

The spectators, who had been on the edges of their seats the entire match, were new standing and cheering.

"What a spectacular match, everyone!" Zeke exclaimed when everyone had been righted and returned to the stands. "That fire technique will definitely come in handy when the time comes to go up against Prince Ostello and his army. Keeping your opponents distracted and limiting the number of attackers that you will have to contend with will be a huge help. Our next dueling competition will be in three weeks and will feature the Griffins and the Pheonix taking on the rest of the school. Next week will be our first stealth competition. Each clan will have a chance to prove how quiet and cunning they can be. The week after that will be the third lapidem match featuring the Pheonix and the Unicorns. Now. Shall we head back to the castle and eat, I hope that our royal guests, the king and queen of Cortis Mundi will join in the festivities as well."

When everyone had eaten their fill, King Sol and Queen Lunam said their farewells and returned to Cortis Mundi. The next two days, the students helped get their new students and the visitors caught up on the things that had already been taught. Training the new students and the temporary travelers was a good way to revisit the things the students had already learned.

Chapter Twenty-One

After their two days off, everyone was up to speed and ready to start learning and preparing for this week's stealth competition. The new students and guests had all got their wands made and had received a crash course in the use of magic and were learning the basics of reading. Zeke had begun helping the guests copy the contents of the school's library.

The students did not know what to expect from the upcoming stealth competition. They knew it would encompass the use of serums, concealment spells, and misdirection. They tried to prepare for whatever Zeke and Barmor would throw at them. The week's lessons focused on the use concealment spells and more advanced serums that would aid them in the challenges, and in life.

The day before the stealth competition, Zeke received a phoenix carrying a letter from Grambine. The letter informed Zeke that Grambine would like a face-to-face meeting as soon as possible, he had new information. The letter said that Grambine would be in the training area of the woods every night and could be found there.

It would still be night there, so Zeke jumped to the clearing in the woods outside Superbia Saltu where the Guardians would meet and train. When he appeared, he opened his eyes to see one hundred fifty wands pointing in his direction. Apparently, he had startled the Guardians. Grambine came forward and told everyone not to attack.

"Zeke, my apologies for the rude welcoming." Grambine said. "We did not know who was appearing here."

"It is quite alright, Grambine." Zeke replied. "I am sure I startled everyone. You said that we needed to talk as soon as possible. I came as soon as I got the letter."

"Yes." Grambine started. "We have learned a lot in the last few weeks. Prince Ostello knows that your school is somewhere north of Mundi Sea, but that is all that he is telling us. The city of Oriens Regnum, on the eastern shore of Eastlund, has vowed to fight for Ostello. They have their own form of magic and have decided not to learn Ostello's. He did not tell us what that kind of magic they use. The prince is very guarded with what he tells us. Although he has narrowed down his search for your school, and he has gained another thirty thousand fighters, I still see a bit of an advantage. Those thirty thousand have not seen how evil Prince Ostello is, and they have opted to not learn his violent form of magic. I think they will abandon him when they see how evil he truly is."

There was a long pause then a heavy sigh, before Grambine continued. "Prince Ostello also keeps talking about how nothing can kill him. I am not sure if he just thinks he is invincible, or if he has actually found a way to not die. I would not be surprised if he has found out how to become invincible."

There was another long pause. Zeke could tell there was more that Grambine had to tell.

"There's more." Grambine eventually continued talking. "Ostello has developed magic that can take over someone's mind. He demonstrated it in front of everyone and taught us how to use it to make someone do whatever we want. When the battle comes, you may find yourself having to fight your own people."

Grambine looked at the ground, as if he had suddenly become fascinated by a small rock by his foot.

"What is it?" Zeke asked.

"His plan is to kill you first." Grambine answered begrudgingly. "He feels that when you are dead your students will lose their leadership and motivation. They will immediately surrender after seeing you die. Those that do not surrender will be tortured."

"That does not sound promising." Zeke said after a long pause of his own. "I have been assuming that he would attempt to take me out first for that reason. Maybe I could challenge him one on one. Our armies promise to stand down when one of us loses. My students would do so out of respect. I am not so sure his generals and the rest of his army would surrender if he fell."

"That would be suicide." Grambine replied sternly. "Prince Ostello has no honor and will order his men to attack as soon as the fight starts. They will kill you and slaughter your students. You do not stand a chance taking him on yourself."

"How are we going to stop him?" Zeke asked.

"I don't think that we can." Grambine explained. "He has become too powerful. I think we should wait. You and King Sol need to tell him you are not a threat and turn yourselves over to him. He will not have a need to attack that way. Then, we buy our time and attack when he is vulnerable."

"Giving up before the fight even starts?" Zeke asked. "If we surrender, he will still kill me. King Sol too. He hates us and sees us as the enemy. If we were to surrender now things would get much worse for everyone else."

"You are probably right." Grambine said.

"For now, though, we do wait." Zeke said. "We wait until he attacks. We have more to fight for. We understand the consequences of losing. If we lose, he will take over the world. When he does attack me, King Sol and his army will be there to help. Then you and the Guardians attack from the inside. I think even though he has become very powerful, and has the larger army, we will still win. We make up for our smaller numbers with our heart."

Grambine began to see Zeke's point of view. They also agreed not to change any plans for the time being. Grambine would continue to gather followers from under Ostello's nose. Zeke would start training his students harder. When Zeke left Superbia, he would go see King Sol before returning to the castle. He wanted to relay the new information to King Sol and see what he thought.

When he arrived at Cortis Mundi, he was almost killed on the spot by King Sol's Royal Guard. After a long conversation, the king and Zeke agreed to intensify their training. The king was very worried about Grambine's new discoveries. They understood that if this went the way that it was going, when it was over, there would be very few people left in the world. Nearly the entire population was fighting for one side or the other.

King Sol agreed that waiting to see how things would play out was best for now. He told Zeke that if Prince Ostello attacked Zeke's school first, the mundians would be there to help. Win or lose, the first battle would be the last battle. Everyone would be fighting, and there probably would not be very many people left afterward.

Zeke returned to the castle with a lot to think about. He would like to find a way to prevent this battle with Prince Ostello without the fight wiping out seventy-five percent of the world's population. Even if there was a way to bring him down without a war, Mahdrin or someone else in his inner circle would take over.

What if it was true, had Prince Ostello discovered how to not die. Zeke would have to spend more time in the library. If there had ever been someone who could not be killed, the answer might be in on of the books they copied from King Sol's library. If Prince Ostello had discovered the answer in his travels, how could they defeat him. When talking with others, Zeke remained confident. Alone, Zeke began to fear the end was near.

When the day of the competition arrived, after lunch everyone made their way to the lapidem field. Barmor had conjured a stone building, that was being patrolled by several different animals. The object was to make it through the building without disrupting any of the animals. Some of the animals would flee if they were disturbed, others would attack the competitors. If the clans scared away the animals or got attacked their score would be affected. Using their ingenuity would be key to getting passed all of the animals.

When everyone was seated in the stands, Zeke began explaining the task at hand. There were many different ways to get through the building, some paths were faster, but the clans would have to contend with all of the different animals to exit. Certain concealment spells, serums, or misdirection would not work on certain animals. The clans would need to know the different animals and what they would be susceptible or immune to. The clans would be timed to get through the building.

The Dragons would go first. The path that they chose through the building took them to a herd of pegasi first. The flying horses were magical creatures that had excellent hearing and could see through most camouflaging spells. If they heard something that frightened them, they would quickly fly away. If the pegasi saw them but were not frightened, they would not flee. If they were heard and not seen, they were guaranteed to scare the pegasi off. The trick would be to remain seen, but not heard, and not to appear threatening.

The six flying horses were on one side of a large room. The room's exit was directly across the room from where the Dragons entered. The pegasi were on the left side of the room. The Dragons decided to use a silencing spell to get past the magical horses. By using the spell "sano", they would be silent when crossing the room. Without making any noise they slowly walked across the room.

When they were about halfway across the room, the pegasi perked up their ears and flicked their tails. They had been alerted to the presence of people walking across the room. Because they could see them and not hear them, all they did was watch the Dragons intently. After they made it more than halfway through and were heading for the exit, the pegasi all settled back down.

The next animal that they had to get passed was a cyclops. The one-eyed giant had excellent hearing and eyesight. Cyclops would attack anything smaller than themselves. They also had a keen sense of smell. Even if the Dragons were not seen or heard, they would most certainly be smelled. There were no rules against attacking any of the creatures that they had to get past, and there was only one cyclops.

With the use of "ligo", a powerful immobilizing spell, they stopped the cyclops in its tracks. They knew that because the cyclops was so large, "ligo" would not last very long. They quickly hurried through the room and past the stationary giant.

Their next challenge was to get through a room with a couple of trolls. The trolls had good hearing and sense of smell but had horrible eyesight. Trolls were notoriously violent and would swing their club just because they haven't hit something in a few minutes. The Dragons used the silencing spell "sano" again and began walking through the room towards the exit.

They were about halfway across the room, when without warning, the two trolls stood and began fighting each other. The students took off running for the exit. One of the trolls had got hit on the head by the other troll's club. The troll staggered backwards, spun half a circle, and fell facedown. The troll landed right in front of the Dragons, blocking their path to the exit. The Dragons quickly ran around the head of the knocked-out troll and made it to the exit.

Next, they faced a small group of unicorns. Unicorns would run away from anything different, but their curiosity would bring them back to see what they had run away from. The Dragon clan used a simple invisibility serum to get past the unicorns.

Their final challenge was a phoenix. Magic spells or serums would not work to get past the phoenix. Phoenix had the magical ability to see through magic. If the Dragons used magic to sneak past the phoenix it would know and screech and fly away. The Dragons knew that the large bird would not immediately fly away just by seeing or hearing people, it had to feel threatened, which it would if it were approached. Unfortunately for the Dragons, the phoenix was sitting right in front of the building's exit. Getting past the phoenix meant they could complete the competition.

Several of the Dragons had extensively studied many creatures including the large, rare, colorful bird. The clan simply walked steadily and confidently up to the phoenix. When they got close to the phoenix, it started to flap its wings. The Dragons bowed deeply and politely told the phoenix that they wished it no harm and simply wanted to pass. The phoenix took off and flew to the other side of the room.

The Dragons set a very hard time to beat of fifteen minutes thirty-six seconds. The Unicorns would go next. The route that they took led them to their namesake animal first, the unicorn. The Unicorns had come prepared with several serums. When they arrived at the room containing the unicorn, they drank three different serums, one that made their movements silent, an invisibility serum, and lasting serum, making the other serums last longer. Those serums would work to get them past everything except the phoenix.

When the Unicorns got to the phoenix, they were unaware that phoenix were immune to stealth spells and serums. They walked into the room, thinking that they were invisible. When they were getting close to the phoenix, it looked at them, let out a squawk, and flew away. By the time the phoenix had returned, the Unicorn clan had finished the competition. Their time was twelve minutes forty-four seconds, with a five-minute penalty for scaring away the phoenix. Their total was seventeen minutes forty-four seconds.

The Centaurs were the next clan to take on the stealth course. The first thing that they had to get past was the phoenix. They also tried to walk by the large red and yellow bird by using the invisibility spell. When the phoenix saw them and got scared it let out a loud screech again and flew away. The loud screech from the phoenix scared the unicorns and pegasi away. They also had trouble with the cyclops.

The Centaurs also used a silencing serum, as well as invisibility spell. They did not realize the acuity of the cyclops' sense of smell. The cyclops smelled the Centaurs' presence and attacked. The cyclops charged the area where the smell was emanating from, kicking and smashing wildly. The cyclops got lucky and kicked two of the Centaur tricksters. The Centaurs' total time with their penalties was twenty-one minutes twenty seconds.

The Phoenix students were the next clan to attempt the stealth course. They had no trouble with their namesake. However, they were not able to get through the room with the pegasi without scaring them off. When they tried to get past the trolls, one of them started running around wildly swinging its club. The troll ended up hitting three of the Phoenix contestants. Their total time after penalties was sixteen minutes eleven seconds.

Then it was time for the Griffins to try their luck. They took their time and would discuss strategy before each room. They were flawless in their approach and made it through the large mazelike building without alerting any of the animals to their presence. Their slow and meticulous approach, however, cost them a lot of time. Their time was fifteen minutes fifty-two seconds. Just a little faster than the Phoenix, but slower than the Dragons.

The Yeti were the last clan to go through the course. As stealth was their area of focus, they were sure to put on a good demonstration. They first took on the pegasi. They recreated the sounds of a peaceful river trail. With the sounds of a flowing river, birds chirping, and a gentle breeze blowing emanating from their wands they confidently walked across the room to the exit on the far side.

When they got to the room with the cyclops, they blasted the cyclops' nose with a powerful smelling spell. All the cyclops would be able to smell was the scent of a decaying carcass. Then they used "sano" and the camouflaging spell, "indespectus". They were now hidden from sight, smell, and hearing, and ran to the room's exit.

When they got to the trolls, they hit the trolls with a euphoria spell, "laetus" making both trolls feel peaceful and euphoric. With the trolls now thinking only of the pleasure they were feeling, the Yeti competitors walked past them to the exit.

When they got to the room with the unicorns, they used "sano" and "indespectus" to hide themselves and made their way across the room unhindered. They reached the far side of the room and exited to the room with the phoenix. When they arrived at the phoenix, they used a very powerful sleeping spell, "soporo" to put the phoenix asleep. While phoenix were capable of seeing through magic they were still susceptible to some magic that was used directly on them. The magic had to be very powerful and would not last very long. The sleeping spell would only give the Yeti a few seconds to run across the room.

Exiting the room housing the phoenix, the Yeti had beaten the Dragons' time by a full minute. They had won the first stealth competition. They returned to the stands where everyone else was watching. When they arrived, Zeke congratulated them on an impressive display.

Then Zeke congratulated everyone else again and commended them on their performances. He was impressed by how much the students had been learning on their own, especially the use of stealth arts, and learning about creatures that they had not studied in their lessons. He told them of his trip to Superbia and Cortis. Zeke told them about the new information that he had learned from Grambine and the other Guardians.

He could see the looks of worry and fear grow on the faces of his students as he told them what he had learned. They knew the threat was real before, but now, his students understood just how afraid Zeke was. He finished off his speech by telling them the next week would be the next lapidem match, the Phoenix and the Unicorns. The week after that would be the next dueling competition, with the Griffins and the Phoenix taking on the rest of the school.

Chapter Twenty-Two

Zeke had been studying Pormin's animal transformation since he heard about it. He and Pormin had been discussing the process at length. They had decided that anyone that wanted to learn how to do the animal transformation, that was older than the age of twelve, would be allowed to. Zeke felt that with the new information that he had received, now was a good time to start the process.

The process would take a month to complete, and they would finish the process just before the first break. The next morning, at breakfast, Zeke informed them of his plan to start the process that afternoon. Everyone was excited for the opportunity to learn the transformation. All the students that were old enough had announced that they were very interested in doing it.

Even though this was supposed to be a rest day, Zeke and the students began practicing the transformation. They all wanted to have all the steps memorized perfectly so that they would not do it wrong.

They had to repeat the phrase "Find my animal side. Reach my animal side. Become my animal side" ten times. While repeating the phrase, they had to start standing up with their arms crossed over their chest, in a final resting pose. Take one step forward with their right leg, while bringing their arms down to a horizontal position with their elbows at their side, as if holding something large and heavy. Then stretching their arms out to the side at shoulder height, while stepping forward one step with their left leg, so that their legs were together again. Then squat while raising their arms over their heads and putting their hands together and interlocking their fingers. From there, they needed to stand while bringing their clasped hands back down to chin level.

Then they had to do those steps, precisely in reverse, ending up back where they had originally started. They had to finish the phrase when they stepped back to their starting location with their arms crossed back across their chest. They had to repeat this process ten times. It was imperative that with each repetition, their steps were exactly in the same spot, at the same time during the phrase. They had to do this sequence every day for thirty consecutive days. Every time they did it, they had to start at exactly the same time each day and in exactly the same spot every day. The other key to success was they needed to visualize their animal side, whatever it may be.

To ensure that everyone started from the same spot every day, Zeke chose an area on the east side of the valley that was out of the way so that it would not be disturbed. He had all the students get a rock and mark it with their name. Those rocks would mark the students' starting location.

They practiced all day so that they would get their timing correct. That night when it came time to start their procedure, they all got in a large circle, with Pormin in the center. They practiced the phrase, steps, and timing three more times before they officially started the procedure. They had started the procedure late enough so that on days that they had afternoon lessons, they could do the transformation procedure after lessons. The weekly competition we be held earlier in the day so that they would finish before they needed to repeat the procedure.

After learning the procedure for the animal transformation, the guests from Miror Austri felt they learned what was needed to go home and begin teaching others. They had learned to read and write, Zeke had taught them to use insta-fly, and they had copied the entire library. They took their leave to start their own school in Miror Austri. They vowed to keep learning all they could from the volumes they had copied from Occulta Vallem's library. They also promised to stay in touch with Zeke and when the time came, they would help defeat Prince Ostello.

That week's lessons and transformations seemed to fly by, before they knew it, it was the day of the lapidem match. The match would start shortly after breakfast. As people finished eating, they all made their way to the lapidem field. The Phoenix would start on the north end of the field and scoring in the gold basket, while the Unicorns would start on the south end of the field and would be scoring in the silver basket.

The game began with a blue stone appearing in the middle of the east side of the field, and the gold basket beginning fifty feet above the Phoenix at the north end of the field, while the silver basket was fifty feet above the Unicorns at the south end of the field. The Pheonix were the first to end with up the blue stone. They were throwing the stone to each other, passing it along until it got to the player that was closest to the gold basket. When the stone carrier went to drop the blue stone, the basket disappeared and reappeared in the northwest corner of the field.

The phoenix quickly pulled the stone back with "sublego" and threw it to the player that was already right next to the basket. The player flew the rest of the way to basket and easily scored ten points for the Phoenix. The next stone was another blue, this time the size of a grape. It appeared in the southeast corner of the field. The silver basket was thirty feet directly above the stone. The gold basket was sitting on the ground in the exact center of the field. Both teams turned and began racing towards the tiny blue stone.

This time, the Unicorns were the first to pick up the stone. Again, just as the player reached the silver basket, it moved. The silver basket was now sitting right next to the gold basket in the center of the field. The Unicorns dove toward the baskets in a tight diamond formation, with the stone carrier in the center of the diamond.

The Phoenix started in a line blocking the baskets as the Unicorns were approaching. When the Unicorns got close, they all broke off in different directions. The Phoenix moved into a circle around the baskets. The stone carrier was able to make flat spin along with a barrel roll maneuver and got by the blocking Phoenix players and scored before the baskets moved again.

The next stone showed up in the middle of the northern edge of the field. This time it was very large and green. The stone was twice the size of a man's head and heavy. The players would need two hands to pick it up and hold it. The baskets were both thirty feet off the ground at the south end of the field. The gold basket was on the eastern edge and followed the edge from the south end to the middle of the field, the silver basket did the same along the western edge.

The Phoenix were able to get the stone picked with "sublego" and carried it with the controlling spell, "tempero". They used the same strategy as before, passing the stone to one another, with "tempero", until it got to the player closest to the gold basket. The final player carried it to the basket, and was successful in getting it in the basket, scoring another fifty points for the Phoenix. He had a little trouble getting the stone into the basket because it was so large.

Then there was another green stone sitting in the southwest corner. This time the stone was smaller, about the same size of a man's hand. Again, the Phoenix got there first and picked it up. As it had worked the first few times, they continued to pass the green stone from player to player, by throwing to each other or using "tempero".

The baskets were at the north end of the field, forty-five feet off the ground. The two baskets were touching and were pivoting in a circle at the contact point. Both teams raced towards the baskets. The Phoenix, passing the stone back and forth quickly, so that no one team member held the stone for more than a few seconds.

When the Phoenix player that was closest to the baskets received the stone, he leaned forward on his broom to push his speed and get in front of the Unicorns. His efforts were in vain, by the time he reached the gold basket they moved again. This time they were sitting on the ground at the south end of the field.

The stone carrier quicky threw to stone to the Phoenix player that was the furthest south. As he was racing southward, the Unicorns were gaining on him. While swerving and dodging the income Unicorn players, other Phoenix were able to race towards the baskets unimpeded. When the other players got closer to the baskets, the stone carrier was able to pass the stone on to the others.

The Phoenix player that was carrying the stone, at the moment, dove and was able to deposit the stone in the basket, making the score one hundred ten points for the Phoenix. The Unicorns had ten points. The stone was now black, in the southwest corner of the field. The stone was twice the size of a man's fist. The gold basket was in the northeast corner of the field, spiraling from the ground to fifty feet in the air. The silver basket was doing the same in the northwest corner of the field.

The Unicorns quickly took possession of the black stone. The Phoenix, seeing that the Unicorns were closer to the stone, all began flying north to play defense as the opposition moved for the baskets. Two of the Phoenix waited near the gold basket in preparation for when the Phoenix got the stone back. While the other three went to the silver basket, to attempt to get the stone back before the Unicorns could score.

The three Phoenix formed a tight wedge-shaped blockade in front of the silver basket. As the five Unicorns drew near, the three Phoenix charged. When the Phoenix began to charge, the Unicorns scattered in different directions. The stone carrier was able to get around the defenders and get the stone to the basket.

After the baskets and stone disappeared, it took the players several seconds to find where they had appeared. It took so long to see where the stone had reappeared, it seemed as though it was an eternity to the players and spectators. The baskets were one hundred feet above the center of the field. They finally saw the next stone.

Floating in the air, sparkling ten feet below the baskets, was the red stone. The stone was perfectly spherical, two inches in diameter. The race was brutal as both teams sped towards the stone and baskets. Everyone was swerving into one another, trying to slow the other team down to reach the stone first.

The Phoenix were the first to reach the stone. As soon as the stone was picked up, the baskets disappeared. The gold basket showed up ten feet above the north end of the field. The silver basket was ten feet off the ground at the south end of the field. Randomly, every couple of seconds, the baskets would switch places.

The Phoenix dove for the north end of the field. They repeated their previous strategy of passing the stone between themselves to avoid having the stone taken or the stone carrier hit by the Unicorn players. When the Phoenix player that had possession of the stone got to where the silver basket was and had to wait for the gold basket to appear.

The silver basket disappeared, but the gold basket never appeared. When the players looked around, both baskets were at the south end of the field. The baskets were on either side of the south end of the field, still switching places, randomly every couple jof seconds. The Phoenix took off to the south and the Unicorns followed.

As the Phoenix raced across the field for the south end of the field, the Unicorns could not keep up. The Phoenix reached the gold basket, and the stone carrier dropped the stone above the basket. As she did so the basket moved again, and the stone fell to the ground. Both baskets disappeared and reappeared back at the north end of the field. Before the Phoenix player that had dropped the stone, realized that it did not go in, a Unicorn player had already summoned the stone with "sublego", and began flying north.

The rest of the players followed him. The Unicorn team took on a tight phalanx formation as they traveled north. The Phoenix tried as hard as they could to penetrate the phalanx but could not break up the tight group of flyers. As they neared where the baskets were, two Unicorns peeled off and went to the east, and three went west.

The Phoenix split up as well and followed, not knowing who had the stone. The two small groups from both teams reached the edges of the field where the baskets were repeatedly changing places. The group of three Unicorns had the stone.

When the silver basket showed up next to the group, the stone carrier dropped the stone from a foot and a half above the basket. Acting quickly, a Phoenix pulled the stone to them with "sublego", and streaked toward the basket, catching the stone on the way. When the Phoenix carrier reached the basket's location, it changed to gold. The carrier charged through the crowd, depositing the stone into the basket, as she flew by. The Phoenix won two hundred sixty points to twenty.

The entire crowd, who had been on the edges of their seats since the beginning of the match, were now standing and jumping. The stands erupted in cheers. The players collapsed in the middle of the field, exhausted. Zeke went down to the field to congratulate the players.

When he arrived in the field, the players sat up and the spectators came out of the stands to listen to what Zeke would say.

"I don't know where to start." Zeke said with amazement. There was a long pause while he thought about what to say next. "Those baskets sure did not stay with the same pattern very long, and there were a lot of green stones. Excellent game everyone. Very well played."

Zeke continued. "Next week will be our next dueling competition, with the Griffins and the Phoenix, taking on the rest of the school. After that will be the next magical skills contest. I am sure that Barmor will have something special planned for everyone. Now we should all get ready for our animal transformation ritual."

Chapter Twenty-Three

They had reached the point where they had gotten what information they could from the library. Although the library was substantial, magic was new and there was limited information available. Much of the library was not related to magic, but Zeke and Barmor had copied it all anyway, so that they would have that information available to them. Now, their lessons were mostly comprised of former Royal Guards that had knowledge or insight that had not made it into the books. The rest of the lessons were taught by Zeke, Barmor, or other particularly powerful witches or wizards that had created their own magic spells.

The magic ranged from new attacks and defensive spells to simple everyday helpful magic, such as making candles float, or learning how to make magical items. Some lessons were just experimenting with magic and trying to learn new stuff. All of the students put forth the best efforts to learn. They all knew what was in store.

Zeke was afraid they would not have the numbers, even if King Sol and those from Miror Austri joined. He was hoping that if the students were able to transform into animals, it could be an advantage. It would also be advantageous if they could get some other creatures and humanoid species to help. While it could help, Zeke had his doubts that they would be able to get any non-humans to help.

Zeke wanted to see Prince Ostello's brutality for himself. That day, after the animal transformation ritual, he would jump to Superbia Saltu and watch the training sessions in the courtyard again. He believed Grambine but wanted to see exactly how brutal the prince had become for himself.

Unfortunately, he would not have a lot of time, as he would have to be back the next day in time for the transformation ritual. He would have just less than a day. It would be early afternoon there when he arrived, and he could stay until late morning the next day.

When it was time to leave, Zeke used insta-fly to jump to the clearing in the forest where the Guardians would meet. From there he could use their tunnels to get into the city and to the courtyard where they trained. When he arrived at the clearing, there was no one around, everyone was in the city, either doing their daily duties or in the courtyard training.

Zeke found the entrance to the tunnels and followed the tunnels into the city. When he got into the city, and was close to the exit of the tunnel, he used the camouflaging spell, "indespectus", to become almost undetectable. The tunnel exited to the basement of someone's house. Zeke moved quickly and quietly to the house and out onto the street.

When he was outside, before he followed the streets to get to the training courtyard, Zeke added "sano" the silencing spell so that he would not be heard. Zeke's spells were working well. As he traveled the streets of Superbia Saltu, no one knew he was there.

When he reached the courtyard, he entered through the gate and stayed next to the wall. Zeke found a place to sit silently and began watching the training sessions. Grambine was absolutely correct, they were using mind control spells on the slaves. The slaves would then turn to attack other slaves. If a slave proved strong enough mentally to fight the mind control spell, they were tortured and killed. If any of the citizens acted like they did not want to attack the slaves, they themselves were tortured or killed.

No one dared to disobey, although Zeke could see that many did not want to be torturing the slaves. Prince Ostello's punishment for disobeying the orders was swift and without warning. Zeke even saw many of the Guardians attacking the slaves without a second thought, purely out of fear.

Unless the slaves had been killed, they were magically healed and attacked again. Ostello's army also used spells to decapitate the slaves or cut off their limbs. When one was done practicing, the limbs would be put back on, and slave righted so that it could be attacked again. There was one thing that Zeke saw, or rather, did not see , that gave him a sliver of hope.

They were only practicing on the slaves. The unarmed slaves, who were not allowed to attack back. When it came time for battle, their hubris would be their downfall. Although they had more numbers than that of Zeke's school, and King Sol's army. They had never attacked someone who could defend themselves and return fire. They would not be ready when they got attacked back. They would be going into battle, thinking that it would be as easy as attacking their slaves.

Zeke thought for a second that he could simply sneak over and kill Ostello now. There was no way that he would make it out of the city, before he got killed, if he did that though. If he attacked, he would lose his camouflaging and silencing spell, and everyone would know who did it. There would be no way to escape. It might be worth sacrificing himself to remove Prince Ostello. Zeke knew that someone else would just take his place. The person that took over for Prince Ostello could be even more dangerous, as they would be seeking revenge.

The prince's closest advisors, and top generals appeared to be more brutal even than Prince Ostello. He seemed to have more self-control. If he killed Prince Ostello now, one of his Royal Guard would just step into the top position. Even if he were to somehow take out the entire upper echelon, most of the citizens had been so brainwashed whoever took up the mantle would continue them down the same path. It seemed a violent war was inevitable.

After the afternoon training session, Zeke made his way back to the Guardian's meeting area in the forest. He waited there until Grambine, and the other Guardians began to show up. The number of Guardians had increased since the last time he had come to visit. They were successfully recruiting, hopefully the new recruits could all be trusted and were not spying on the Guardians for Prince Ostello.

Unlike the city-wide training with everyone, the Guardians were actually leaning how to defend themselves. They would spend their nights learning and practicing how to block and deflect spells, as well as healing those that had gotten injured. On his last visit, Zeke had taught them how to use the art of insta-fly. That was something that only a few of the prince's Royal Guard knew how to do, and they were not teaching it to the others.

When Zeke mentioned the increase in numbers to Grambine, he admitted they had been able to more than double their numbers since Zeke's last visit. Grambine also informed Zeke that there were other groups of people throughout the city that were gathering in defense of Prince Ostello. There was always chatter when walking to the training courtyard and during training. Prince Ostell's numbers were dwindling by the day. However, they were also growing more powerful.

Zeke wanted to know more about the other groups. Grambine told him that he had heard that there were many other groups like the Guardians. They had their own meeting spots, but Grambine was not sure exactly where they were. He surmised that some were in other places in the forest, or possibly underground somewhere. One thing he knew for sure was dissent for Prince Ostello and his dark, evil ways, was rising all across the city.

The next morning during the training session in the courtyard, Zeke was there, again, camouflaged and silenced. Instead of sitting at the edge of the courtyard, this time he slowly wandered through the ranks and files of the trainees. He was trying to listen for chatter to see who was talking about fighting back or disagreeing with Ostello. Grambine was right. About a third of the morning session was murmuring about how they wished things were better and trying to figure out a way to get out from under the prince's rule.

If all of the people that sounded like they were against Prince Ostello, actually stood against him when the time came, the prince would be greatly outnumbered. If he could somehow convince them to leave before Prince Ostello began his attack maybe he would see that he did not have the numbers. Zeke was sure that most would be afraid to leave, thinking that Ostello would retaliate. They would be more open to leaving if they knew that King Sol would take them in, which would also take some convincing on Zeke's part.

Zeke returned to Occulta Vallem Magia, with plenty of time to prepare for the day's transformation ritual. After the ritual Zeke would go talk to King Sol again. He felt the king needed to know about the level of dissention in Superbia Saltu. There may still be a way out of this without a war that would decimate the population.

When Zeke jumped to the Cortis Mundi that evening, he did not need to make a startling appearance. He arrived just outside the city walls next to the port. As he walked through the city streets towards the palace, he got looks of recognition from the mundians. Zeke arrived at the palace walls and informed the Royal Guards that he was there to see King Sol. They promptly let him in and sent him unassisted to find the king.

Zeke easily found King Sol and Queen Lunam in the Royal Courtyard.

"Zekious." King Sol said, smiling when Zeke entered the courtyard. "To what do I owe the pleasure? How are you doing this evening?"

"I am here with news of Superbia Saltu." Zeke replied. "The level of dissention there is on the rise. There are groups of rebellion all over the city that are beginning to secretly band together."

"That is good news." King Sol said. "Maybe they can all come together as one and put an end to my son without there being a war."

"They do not have those kinds of numbers yet." Zeke replied. "However, it may be enough that if they were to openly join us, it may be enough for him to see how outnumbered he is and he may back down."

"Or, possibly when he does attack," King Sol started. "And they change sides then, it may be enough to get him to stop his attack."

"I think, at that point it will be too late." Zeke countered. "He is using mind control as well. I believe that when he attacks, he will have most of his army back to believing what he is doing is the right thing. He does have a few weaknesses though. He is not teaching his army to jump, that power is kept to small few. They are only attacking the slaves, the slaves that are not taught magic. If the slaves accidentally do pick up the magic that is being used on them, and use it to defend themselves, they are tortured or killed. His army will not be accustomed to a full-fledged battle where we are attacking back. Grambine also told me they have not discovered any means of flight. We have our brooms. They will also be key during the battle."

"That does us give a little more of an advantage." Sol agreed. "If anyone there is willing to leave the prince and join me, I would welcome them with open arms."

"As would I." Zeke replied. He was caught off guard by how easy it was to convince King Sol to take in dissenters from Superbia.

After their conversation, Zeke would return to Superbia. He would try to find out where the other groups were gathering. If he and the Guardians could consolidate them all under one banner and convince them to all leave at once it might be enough to stop the war. Zeke and King Sol also discussed alternatives just in case they could not convince enough people to leave Prince Ostello.

First, they agreed to weekly meetings, to discuss the news that they learn each week. Second, King Sol would start teaching animal transformation to those that would want to learn. They would also start sharing new magic that each had learned so that everyone knew as much as they could going into the battle. They agreed that everyone needed the biggest advantage that they could, just in case they were not successful in getting Prince Ostello to see reason and back down.

Zeke returned to Superbia Saltu and met with Grambine once more. He explained to the Guardians that both he and King Sol would take anyone that wanted to change sides. He told them that he wanted to find some of the other groups so that he could tell them the same thing. It would be best if those that wanted to leave, all left at the same time. When Ostello found out that people were leaving him to go the other side, it probably would not go very well for those that stayed.

The Guardians explained that there was a very strict curfew. If anyone was caught on the streets after dark they would be killed on the spot. The enforcers were all sensers, so if Zeke were to use his "sano" and "indespectus" spells, they would know he was there. Zeke thought that he might be able to use serums. The Guardians had their doubts that Zeke's serums would work, the sensers can feel any use of magic, and as magic was not allowed during curfew, they would more than likely be able to know that someone was using magic.

Zeke surmised that, like the Guardians, the other groups may be using somewhere in the forest to gather and train. The forest was far too large to search very much of it in one night. But he had brought his broom. He told the Guardians that he would fly around above the forest looking for lights and make note of where he saw activity below.

As he flew over the forest, he was right. He saw lights and heard voices in about twenty different spots spread out through the forest. All far enough from the city that they could not be felt by Ostello's Royal Enforcers. When Zeke returned to the clearing where the Guardians were, he described in detail where the other groups were. Although the Guardians were excited to know where the other groups were meeting, they were more interested in his broom.

They were asking him a lot of questions about the broom. He explained how Barmor had developed them, and how everyone at his school, and most of the mundians, had built their own. They all wanted to ride it. Zeke would not allow them to ride it, because there was not enough time for everyone to ride. He told them how to make their own. He told them that it would be best if no one that sided with Prince Ostello saw anyone flying. Flight was one the few advantages that they had over Prince Ostello.

Now that they knew where the other groups were, they would be able to jump there to discuss working together. Grambine and the other Guardians would start trying to meet with the other groups of defectors over the next week. Zeke, Barmor and King Sol would return next week. Hopefully by then most of the groups would all be willing to sit down with them.

Zeke returned to the school. When he arrived, the sun was just starting to come up over the eastern cliffs of the valley. It was starting to get cool even on the valley floor, as winter was quickly approaching. The mountains were already covered in snow. In fact, the valley floor was about the only place nearby that was not already covered in snow. As sessions returned that morning, everyone's focus remained intense.

That week they intensified attack and defense classes, as well as battle strategy. In both classes they began working hard on engaging multiple assailants at the same time. Changing from one target to another while being attacked from all sides. They also worked a lot with one-on-one dueling all week as well.

The night before the dueling competition, when everyone was seated before they started eating, Ridmeus stood and asked if he could address the school. Zeke told him that would be great.

"We have been working all week on combating multiple enemies at once." Ridmeus began. "In the previous dueling matches we have all begun using our brooms which is a good strategy, however, we have not done much fighting on the ground. In the battles to come we may not be able to use our brooms and we need to know how to work from the ground as well."

He paused while everyone considered his words. When the murmurs of agreement began, he continued. "Let's make this one a little more interesting.

No brooms. No building cover to hide behind. Let's see how it turns out if we just stand and face off. It may hurt my chances as I am on the grossly outnumbered side, but it will give us a good look at how we might fair against a larger army."

"That sounds like a good idea." Zeke said over the shouts of both agreement and disagreement. Zeke allowed the dining hall to quiet down again before repeating himself. "That sounds like a really good idea. The brooms will be advantageous when it comes time, and we have seen several different strategies involving the brooms, but we have not done much without the brooms or without making your own cover."

After Zeke had spoken, the murmurs of disagreement among the students changed to agreement. They all agreed that tomorrow during the competition, it would be wands only, and they would not be conjuring any cover. The whole battle would be fought on the ground, facing off with each other toe to toe.

After dinner the Griffins and the Phoenix met in a large empty classroom to work on their strategy and get some last-minute practice in. The rest of the students found their own empty classroom to do the same thing, all of their practice so far had mostly been involving brooms.

With the transformation ritual taking up the late afternoon, Zeke and the school had decided to have an early breakfast. The dueling competition would start in late morning, and they would forgo lunch, until after the competition. When it was time, everyone headed for the lapidem field. King Sol and Queen Lunam arrived while everyone was filing into the field.

The red team, the Griffins and the Phoenix, started on the north end of the field. The rest of the school would be the blue team, and they would start on the south end of the field. There were about twice as many on the blue team as there were on the red team. When Zeke shouted to start the match, both teams charged forward.

When they reached the center of the field the red team broke off into pairs. The pairs lined up back-to-back, forming two lines. The blue team formed a circle around the red team. Spells erupted from both teams. Both teams started out blocking and deflecting the incoming spells very well.

Ridmeus was doing an excellent job of deflecting the inbound spells back at the blue team. In the first few minutes of the match, he was able to connect with eight different adversaries, taking them out of the fight. The blue team was able to get their injured fighters back in the match right away, due to their advantage in numbers. Whenever a red player was eliminated next to Ridmeus, he was quick to break the spell or physically heal them, bringing them back into the fight.

Because of his ferociousness and ability to keep his teammates in the fight, Ridmeus, had become a prime target of five fighters from the blue team. With that many adversaries focusing on Ridmeus, the other red fighters had fewer blue fighters to contend with. The red team could eliminate more blue fighters, but the blue team was still able to tend to their downed team mates quickly.

After the battle had been raging for nearly ten minutes both teams had all of their fighters standing again. Without warning, all of the red players jumped to the outside of the circle created by the blue team, appearing behind the fighters. They were able to eliminate almost half of the blue players.

The surprise attack had the blue team scrambling. Most of the remaining blue fighters began attacking the red team one on one. Two blue fighters left the fight and began breaking the spells on their downed blue teammates. As a blue fighter was brought back into the fight, they quickly joined their teammates that were dueling with the red fighters.

In just a few moments the blue team had all of its team members back in the fight again. Ridmeus was fighting against four blue fighters, the rest of the reds were battling with two blue challengers. The battle continued this way for several minutes. Neither team was able to land an attack on the other.

Although the red team was outnumbered more than two to one, they were able to hold their own. They were able to block or deflect every incoming attack. Every time they were able to eliminate a blue fighter, the blue team was big enough to send a teammate to bring the injured player back right away. The red team knew that if they did not start to eliminate the blue fighters permanently, they would soon start becoming too tired to fight effectively.

Neither team was able to push the other team back. Ridmeus finally used a spell that he had been working on in private. With the word "brastes" the ground around him began to heave and roll. The earthquake spell knocked most of the blue team off their feet. The red team acted quickly attacking the blue team while they were distracted. The attack took out more than half of the blue team.

Now with the numbers even on both sides, the red team pushed forward. The blue team did not have time to spare anyone to go revive their fallen teammates. Even though the larger blue team had lost half of their force they were still surviving one on one against the red team. The red team had forced the blue team into a small group and formed a circle around them.

Now with the blue team surrounded and nowhere to go, the red team had full control. Or at least they thought that they did. When the blue team had gotten surrounded, during the flurry of smoke and sparks of all the attacks and parries, two members from the blue team jumped out of the circle of red fighters. Again, they began reviving their blue teammates that had been eliminated during the earthquake attack.

The now revived blue fighters had rejoined the fight, attacking the red team from behind. When the blue team was back to full fighting force, the red team was caught in a crossfire. They were in trouble. In a final stand, the red team began a jump then attack and jump again strategy.

They would jump randomly and throw a few quick attacks. When the blue turned to find where they were, the red team would jump again. They would jump behind the enemy combatants and attack. Each attack and jump would result in a few blue fighters to get taken out, and each time the blue team would be able to revive a couple.

After several rounds of their new strategy, they were once again making a dent in the blue team's numbers. The blue team also got wise to the red team's tactics and began using them as well. The lapidem field was filled with sparks and wisps of different colored smoke from the attacks all over the field. The field was also filled with the faint sounds of pops and snaps of people jumping erratically. With everyone now using the same tactics, it was hard for Zeke and the other spectators to tell who had the upper hand.

The attack zend jump strategy was so fast paced, that if anyone from either team stopped to revive a fallen teammate, they themselves would get taken out right away. After several minutes, it appeared that the red team was again taking the advantage. There were more blue team players laying on the ground than there were red team players.

The battle continued like this, and eventually the active red players once again outnumbered the blue players still in the fight. When that happened the red team quickly claimed victory. When the battle was over, the remaining red players, drenched in sweat and gasping for every breath, fell to their knees or sat down in exhaustion. Zeke, Barmor, and the king and queen jumped to center of the field and began helping revive the fallen players.

Zeke and the others waited for the players to catch their breath after all the students had been revived. There were words of congratulations among the players as they gathered around Zeke. When everyone had caught their breath and sat down around the center of the field, Zeke started his customary speech.

"Let me just start by saying," He began. "That was some of the most impressive fighting I have seen yet. It was amazing seeing you change tactics so quickly and smoothly. Keep up the good work. Having the ability to change things up on the fly and having many different strategies is very important. Both sides made a very good come back when you were on the verge of defeat."

"Next week will be our next skills contest." Zeke continued. "Barmor has been working hard to test your skill. The week after that will be our next lapidem match featuring the Yeti and the Centaurs. The week after that will be another dueling contest. At the start of that week, we will decide on the teams. We will be finishing the animal transformation ritual, or the animesco ritual as I've started calling it. I am hoping for some very interesting animescia."

"Before we take a break until tonight's animesco ritual." He added after a short pause. "I went back to Superbia Saltu and watched more of their training exercises. I also spoke more with Grambine. There are several groups banding together that are beginning to see how evil Prince Ostello and his people are getting. Grambine and the Guardians knew that there were some but were not sure how many or where they were meeting. I did some scouting on the broom and saw maybe twenty more groups that were meeting in different places in the forest. Grambine and the Guardians are going to attempt to make contact this week. Next week when King Sol and I visit again, we hope to get better numbers. Sol and I have both agreed to take anyone and everyone that want to leave and join one or the other."

"I have found a few advantages that we have over them." He added. "Firstly, they have not developed a broom or anything else that can fly. Secondly, they are training on the slaves. The slaves are not allowed to practice magic. If they do, they get tortured or killed. Prince Ostello's men will not be accustomed to fighting against people that actually fight back. The prince still thinks we are not a threat, but still wants us out of the way. We are just a steppingstone to get to King Sol. We are just practice to him. And, with any luck, we will have some animescia."

That night after the animesco ritual, everyone had a surprising result. With the final step of the ritual, everyone began to transform. The transformation was fleeting but it was there. For a fraction of a second, everyone started to transform. Their bodies began to change shape, some showed hair, others showed feathers. Everyone was excited that all of this repetition was not for nothing.

King Sol and Queen Lunam stayed to watch the ritual. Zeke explained to them that the ritual had to be repeated at the same time, in the same location, in the same way every day for thirty days. He told them about Pormin, who studied and perfected the transformation ritual. Pormin even demonstrated his transformation for them. King Sol was eager to begin studying the animesco ritual and trying it himself and teaching it to his people.

After the ritual, they all convened in the dining hall for a fantastic meal. After dinner, King Sol and Queen Lunam returned to Cortis Mundi feeling more optimistic about the upcoming battle. After seeing the day's display of skill and knowing what they and Zeke were teaching, that Prince Ostello was not, they felt that they stood a good chance, even though they were outnumbered.

Chapter Twenty-Four

Early the next morning, Zeke jumped to the clearing in the forest outside Superbia. There, it was still the middle of the night, and Grambine and the others were still training. When Zeke arrived, Grambine and a few others came over to greet him. Grambine explained that there were twenty other groups that were opposed to the dominative and evil teachings of Prince Ostello. On average, each group had a thousand members. The next night each group would send a delegation to meet with the Guardians, Zeke, and King Sol. Grambine felt confident that they were prepared to defect.

The thought of taking twenty thousand fighters from Ostello made Zeke even more hopeful about their success. However, having that many people disappear from Superbia Saltu would surely upset Prince Ostello. He would certainly retaliate. If he still did not know where Zeke's school was, King Sol would probably catch the blunt of that retaliation. However, if they stayed and the prince was unaware that they were leaving and they could switch sides at the beginning of the war. He would be caught by surprise.

After meeting with Grambine, Zeke jumped Cortis Mundi to meet with King Sol. He told King Sol about the number of defectors from Superbia. King Sol was impressed that there were that many that were not aligned with Prince Ostello. Zeke informed him that, while that number sounded large, it was only two percent of the Superbian population.

With such a low percentage, King Sol began worrying that he may have two percent of his people that were not happy with his rule. He had his Royale Guards call an emergency city meeting in front of the pyramids. When everyone arrived, he asked if there was anyone that was not happy with him and the queen. He assured them they would not be harmed and allowed to leave to go seek their own life or join Prince Ostello. He asked if anyone would like to leave to please come forward. No one moved.

There were shouts from throughout the crowd. Everyone began chanting "King Sol. King Sol" in unison. King Sol informed his people that if anyone ever felt that he was not the best leader he could be, to please let him know what he was doing wrong. He may be the King, but he wished to always be the best leader that he could be.

When the king was satisfied that his people were not planning a rebellion of their own, he asked them one last question. He had an idea that may prove absolutely insane, but it may be how they would save the most lives.

"How would you feel about taking the fight to them? I am aware that if we attack, we are the aggressor. That being said, if we attack him before he is ready, we will have the element of surprise. There are twenty thousand witches and wizards that will join us in taking him down. The battle will not be easy when it does happen, but if we can control when and where it starts, at least we will not be waiting for it to start. We will not be the ones getting caught by surprise. So, what will it be? Do we wait, or do we prepare to fight?

The whole city erupted with cheers, and shouts of "FIGHT. FIGHT. FIGHT." King Sol told Zeke they would begin making preparations to take the fight to Prince Ostello. He would start the animesco ritual that day. After the students of Occulta Vallem Magia, and the mundians had all finished their animescia ritual, if Prince Ostello had not already attacked, they would.

Zeke was caught off guard by this sudden change in plans. Had he not heard the chanting, and seen the mundians cheering for battle, he would never have believed it. It was spectacular seeing that many people excited about going to war.

Zeke jumped back to the Guardians' clearing. By this time there was no one in the clearing. Zeke hurried through their tunnels and found Grambine in his house. He informed him of King Sol's plan that if war was not already going in thirty days, they would attack Prince Ostello. He also told Grambine that if the groups of citizens that would not follow Ostello left, it could kick off the war before Zeke and the mundians were ready. If they stayed and kept training, then switched sides at the beginning of war, it would be more beneficial to everyone.

Grambine agreed but warned Zeke that none of the other groups had ever learned any kind of defense, that Prince Ostello had always felt his superior numbers would win him the world. Prince Ostello felt the people were expendable. Zeke told Grambine to begin teaching them what Zeke had shown him about defense, and Zeke would keep coming back in the meantime to teach as much as he could. King Sol would be doing the same. Together, they could all stop Prince Ostello's march for world power.

When Zeke returned to the castle. He prepared a letter that said that if Prince Ostello had not attacked in thirty days, Zeke and his students alongside King Sol and the citizens of Cortis Mundi would take the war to him. It was their best hope for the fewest casualties. He gave the letter to Longtail, to be delivered to Miror Austri.

That evening, after the animesco ritual, Zeke asked everyone to take a seat. He had some news to share.

"This morning, I met with Grambine, from Superbia Saltu again." He started. "He said that there are twenty thousand people, in twenty different groups, there that are banding together against Prince Ostello. Grambine has arranged a meeting with a delegation from those groups. King Sol and I will be attending that meeting."

"After I left there, I went to go speak with King Sol again." He continued. "After I told him that there were that many superbians that were against Ostello, he was afraid he may have a large number that were secretly against him, so he called a meeting of his citizens. After they assured him that they were all happy with the style of his rule, he proposed a new strategy."

"He asked the mundians if they felt we should wait until Prince Ostello attacked us," Zeke began telling them the new plan. "Or if we should make a preemptive attack of our own. They all agreed to attack Ostello before he had a chance to attack us. I did not like the idea at first. I have been weighing the advantages and disadvantages of both strategies all day. After much consideration, I now believe it is the right play. He is going to start teaching the animesco ritual today, as well. In thirty days, when the mundians have completed their ritual, we will attack Prince Ostello in Superbia Saltu. Unless of course he has already attacked us. If we do it this way, nearly our whole side with be able to transform into animals. Yes, if we attack, we are seen as the aggressor. But, by attacking first we can catch them by surprise. It is King Sol's belief, by doing it this way we can minimize overall casualties as we are not attacking to kill them, only stop them. How do all of you feel about attacking first?"

Murmurs erupted through the students sitting on the ground. Most were positive, but there were few that did not think this was the best idea. The students began discussing the change of plan amongst themselves. After a several minutes the students began stand up and saying, "We will attack first then."

"What are going to do with them after we stop them?" Ridmeus asked. "What are we going to do with Prince Ostello? I understand we do not want to kill them. I know that I do not wish kill anyone. But we cannot simply defeat them and expect them to fall in line. It would only be a matter of time before Prince Ostello and his truest believers fall back into their evil ways."

"I see your point." Zeke answered. "I have been trying to find that answer since we started down this path. I have not come upon the correct answer yet."

"We could design a fortress of sorts to house them." Barmor said stepping forward. "I have also been thinking the same thing. The only thing I have come up with is a large strong fortress. The fortress will be imbued with different sorts of magic, preventing them from using their own magic to get free. Just like the castle, we can find gnomes willing to feed them. Those with evil tendencies can be given a choice, the fortress, or death. If they chose death, we will do what is necessary."

"That should work." Zeke agreed.

Early the next morning Zeke returned to the Guardians' clearing. The delegates from the other groups were already there. King Sol arrived a few minutes later. They, along with Grambine, took turns explaining the new plan. When the delegates stated that they only knew how to attack violently, Zeke told them that he would begin teaching them less than lethal attacks to subdue the enemy, along with defensive spells. King Sol informed that he would send sixty of his Royal Guard and strongest citizens over to help teach them.

They went on to explain that the key to this approach would be secrecy. In their day-to-day lives they had to act as though nothing was happening. Train hard at night learning the light and pretend to enjoy learning Prince

Ostello's dark form of magic during the day. It was imperative that no one aroused suspicion or got caught talking about the revolution. Grambine assured them that that would not a problem, as no one was allowed to talk out of turn, they would be tortured or killed.

That night after their animesco ritual, Ridmeus asked if they could have another school meeting. Zeke and Barmor happily agreed. Ridmeus said that after last night's meeting, he and the other Griffins had their own discussion.

"We would like to make a suggestion." Said Ridmeus. "How would you, Zeke and Barmor, and the rest of the school feel about foregoing the skills and stealth competitions until after the war. Maybe even lapidem. We will continue the dueling competition and focus our attention on preparing for the war. We enjoy and understand that skills and stealth competitions are necessary for progressing the world, but if we do not win this war there will be no world to progress."

"That isn't a terrible idea." Zeke answered. "We can keep the dueling contest, that is a great way to practice. And Lapidem does help promote battle strategy. How does everyone else feel about forgoing the stealth and skills contests for the time being?"

Everyone agreed. Preparing for the war was the only thought right now. If they were victorious, they would be more than happy to bring back challenges between the clans, but for now, Ridmeus was right. They needed to focus on preparing for the battle of their lives.

"Since that is settled." Zeke said. "We will move our next dueling competition up to the end of this week. We have tried two clans against four twice now, and both times the smaller team has come out victorious. This time we will make it very difficult. We had planned to go five on one with no revivals, but we will reserve that for next time. You truly want to plan for the war, we will do a free for all. Every man for himself. No clans, no revivals, no killing, and no help."

"How is that going to prepare us the war?" Dalvo asked "During war we will have teammates."

"During the war," answered Zeke. "Yes, you may have friends, but the superbians will not hesitate to kill you. We have figured out how to break the spells that we know, but we cannot bring back those who have died. If you fall during this war, you are gone. And this war is going to be absolute chaos, you will need to know what is going on all around you. This will help with that."

"Oh, that makes sense." Dalvo answered.

The rest of the week, everyone trained harder and longer. Every spare moment the students were trying to figure out new spells. They stayed longer in the library every night, studying. Even Zeke and Barmor intensified their studying and practice. Little did the rest of the students know they would be joining them in the dueling contest. After all they would be a part of the war, they might as well test themselves against their students.

That week Zeke and Barmor also spent a lot of time jumping back and forth between Occulta Vallem Magia, the Guardian's clearing, and Cortis Mundi. They were making and revising battle strategies with King Sol, Grambine and the delegates from the other groups. They also discussed the creation of a fortress of sorts to hold those of evil intent. They began calling it Phylaca Malignus.

Chapter Twenty-Five

The morning of the day before the free for all duel, Longtail returned with word from Miror Austri. The letter said that they had been working hard and learned much magic. As promised, they would be there to help when the time came. They all had brooms so they would fly to Superbia Saltu.

From where their homeland was, they could fly to the northeast to reach Superbia. They estimated that the flight would take two days. They would leave on day twenty-five and set up camp in the forest south and west of the city. Arriving a few days before Zeke and King Sol were to start their attack, would give the Mirori a couple days to rest and scout.

Zeke thought that would work great. The Guardians and the other groups of revolutionaries were scattered north of the city. Their tunnels would give great access to sneak in and out of the city if they needed. King Sol and the mundians could sail upriver and attack from the east. Zeke and the students could attack from the air, aboard the Cherry of the Sky.

On the morning of the free for all, King Sol and Queen Lunam arrived from Cortis Mundi. Grambine and the other delegates also arrived from Superbia Saltu. Zeke had given them permission to come watch the free for all and explained how to get past the protections put in place to guard the valley. They were all excited to see what the students at Zeke's school could do, all facing off against one another. The visitors also did not know that Zeke and Barmor would be joining the fight.

Zeke was the first at the lapidem field before the dueling competition began. With a wave of his wand, he covered the field in a deep thick darkness. When everyone else arrived, he instructed everyone to pick a place on the field by themselves. When everyone had chosen a place to start, Zeke would lift the darkness. Everyone made their way through the darkness and the guests took their seats in the stands.

Everyone waited in silence until Zeke lifted the darkness. It was complete chaos when the match started. Nearly everybody immediately began with a jump and attack tactic. There were many casualties in the first fifteen seconds. After that, the fight settled into many one-on-one duels, still with many fighters using insta-flight to their advantage, and others had taken to the air with their brooms.

When one player won his current duel, it was easy for them to find another target. If they did not immediately see someone not fighting, they simply attacked someone who was not paying attention. The battle continued until only Mevlar, Dalvo, Zeke, Ridmeus, and Markar were left standing.

Either they were the five best fighters, or the luckiest. The four students considered it a badge of honor to be the one that eliminated their teacher. They all began working as a team to take out Zeke. They were all on their brooms at the time, but they were too well matched on their brooms, and they took the fight to the ground.

Even with four attackers coming after him, Zeke was able to fend them off. Zeke would block or dodge every attack, then send an attack of his own. The four students were also good enough to either block or dodge the incoming attacks from Zeke. After several minutes of not being able to catch Zeke off guard, Markar tried to change things up.

Markar waited until he thought he could throw a sneak attack at Ridmeus. Ridmeus, Dalvo, and Mevlar, with the nature of the battle being only one winner, knew that any one of the others could break the unspoken alliance at any time. Ridmeus was ready for Markar's surprise attack and jumped out of the way. The fight then broke off with Markar and Ridmeus going toe to toe. Dalvo and Mevlar were still trying to bring down Zeke.

Both battles raged separately. In the battle with Ridmeus and Markar, neither one of them could get the upper hand. Every spell sent from either fighter was blocked or parried. Meanwhile, Dalvo and Mevlar would wait until Zeke's attention was on the other and try to attack when they thought that they could catch him off guard. The two fights seemed like they would never end. Everyone was moving so fast that the lapidem field was just a blur, and the spectators could not track most of the action.

Markar tried to turn Ridmeus to stone, Ridmeus jumped behind Markar and tried to freeze him. Markar jumped to the side. The fight had been so physically demanding that everyone was getting fatigued and short of breath. When Markar jumped to the side, he stumbled as he reappeared. That gave Ridmeus the time to attack again with another "refrigero". Markar recovered from the stumble just in time and rolled out of the way. Ridmeus followed up with a rigid body spell, "rigesco". Markar blocked the incoming spell and parried with the "gelata" spell.

Ridmeus also blocked and deflected the "gelata" back at Markar, and immediately followed it up the pushing spell, "trudo". Markar had gotten too tired, and his reflexes were too slow. He got hit by his own jelly limb spell, then his limp body got pushed back fifteen feet, by Ridmeus' follow up attack. The fight was now down to four remaining fighters.

Ridmeus made his way to where Zeke was defending himself against Dalvo and Mevlar. Ridmeus tried to decide when to assert himself into the fight at the most opportune time. Before he could though, Dalvo tried to pull him into Zeke with "sublego". Ridmeus jumped out of the way and reappeared behind Mevlar.

When Ridmeus appeared, he attacked Mevlar with the knotting spell, "nodum". Mevlar blocked the attack over his shoulder and jumped to the side of Ridmeus. Ridmeus was ready for the jump and sent a "trudo" at Mevlar as soon as he appeared. Mevlar blocked the spell and retaliated with the senseless spell, "excors". Ridmeus used "averto" to block the spell and send it back at Mevlar as he did with Markar. Mevlar was still fresh enough to have quick reflexes and blocked his own spell coming back at him. Ridmeus went on the offensive, and started sending spells in rapid fire, hoping to tire Mevlar out.

Mevlar continued on his own offensive. Both men would attack and jump, trying to push their opponent to their physical limits. As all four remaining fighters were nearly equal in their knowledge and skill, winning the competition would come down to who had the most physical endurance. Every time they jumped, and every spell they cast took a little more out them.

Zeke and Dalvo were using the same tactics, trying to make the other one tired enough to make a mistake.

Ridmeus was starting to get very tired, he was afraid that he was not going to have enough energy to defeat Mevlar and Zeke. Mevlar was also getting very tired. They were fighting purely from adrenaline. If Dalvo and Zeke were starting to get exhausted, they were doing a good job hiding it, they both appeared strong.

As Mevlar was starting to faulter, so was Ridmeus. Mevlar cast a freezing spell at Ridmeus, who jumped out of the way and countered by attempting to turn Mevlar into stone with "muto silex", but Mevlar blocked it. Ridmeus decided to stop trying to jump and catch Mevlar when he reappeared. If Mevlar kept jumping he was sure to get tired faster, Ridmeus would simply listen for the faint sound that was created when someone reappeared after jumping and line up to attack. It took several attempts, but it finally paid off.

Mevlar appeared, Ridmeus used "trudo" to knock him backwards. The attack found its mark, Mevlar fell backwards and slid several feet on his back. Ridmeus followed up quickly with "rigesco". Mevlar rolled to feet just in time to dodge the attack, but before he could counter, Ridmeus sent another rigid body spell, hitting Mevlar in the chest. Mevlar's body went rigid, and he fell face down.

In the final moments of the battle between Zeke and Dalvo, Dalvo was sending spell after spell at Zeke as fast as he could, Zeke would simply step to the side and block the attack, trying to send the attack back its caster. Dalvo's next attack would already be on its way. The reflected and the fresh spell would collide in midair. Zeke deflected a spell back at Dalvo and it missed the incoming spell. Before Zeke could try to block the new incoming spell, he was wrapped in vines from his ankles to his shoulders and toppled over backwards.

Ridmeus turned to join the battle between Dalvo and Zeke, just as Zeke got tied up with vines by "notovitis". Ridmeus wondered to himself, was Zeke out of practice because he had been traveling too much or was he taking it easy on Dalvo because it was not fair for the founder of the school to win the competition and let Dalvo win. Either way, Ridmeus now had to contend with Dalvo, and he could barely stand on his own feet, and Dalvo still look as though he simply walked across the valley floor.

Dalvo and Ridmeus stood at the center of the field about twenty feet apart from each other. Ridmeus' clothes were soaked in sweat, and he was gasping for breath. Dalvo only had a few droplets of sweat on his forehead and his breathing was calm. Dalvo was confident that he would be victorious, with how tired Ridmeus was looking, and after all he was able to single handedly take down Zeke. Although Ridmeus was exhausted, he too was confident that he could still win. He had a few tricks up his sleeve that he had not told anyone about.

Dalvo began with the attack and jump tactic, hoping that Ridmeus would follow suit and tire more quickly, but Ridmeus would block and deflect waiting for the right moment to attack, he was going to conserve what little energy he had left. Dalvo kept trying to get the angle and surprise Ridmeus. Ridmeus, just as he was doing with Mevlar, would listen for the sound, sidestep, and attack or block.

Ridmeus gathered every last ounce of energy he had left. He knew that what he was about to do had required more energy than he had left, but it was his last chance. If he did not stop Dalvo soon, he would not even have enough energy to block. He waited until Dalvo appeared after a jump and sent an attack toward him. Ridmeus jumped behind Dalvo, then he jumped again before fully reappearing. Then he did it again and again. The next thing Dalvo knew, there appeared to be ten different instances of Ridmeus appearing and disappearing all around him.

Dalvo did not know what was going on, or where Ridmeus really was. The flurry of Ridmeus jumping around Dalvo in a circle continued for about a second and a half.

"Refigero". Ridmeus said. Dalvo had been hit by the freezing spell in the chest from directly in front of him. Dalvo was encrusted in ice and fell backward. Ridmeus collapsed to knees then rolled over to his back. The match was over, and Ridmeus had come out victorious.

King Sol, Queen Lunam, and the visitors for Superbia Saltu came down from the stands and began breaking the spells that people had fallen to. As students got revived, they began helping others. When everyone had been released from their spells, they all gathered together around Ridmeus and Dalvo. When Ridmeus was able to catch his breath and breathe normally again, he sat up. Dalvo was standing next him, his clothes now dripping with sweat.

"How did you do that?" Dalvo asked. "How did you make it look like there were ten of you all around me?"

"I call it mirage." Ridmeus answered. "Normally I can do it longer, but it is a one-use process because it uses so much of my energy to do it, so I saved it for the end. I am surprised that I was able to make it work. I make it appear there are copies of me by jumping extremely fast. You see multiples of me, not knowing where I really am, giving me the chance to land an effective attack. Why are you sweaty now, when I dropped you, you barely had any sweat?"

"When you were fighting Markar," Dalvo replied. "I cast a drying spell on myself, giving the illusion that I was not sweating so everyone else would think that I was not getting tired. It also helped me keep my confidence up. Zeke, did you let me win on purpose?"

"What?" Zeke asked as though caught off guard. "No. No way would I *let* you best me. You did that all on your own. I got tired and made a mistake. Plain and simple."

By this time Ridmeus and Dalvo were able to stand up. Everyone gave their congratulations. Zeke reminded them that that next week would be the next lapidem match, the Dragons would take on the Phoenix, and they were almost halfway through the animesco ritual. Now it was time to rest and prepare for that evening's ritual.

Chapter Twenty-Six

After that dueling competition, everyone saw how important physical stamina was during battle. They all took it among themselves to condition themselves better, physically. They all began running around the valley twice a day, once in the morning, and once at night after the animesco ritual.

At the start of the next week, Zeke continued to jump back and forth between the Guardians' clearing and Cortis Mundi to meet with their allies. Their main topic of discussion was obviously the upcoming battle for the health and prosperity of the world. They discussed battle strategy and how everyone was progressing with their magical knowledge. They also discussed how and where to build Phylaca Malignus, the prison to house the worst offenders.

They agreed that their best option to keep the worst sort of people was far from other people. Zeke suggested building their dungeon somewhere in the far north beyond the ice wall, the others agreed. Zeke told them that from his castle, he could get to the ice wall in a short amount of time either by broom or on Longtail.

It was decided that Zeke would begin scouting beyond the ice wall in the far north to find a place to build their prison. The first day that he began looking he rode Longtail to scout, Barmor also came along on his broom. The ice wall was over a mile high and as far as Zeke knew no one had ever been beyond the wall. When they arrived at the ice wall, they realized it was not a wall. It was, in fact, a layer of ice. A sheet of that was more than mile thick.

That would be perfect, they could build the dungeon into and under the ice. With a large maze of tunnels, it did not really need to be guarded. Even if someone figured out how to get out of the dungeon, they could get lost in the tunnels. The tunnels and dungeon would be enchanted so that no one could perform magic. They could choose any spot that they wanted several hundred miles north of the edge of the layer of ice.

It only took the two of them a week to carve the castle out of a stone cliff when they had a lot less knowledge, if they brought some of the others to help, they would be able to carve the dungeon out of ice with the knowledge they had now a lot faster. At the next meeting, Zeke would relay their plan on where and how to make Phylaca Malignus.

Back at Occulta Vallem Magia, if the students were not at lessons, they were practicing what they had learned or trying to develop new magic. While they were developing new magic, Dalvo invented a spell, "inpulsa", that would send a bolt of lightning. They found out that when the lightning was cast, the people that were in the immediate vicinity to it were not able to perform magic for a short while, and all magic in the area stopped. Apparently, there was something about the electricity in the lightning that disrupted the flow of magic. Because of the damage that it could cause they decided to only use that one on enemies.

Every evening when they did their animesco ritual, everyone's transformations were becoming clearer and more pronounced. Some of the students were starting to know what they were going to turn into. Zeke was sure that he was going to transform into a dire wolf. While Barmor knew that he was turning into a saber-toothed tiger, his teeth were beginning to stretch into long fangs.

Everyone was up early, the morning of the lapidem match. Everyone except the Dragons and Phoenix got their morning exercise in before the game was to start. The players did not do theirs, so they would be fresh for the lapidem match.

When the students began filling the stands, the king and queen were already there as were the delegates from Superbia Saltu. The Dragons took the south end of the field and would be scoring in the gold basket, the Phoenix took the north end of the field to score in the silver basket. A long narrow black stone appeared in the center of the field, A silver basket appeared thirty feet above the Dragons, and a gold basket thirty feet above the Phoenix.

The Phoenix were the first to gain control of the black stone, by using "sublego" to pull it toward them and racing to meet it on their brooms. Once they had control of the long narrow black stone, they took on a tight vee formation, with the stone carrier in the center of the vee.

The Dragons got ahead of them and formed a tight group of their own and rushed the incoming Phoenix. The two teams met head on with a crash. All but two of the Phoenix got injured and fell off their brooms, including the stone carried. The Dragons picked up the stone and rocketed toward their gold basket.

The Dragons reached the basket before the Phoenix could get their injured teammates off the field and send in replacements. When they were above the basket and dropped the stone to score, the baskets switched positions. The Dragons could not retrieve the stone before it was in the basket, scoring five points for the Phoenix.

Another black stone, this time about the size and shape of a potato, showed itself on the south end of the field. The baskets were in the center of the, orbiting each other twenty feet above the ground.

Again, the Phoenix seized early control of the stone. This time they repeatedly passed the stone between players as they raced to baskets. The Dragons arrived at the baskets at the same time as the Phoenix. When the stone carrier reached the baskets, she dodged the two incoming Dragons, and easily deposited the stone into the silver basket. Another five points for the Phoenix.

A third black pear-shaped stone glinted on the north end of the field. The gold basket was along the eastern side, just short of the north end of the field, forty feet off the ground. The silver basket was in the same position on the western side of the field. This time the Dragons were the ones to claim possession of the stone.

As the Dragon stone carrier rounded on the basket, both of the baskets moved to ground, in the center of the field, just short of the south end of the field. The stone carrier threw the stone south and used magic to guide it to the far end of the field. As the stone was in the air, one of the Dragons flew off the field. Then one of the Dragons that were watching from the south end of the field stepped onto the field and caught the stone.

The new stone carried moved toward the baskets and threw the stone into the gold basket. The stone hit the rim of the basket, bounced, and landed in the silver basket, scoring again for the Phoenix. The Phoenix were now leading fifteen points to zero.

The fourth stone was another black stone the size of a loaf of bread and three times as heavy. The stone again appeared in the north end of the field. The new Dragon player left the field, and the player that had left before, stepped back on. He began racing toward the large black stone, on his broom. He had to use both hands to pick up the heavy stone and flew, unsteadily toward the baskets that were floating fifty feet above the center of the field.

The Dragon reached the gold basket and dropped the stone. The Phoenix that was closest to the silver basket used a perfectly timed "sublego" to steal the stone as it was dropped. The Phoenix player caught and dropped it in the silver basket. Another score for the Pheonix. Although the Dragons were a little frustrated that they had not yet scored they were not afraid that they would lose as the red stone was worth one hundred fifty points

The first blue stone, the size of an apple, was twinkling halfway between the north end and the center of the field. The baskets were fifteen feet off the ground, halfway between the south end and the center of the field. The baskets were traveling back and forth between the sides of the field. The Phoenix picked up the stone and formed a small tight group passing the stone between the players.

The Phoenix took an early lead racing toward the baskets, with the Dragons trailing behind, unable to catch up. As the Phoenix arrived at the flightpath of the baskets they met the silver basket on the edge of the field, and easily scored another ten points. The Phoenix were now leading thirty to zero.

Another blue stone appeared in the center of the field. This one was the size of the head of a pegasus, but as light as a feather. The gold basket was bobbing up and down from thirty-five feet to forty feet off the ground in the northeast corner of the field. The silver basket was doing the same on the northwest corner of the field.

The Dragons were able to get to the stone first. The stone was too light to be physically thrown between teammates so if they passed it, they had to do it by magic. They flew unhindered to the basket. When the stone arrived at the gold basket in the hands of Dalvo. He used both hands to set the stone into the basket. He released the stone inside the rim. The stone was so light that it fell slowly, and the basket moved before the stone reached the bottom.

The Phoenix retrieved the light stone as it floated towards the ground and took off in the direction of the center of the field where the baskets were now hanging forty feet off the ground. The Dragons were slow to catch up, frustrated that yet again, the basket moved or changed before they could score. The Phoenix quickly made it the silver basket and scored again. The Phoenix had forty points, and the Dragons still did not have any.

Then a third blue stone arrived on the ground in the middle of the field. The silver basket was twenty feet above the ground at the south end of the field, and the gold basket was twenty feet off the ground at the north end of the field. Every few seconds the baskets would instantaneously switch positions.

Dalvo dove and scooped up the squirrel sized blue stone for the Dragons. He rushed for the north end of the field, well ahead of the other players on the field. When he arrived at the basket, it was still silver. He waited a few seconds, and the basket changed to the gold basket. Dalvo dropped the stone into the basket, and it immediately changed back to silver. The Phoenix were awarded another ten points.

Then a green stone appeared on the ground directly below where Dalvo was. By the time he could dive to retrieve the small green stone, the Phoenix had already picked it up. The baskets were sitting on the ground on either side of the stone. The stone got placed in the silver basket, making the score one hundred points for the Phoenix. The Dragons had still been unable to score.

Another green stone appeared back at the south end of the field. The baskets reappeared right where they were a moment before. Three players from each team raced to the far end of the field. One player from each team stayed near the baskets, while the remaining players went to the middle of the field. Whichever team was able to collect the stone would be able to pass it to the players that were closer to the baskets, getting the stone to basket quicker.

The Dragons were the ones to collect the stone. When the stone carrier had a clear throw, she passed it to the player in the middle of the field. The middle player used "sublego" to get the stone more quickly, and immediately turned and passed it to Dalvo waiting near the baskets. As the stone was thrown, the players from both teams waiting at the baskets used "sublego" at the same time.

The Phoenix player won the magic battle over the stone. When the player caught the small green stone, he threw it into the silver basket. The Phoenix were now leading by one hundred fifty points. The players waited for the next stone to show up.

There was the red stone, rather, the red pebble, in the middle of the field. The gold basket was ten feet off the ground at the north end, while the silver basket was the same at the south end.

The Dragon player that was waiting in the middle of the field swooped down and collected the tiny red stone and flew north. He used magic to send the red pebble to Dalvo that was still at the north end of the field. Dalvo caught the stone and evaded the incoming Phoenix player.

When Dalvo arrived at the basket, he placed the stone in the basket all the way to the bottom, making certain the basket was still gold and still there, assuring that they would score. When he released the stone, everyone thought the game was over. It took them several seconds to process the final score. When they looked at the scoreboard to see if it was enough to win. It was a tie.

In the event of a tie after the red stone had been used, the game would go into sudden death. One more stone and only one basket. The score would go to the last team to touch the stone before it entered the basket. There sitting on the ground in the center of the field was another black stone. Floating in the air forty feet above the stone was a solitary basket.

The Phoenix were the first ones to pick up the stone. As they charged toward the basket, the Dragons charged at the incoming Phoenix. There was a loud crash as all ten players clashed together. Three Phoenix and two Dragons were on the ground, including the stone carrier. Dalvo retrieved the stone with "sublego" before anyone could react to the crash and flew to the basket. He deposited the stone into the basket, winning the game for the Dragons.

As the basket and stone disappeared, the players landed at the center of the field and began helping those that got injured during the game. Zeke and the spectators joined the players at the center of the field. When they arrived, Zeke congratulated them on a game a well-played and praised the Dragons for not giving up when baskets kept changing and moving at the worst possible time.

He finished his speech by telling them about next week's dueling competition. It would be all clans against each other. No revivals. The clan with the last remaining fighter would win.

After the speech, they had their animesco ritual. During the ritual, the student's transformations lasted almost a second. They were really seeing what they were going to transform into. There were going to be many different animals, including wolves, tigers, eagles, and even a dragon. Everyone was excited that in just over a week they would be able to transform whenever they wanted. Zeke and Barmor felt they needed something positive to look forward to, with the war for the world looming in the future.

At the beginning of the next week, Zeke, Barmor, King Sol, Queen Lunam, along with Grambine and some of the delegates from the other rebel groups met at the place on the ice shelf where they decided to build their magical dungeon. They began by digging a maze with hundreds of miles of tunnels. There was only one entrance and one correct path that reached the center. In the center of the tunnels, they began building the dungeons.

They carved small cells into the ice. The cells were all along long hallways. Each hallway had thirty cells, and there were ten hallways for each level. They started with five levels of hallways for the time being. If they needed more cells, they could carve deeper into the ice. As they were carving the dungeons of Phylaca Malignus, a tribe of ice gnomes came to see what was happening. The ice gnomes were about a foot tall, had large bulbous eyes, tall, pointed ears, and almost nonexistent noses. After Zeke explained what they were doing he asked if the ice gnomes would be willing to be the custodians of the dungeons. The ice gnomes were excited to have a purpose in life.

To keep the prisoners contained, they covered the entire complex with spells to block magic. Before someone was sent there, their wand would be taken, and no one would be able to perform magic on the premises, except for the ice gnomes. Their form of magic was simple and not blocked. There were sound deadening spells placed on the entire complex so that even if someone was talking, no one would be able to hear. The only thing anyone would hear was their own voices. The prisoners would remain in their cells for their entire stay.

There would only be one small candle placed at both ends of each hallway. The darkness, quiet, and being restricted to their cells would ensure that no one could even begin to plan an escape. In the very rare circumstance that anyone could actually get out of their cell, they would die before they found the only path to get out of the complex.

Their sentences would be determined by their crimes. After their sentence was complete, a prisoner would be evaluated again, if they acted like they would fall back into their evil ways, they would be resentenced. The sheer torturous nature of Phylaca would detour most people from ever wanting to go there.

Making the prison took them less than a day. They had it completed before they needed to return for their animesco rituals that evening. After that night's ritual, Zeke and his students would only have a week's worth left while King Sol and the mundians would have two weeks left.

Zeke's students spent the remainder of the week working hard on practicing for the dueling competition the day after that. The day of the competition, Zeke covered the field in a thick black darkness again. The clans all took a spot in the darkness and waited for the fight to commence.

With one of the rules for this match being no revivals allowed most of the players began fighting on their own, not thinking about working as a team. The Dragons and the Griffins were the only ones to start the match working at teams. Only after half of the other clans' players had been eliminated, did they start working as teams. By that time the Dragons and Griffins had good strategies and easily took out the remaining clans.

Everyone already expected the Dragons and Griffins to be the final two clans as they were the biggest and most well-rounded clans. Even though they were really closely matched, both clans were able to eliminate the other players until it was down to just Dalvo and Ridmeus again.

"Are you ready for rematch?" Dalvo asked.

"Absolutely." Ridmeus retorted. "I have some more new magic that I need to try out. Let's give them another show, shall we."

They both had an easy battle until now, so neither of them was showing any signs of fatigue. As the one-on-one duel began, they both started with the attack and jump strategy. Ridmeus quickly realized that with both of them being less fatigued, their reflexes were a lot quicker than last time. He decided to take on a more conservative, wait and defend strategy. As Dalvo continued using the jump and attack tactic, Ridmeus would listen for the sound of Dalvo reappearing and turn to block or deflect the incoming attack. He would occasionally jump to a new location immediately after seeing Dalvo disappear.

By jumping after Dalvo disappeared, he would reappear after Dalvo, giving Ridmeus an extra split second to attack or block. Dalvo was still quick enough to block Ridmeus' attacks. They both realized that sticking to just one plan of attack was not going to work, they were too predictable to their opponent. They both began changing tactics after every attack, trying to be as unpredictable as they could be.

Ridmeus was waiting for the right time to use some of his new spells that he had created. He had several new magic spells, one of them would spin the receiver on all three axes. Another one would make the target move in slow motion, no matter how fast they tried to move. Apparently, Dalvo had been working on new magic as well.

Ridmeus got lucky and deflected a spell back at Dalvo. The result was something that Ridmeus had not seen happen before. The spell had come at him fast, in the form of a bright white spark. Ridmeus hit it just right with a deflecting block and sent it back and before Dalvo could get out of the way it hit him. When the little white spark returned to Dalvo, it turned into a large bright white light. The light was brighter than the sun. There was also a loud shrill crack sound.

The sound and bright light dazed Dalvo and made him stagger backwards a couple steps. Even though Dalvo was thirty feet away from Ridmeus when the spell hit its creator, it was still bright and loud enough to disorientate Ridmeus. He had been blinded and his ears were ringing. Ridmeus was able to recover almost a second before Dalvo regained his senses.

Ridmeus sent another new magic spell toward Dalvo, taking advantage of the situation. The spell's intention was to overwhelm Dalvo's mind with a multitude of thoughts and anxieties, so that he could not focus well enough to perform magic. However, Dalvo's battle sense were attuned enough, so that as soon the light shined and the sound cracked, he cast a powerful shield around himself. The shield held long enough for him to regain the use of his eyes and ears.

As the battle raged on, they both realized that their physical conditioning that they had been doing was also proving to be very beneficial. Neither of them was tiring as fast as they had during the free for all duel the previous week. As they were not thinking about how tired they were getting, they were able to focus better on the battle. They were able to have multiple plans, looking several steps ahead. Each different plan would be determined by what strategy the other would use.

Neither fighter made any mistakes that they could not recover from. Shortly after Dalvo got hit by his own sunlight spell, Ridmeus was a little slow blocking a "refrigero" and got froze. Luckily, he had figured out how to break some debilitating spells affecting himself, including "refrigero". Dalvo had thought that he avenged his defeat from the last dueling competition when he hit Ridmeus with the freezing spell and was caught off guard when Ridmeus was able to break free and stand back up.

The spectators also thought the battle was over and began cheering. There was a rule stating no reviving teammates. However, there was no rule about breaking spells done to one's self. Zeke and Barmor were very pleased to see Ridmeus had figured out how to break magic done to you. They both made mental note to have him show the rest of the school.

When Ridmeus had gotten back to his feet, he immediately attempted to send Dalvo spinning every which way with his new spell, "totus verso", but Dalvo was able to jump out of the way at the last second. Dalvo reappeared directly behind Ridmeus and sent his new spell that he had been working on, "nemosensus". The spell that would have made it impossible for Ridmeus to formulate any thought hit an invisible shield and bounced directly back to where it was sent from. Dalvo was lucky enough to have jumped to a new location immediately after sending the spell and disappeared before the spell got back to him.

After last week's free for all competition and seeing Ridmeus' mirage technique, Dalvo had been practicing it himself. When he was well rested, he could continue it for just over a full minute. Thinking he could beat Ridmeus at his own game, Dalvo started jumping in a circle around Ridmeus, creating the image of a dozen copies of himself.

Seeing what Dalvo was attempting to do, and knowing how much energy the technique used, all Ridmeus had to do was wait. It would not take long before Dalvo would be completely exhausted. When he saw the number of copies starting to decrease, Ridmeus knew that Dalvo was about spent.

Ridmeus waited until the last copy faded, and there was only one Dalvo remaining and tried to jump out of the circle Dalvo and his copies had made. He could not jump. He could not even move his feet. It was as if his feet were stuck to the ground. Dalvo had figured out how to keep the mirage technique going and still cast a spell. He had hit Ridmeus with some sort of anchoring spell,

Until he figured out how to break free from the anchoring spell, Ridmeus could not move his feet, but he still had the use of his hands and his mind. Hopefully Dalvo had expended too much energy and would have slowed down reflexes. Ridmeus also hoped he could fight and defend himself without being able to move his feet, Dalvo only had to get lucky once.

When Dalvo stopped moving, Ridmeus could tell he was visibly tired. His repeated jumping had taken its toll on him. He was not going to last much longer. There was a flurry of attacks and parries from both fighters. Ridmeus would block, and counter with another attack. Dalvo would deflect the spell back at Ridmeus. Ridmeus fell over twice trying to physically dodge an incoming spell and lost his balance. Dalvo was running on pure adrenalin.

The battle seemed to continue for a very long time, both fighters had their own version of disadvantage that they had to overcome. When Ridmeus had an opportunity to think, he would try to find a way to free is feet, but Dalvo was still pretty relentless in his attacks. Then his chance to get free finally arrived.

Ridmeus was able to deflect a spell back at Dalvo, and Dalvo was too slow to block it and got struck by his own spell. Dalvo looked as though he had been crucified on an invisible cross. With Dalvo not being able to attack for a couple seconds, Ridmeus was able to break his feet free, and was able to move, and more importantly jump, again. Ridmeus immediately jumped behind Dalvo, preparing to attack again. However, Dalvo had freed himself from the imaginary cross and had also jumped to a different spot.

In the brief time that it took Ridmeus to find where Dalvo had gone to, Dalvo had reappeared and sent an attack at Ridmeus. At the last fraction of a second, Ridmeus blocked the inbound spell from Dalvo and deflected it back at him. Dalvo's reflexes had finally failed him, and the spell hit him in the stomach. Dalvo started laughing uncontrollably. While he was laughing and could not focus enough to defend himself, Ridmeus hit him with an extremely powerful sleeping spell. The spell was almost unbreakable because it would put the target into a deep sleep, both the mind and the body.

Ridmeus had proven himself again. He had won, what could possibly be, the final dueling competition. Everyone in the stands gave him a standing ovation, while he began freeing the other students. As students had gotten revived, they began helping free the other students. When all the students had been revived, they all returned to the stands.

When everyone returned to the stands and had sat down, Zeke gave his customary speech, starting with congratulations. After he gave the students their congratulations, Zeke talked to them about next week's events.

There would not be any more group lessons until after the war. They would continue their animesco ritual until their transformations were complete. While they were waiting for King Sol and the mundians to finish their ritual, the students were to continue practicing on their own or in groups. Zeke, Barmor and the more knowledgeable students would be available for help if anyone needed more instruction. Zeke asked Ridmeus to show the others how he broken the spell affecting him. After the speech, they all made their way to the side of the valley where they performed their transformation ritual.

Chapter Twenty-Seven

The next two days were spent practicing and testing each other. The older and more advanced students wandered from group to group, helping the younger students. Dalvo, Ridmeus and the others that had created their own magic taught some of their new spells to the other students.

The students were also talking about what they were going to transform into, and what they would look like. Even though their transformations were not complete, they were starting to show, so most students knew what they were going to become. Everyone was getting excited to see what they could do with their new animal transformations.

According to Pormin, they would need to practice with their animal forms. The students would have to learn how to control their new animal forms. From walking to flying, even learning how to balance themselves would take a little practice. Pormin told them it took two full days to learn how to fly efficiently.

When the time finally came, Zeke and the rest of the school met at that animesco area for their final ritual. Zeke explained that when they completed the final steps of the ritual, their first full transformations would take place. From that point on they would only have to visualize their animesco form and feel their transformation take place. To return to normal all they would have to do was visualize their human form. They would be able to change their form whenever they wanted.

As they all took their places and waited for the ritual to begin, Zeke wondered if they had given themselves enough room for their transformations. They were committed now, due to the precision required in the transformation, they could not move now. When everyone was in their place and it was almost time to start, Zeke counted down from five for the final transformation to begin.

"Five,,,four,,,three,,,two,,,one,,,". Everyone started performing the movements and reciting the words for the last time.

"Find my animal side. Reach my animal side. Become my animal side." They all said in perfect unison.

When they finished the ritual, there was a series of pops, cracks, and claps as everyone's transformations took place. That was followed by the sounds of many different animals. There were several types of roars and growls, there were also howls, chirps, and squeaks. Zeke looked around and saw all the animals in front of him.

The animals in front of him ranged from small insects all the way to a large bull mammoth, and even a dragon. There were even animals where the younger children had been watching from. Apparently, the young children still followed the ritual on their own even though they were not allowed to. It worked out, they had all successfully transformed into animals as well.

As Zeke had suspected, he had transformed into a giant dire wolf. His wolf form was fifteen feet from his nose to the tip of his tail. He was five feet tall at the shoulders. His fur was swirled with black, gray, and white. He had long fangs and sharp claws. His tail was long and bushy.

Barmor was standing next to him in the form of a small red and white monkey. He had been wrong in assuming he would become a sabertooth tiger. He stood about two feet tall, and his tail was as long as his body. He looked as though he was wearing a red tuxedo, all red except for his small chest and stomach, which was white. Barmor was looking himself up and down and checking out what the other students had become as well.

Where Ridmeus had been standing stood a cheetah. He was amber in color with back and orange spots. He had retractable claws on both front and rear paws. The claws were about 4 inches in length. The cheetah was about ten feet from nose to tail tip and stood just under four feet tall at the shoulders. Ridmeus was looking at his paws and extracting and retracting his claws while flicking his tail.

Dalvo was next to Ridmeus unfurling his massive dragon wings. His skin was a dark blue with red spikes on his head, neck, and chest. He also had red plates running along his spine. Dalvo's dragon form stood about seventeen feet tall. When he stretched out his wings, he had a wingspan of twenty-five feet. On his small arms, he had three talons that were about five inches long. His hind feet were like hands as well, they had long fingers with claws for grabbing and holding.

Mevlar was a large woolly mammoth. He had thick long black hair. He stood twenty feet tall at the shoulders and had two long black tusks that were fifteen feet long each. Mevlar was shaking his head and swinging his trunk and tusks.

Markar had taken the shape of an ice cave bear. He had long white hair with flecks of black interspersed throughout. He was eight feet tall at the shoulders, and when he stood on his hind legs, he stood more than fifteen feet tall. On his large paws he had claws that were six inches in length.

As Zeke looked around, he was amazed at all the different animals that his students had transformed into. He could not help but feel a little proud at how far his students had come since he had started the school. After he had looked at himself and the students, he began trying to walk around.

It took him several minutes to figure out how to walk in his wolf form. He was very unsteady on his new legs. When he first started walking, his gate and the motion of his legs did not feel natural. Slowly he was able to finetune his motions and was able to walk smoothly. After walking around for several more minutes he began experimenting with faster gates. Soon he was running and jumping around the valley floor.

While Zeke was trying out his wolf form, Barmor was figuring out how to be a monkey. In a short amount of time, he had figured out how to use his limbs to walk, run, and grab. He did not have much trouble as a monkey was pretty similar to a human. He took off running for the trees to try his luck at climbing and swinging.

Ridmeus was quickly becoming accustomed to his cheetah form. In a few short minutes he was running laps around the valley floor at top speed. Zeke, the dire wolf could not keep up with him. Ridmeus jumped up into a tree and waited for Zeke to pass below him.

Dalvo was having more trouble getting used to his dragon from. He could walk easily enough. However, it took him a while to figure out the use of his wings. He could spread them out and fold them up, but he was having a hard time getting them to flap evenly. It was going to be a while before he would be able to fly. He was also trying to figure out how to breathe fire, that too was going to take a while to perfect.

Mevlar and Markar did not have trouble getting used to their animal forms. In a short time, they were chasing each other, and other students around the valley. After Zeke had had enough running around, he started practicing changing back and forth at will. After one cycle of changing to human and back to wolf, he found it very easy.

The students continued getting used to their new animal forms long into the night. The next morning at breakfast Zeke talked to the school about the week's itinerary. It would be a week before King Sol and the mundians had finished their animesco ritual. Zeke wanted to know more about what was going on with Prince Ostello, and check with King Sol. The students were to continue practicing and helping each other on their own. Zeke would be doing a lot of traveling the next several days.

First, he would go to Superbia and check with Grambine and the delegates of defectors. While he was there, he would try to gather as much information as possible about Prince Ostello. Then he would go visit King Sol and Queen Lunam. There was still a lot that they needed to discuss. Finally, He would go to Miror Austri and see how they were progressing.

The next morning, when it would still be after dark in Superbia Saltu, Zeke jumped to the clearing where Grambine and the guardians met. When he arrived, Grambine was there with a few of the Guardians. They greeted him and Zeke told them about finishing their animesco ritual. He told them about the animals that he and his students could now turn into and demonstrated his transformation into a dire wolf.

After the demonstration, they discussed the upcoming battle. They talked about battle strategies, and how they would hope the battle to go. They still agreed that the Guardians and the other dissenters would remain to appear loyal to Prince Ostello until after the battle started. They discussed the advantages of a nighttime attack.

The Guardians and the other dissenters had learned the insta-fly technique to jump to another location, but Ostello was not teaching all of his followers how to do it. Grambine had the idea that in the middle of the night Zeke, along with his school, the mundians, the dissenters, and the Mirori could all jump into the palace and attack at the same time. He felt that, by the time the rest of the superbians knew their city was under attack, they could already have Prince Ostello and his Royal Guard taken out.

He was certain that if their leaders were all gone, and the superbians saw that they were not only were they outnumbered, but several thousand of the attackers were other superbians, they would back down. Zeke warned to keep the plan between Grambine and the trusted delegates, Prince Ostello may have spies embedded in the dissenters. Grambine and the delegates would tell everyone immediately before it was time to attack.

Zeke agreed that a night attack would give them the best hope. He also believed that if the rest of the city saw that their leaders were no longer able to fight, most of the citizens would give up. There may be some that were proud or ambitious that would stand and fight, but it would be considerably less than taking on the whole city. With a little luck they would be able to take over the palace and stop the prince and his Royal Guard.

After leaving Superbia Saltu, Zeke jumped to Cortis Mundi. There he spoke with King Sol and Queen Lunam, who also agreed a nighttime attack would be best. However, they were worried that simply bringing down the leadership would not be enough to make the other citizens want to surrender, even if they were outnumbered. They actually felt that being attacked in their home, with a surprise attack taking out their leaders would actually give them more pride and drive to fight harder.

Zeke understood where they were coming from. If someone came into his house, he would surely fight harder, but he still felt that when they saw that their leaders had been taken out, they would surrender. Zeke also thought that there were others, besides the Guardians and the other dissenters, that were against Prince Ostello. They would quickly stand down as soon as Prince Ostello and his Royal Guard were brought down.

King Sol and the mundians still had six more days to complete their animesco rituals. After their transformations were completed, King Sol felt that Zeke and the school, along with the Mirori should meet at Cortis Mundi and travel to Superbia Saltu together. Before they would travel to Superbia, they could devise a more solid battle plan. It was already agreed that the Guardians and other deserters would stay in their homes until the battle started, then would attack from within the ranks of the superbians.

When the citizens saw other superbians fighting with the attackers, it might make other citizens join the attackers.

Zeke thought about staying to watch their animesco ritual but decided against it. While he was curious as to what kind of animals the mundians would be transforming into, but he could wait to see them until their transformations were complete. He jumped to Miror Austri to check in with their progress.

It was late in the afternoon when he arrived at Miror Austri. When he saw him coming along the beach, Forvy approached and greeted Zeke enthusiastically. Zeke told him that he had come to discuss the upcoming battle against the superbians. Forvy said that he had bad news.

"We will not be joining you." Forvy began. "After much deliberation, we have decided that we do not want to be a part of this battle. We are a peaceful people. We understand that if this Prince Ostello is not defeated, he will come to get us to join him. Which we will not. It is better for us to be killed than to not remain peaceful. We are fully prepared to remain peaceful or die."

"You vowed to help, when the time came." Zeke snapped. "The time is now."

"My very deepest apologies." Forvy replied calmly. "We did vow to help. But our beliefs will not allow us to join the fight."

"I respect your beliefs." Zeke replied. "I hope we are able to stop him without your help. Our fight was going to be really hard with you, now we will need a lot of luck without, but you have made your decision. May I ask though, why you have changed your mind? Why did you tell me you would help when you knew your beliefs would not allow it?"

"Originally, we had agreed to help because we felt it was our only choice." Forvy answered. "We also felt that the battle was a long way off, and deep down, we had hoped that you would be able to stop the battle and we would not be forced to fight. Now that the fight is eminent, morally, we cannot participate. We regret that we had originally said that we would help but are backing out now that you actually need us."

Zeke was let down, and was secretly angry at them. They had promised that they would be there when the time came. Now that the time had come, and they were going back on their word. Zeke was worried that now they would never stand a chance. Although he was let down, Zeke also understood not giving up on their beliefs. Their beliefs of ultimate peace were as strong to them as his beliefs were to him. Those of doing the right thing for the betterment of the world, no matter the personal consequences.

With a heavy heart, he returned to Cortis Mundi to inform King Sol of the Mirori's decision to not participate. After a short discussion with the king and queen, his optimism had returned. With their combined knowledge along with their animesco abilities, they still believed, although the battle would be hard fought, that they would come out victorious.

After discussing the battle some more and changing the plan slightly to compensate for the Mirori not being there to help, Zeke returned to Occulta Vallem Magia. When he was back home, he and his students continued their practicing and training amongst themselves for the next few days until the mundians had completed their animal transformations. One the night of the mundians final animesco ritual, Zeke and the rest of the school jumped to Cortis Mundi.

Chapter Twenty-Eight

Shortly after they arrived at Cortis Mundi, King Sol and the mundians began their final animesco transformation ritual. As Zeke watched the final steps, the transformations began. King Sol turned into a black and gray giant spider. Queen Lunam was now a giant black and red hornet. The rest of the citizens of Cortis Mundi ranged from small mice to a couple large dragons, and everything in between.

They spent that evening and most of the next day figuring out their transformations and how to use them. When everyone had got a handle on using their animesco forms, the King and Queen, Zeke and the rest of the school, along with the top generals of King Sol's Royal Guard sat and discussed the finer points of their attack.

When it was the middle of the night at Superbia Saltu, they would jump to the palace there. Most of the mundians would jump to the outside of the palace, and stand guard, keeping the superbians out. Zeke and his students, along with some of the mundians would jump inside the palace. They would work their way through the palace in hopes of capturing Prince Ostello, and his inner circle of Royal Guards. Dalvo and rest of the people that could transform into dragons would stay on the outside the of the palace just in case they needed extra help from them. They would leave the next afternoon, when it would be the middle of the night in Superbia Saltu.

There was not much rest that night, everyone was too nervous and worried about the upcoming battle. With the majority of the world population involved, this battle was surely to nearly wipe out the human race. Most of them spent time with their friends and family. When it was time for the attack, they began jumping to the Royal Palace of Superbia Saltu.

Zeke, King Sol, Ridmeus, Barmor, and Longtail, arrived in the center of the palace courtyard and lead the attack. In the beginning, it appeared the surprise attack was going to work. As they began appearing in the courtyard, they quickly, and as quietly as possible, began taking out the patrolling guards. They made their way across the palace courtyard and to the steps of the fortress.

Once they were inside the fortress, Longtail took to the air to patrol the sky and attack as needed. King Sol took a contingent of fighters down the first hall on the left. Barmor did the same going to the right. Zeke and Ridmeus with more fighters continued straight ahead. Further ahead, they came to a flight of stairs going up, leading to the barracks, and living quarters of the fortress.

The left and right halls rejoined in the back of the fortress. King Sol and Barmor rejoined their forces. Together, they followed Zeke up the stairs. Every sentry they came across was quickly subdued before they could sound any type of alarm. Until they reached the barracks.

When they arrived at the first Royal Guard barracks, several of the guards quickly escaped, and sounded the alarm. Fighting in the tight confines inside the fortress would not be conducive to success. At the sounding of the alarm, Zeke and the others jumped back to the courtyard. Shortly after they arrived back in the courtyard, so did Prince Ostello and the rest of the Royal Guards.

Prince Ostello was six and half feet tall had blonde shoulder length hair that looked tangled and the long sides framed his face. He was clean shaven, had hard set jaws and a strong square chin. He looked like he was in late thirties. He wore a black cloak, over black pants and shirt, with the hood back, resting on his shoulders. He looked confused and furious at the same time.

When Prince Ostello saw his father, he became even more enraged. Ostello sent Mahdrin and three more of his top guards to attack King Sol. Zeke was sure that he heard the prince say, "Bring me his head." Zeke continued through the waves of the Royal Guards, making his way toward Prince Ostello.

While he was fighting through the crowd in the courtyard, Zeke could hear the battle beginning outside the palace walls. It did not sound as strong of a battle as they were facing inside the walls. When he glanced up, Zeke saw Longtail and other flying creatures swooping down and picking up unsuspecting superbians and dropping them from just high enough to knock them out or they would throw them into walls.

Zeke kept making his way toward where Prince Ostello was fighting. When he made it to Ostello and prepared to challenge him, Ostello began to taunt Zeke.

"You must be Zekious?" Prince Ostello asked sharply. "You must be the one that thought it was good idea to teach magic to everyone and start a school. I see you were able to convince my father that everyone should be allowed to learn magic."

"Actually." Zeke answered. "You did all the convincing, yourself. Once we heard about you wanting to control the whole world and he saw how evil you had become, he felt the only way to stop you was to allow everyone to learn it. He had actually banished me and my students. We were going to leave you alone. Then we saw the evilness in your heart and knew that you had to be stopped. Give up, tell your people to stand down. Let's talk and figure out how to all get along."

"Stand down?" Ostello shouted. "YOU attacked ME. In the MIDDLE the NIGHT. We are fighting to protect our home. We will not stand down until every one of you are dead. Starting with you." As finished talking he waved his hand, sending red sparks, green smoke, and a flash of blue light flying at Zeke.

Zeke responded quickly, blocking all three spells at the same time. He quickly attacked back, attempting to knock Prince Ostello off his feet. The pushing spell hit Ostello in the chest. He flew backwards landing on his back. Zeke instantly followed up with the jelly limb spell.

As soon as Ostello landed on his back he jumped behind Zeke. Zeke saw him disappear and he jumped himself, to where Ostello had just disappeared from, facing back to where he had been. When he reappeared, he saw Ostello standing where Zeke had just left. Zeke jumped again, so that he would be standing directly in front of the prince. When Zeke reappeared again, Ostello was still there. Zeke punched him in the face, then immediately tackled him.

Ostello was skilled in hand-to-hand combat, as well. When he got tackled, Ostello was able to use the tackle against Zeke. He rolled with the tackle and stuck his legs into Zeke's stomach and launched him as he rolled. As soon as Zeke was clear, Ostello Jumped again. While Zeke was in midair he jumped as well.

They both reappeared where they had originally started their fight, facing each other again. Ostello had drawn his wand by this point, with a single wave, he sent three more simultaneous attacks at Zeke. Zeke sidestepped and rolled to the side. As he came to his feet, Zeke sent a "rigesco" flying towards Ostello. Ostello jumped to avoid the hit.

Zeke stood his ground, waiting to see where Ostello had jumped to. Zeke was beginning to think he may have gravely underestimated the prince. Casting multiple spells at once was not something Zeke had expected. If he survived, that would be something he would have to look into mastering.

Ostello reappeared just to the left of where he had been standing. Zeke began a fast-paced attack, jump, attack strategy, attempting to keep Ostello on his heals. Ostello was forced to dodge or block Zeke's barrage of attacks. They continued the fast-paced attack and move tactic for several minutes, then Zeke changed to a more defensive strategy.

Zeke did not want Ostello getting too used to any one particular fighting strategy, he wanted to keep him guessing. Zeke began waiting and defending himself from whatever Prince Ostello would throw at him. When Prince Ostello saw that Zeke had quit jumping, he took the opportunity to attack.

Ostello charged at Zeke, waving his wand wildly, sending an endless string of spells at Zeke. Zeke began blocking and deflecting the onslaught coming at him. Every so often he would have to step to the side. He would also send his own spells back if he had the chance between attacks. After several more minutes of this continuous defense, it was time to change it up again.

With the fight staying on the ground, neither of them was showing signs of tiring, nor were they making any mistakes that they could not overcome. Zeke thought about using his dire wolf form but as a wolf, he may inadvertently kill Prince Ostello, and he only wanted to stop him. He thought it best to take the fight to the air. If Ostello did not have a way to fly, Zeke would gain the advantage. He would be harder to hit. If Ostello did have some means of flight, the fight would still be pretty equal but with more chances of one of them making a mistake.

Zeke called for Longtail. If the griffin was too busy, Zeke did have his broom, but Longtail would give him more of an advantage. The griffin could fly himself without Zeke having to concentrate on the flight, just attacking. There was also the added bonus of Longtail being able to attack as well. Longtail had not even landed when Zeke quickly jumped onto his back and the took to the air. As he circled around Ostello, sending spells trying to catch him off guard, Zeke saw the look of bewilderment on Ostello's face.

Prince Ostello watched Zeke fly around him on the griffin, he was almost hit several times by Zeke's spells. Ostello was surprised by the fact that someone could actually ride on a griffin. As he was dodging and blocking Zeke's incoming spells, Ostello got a glimpse of several others flying on brooms. In that moment he realized that the mundians and the students at Zeke's school had a broader knowledge of the use of magic, than he gave them credit for. For the first time, Ostello realized that they might lose.

As Zeke was flying around on Longtail, he was able to see how the battle was going. In the courtyard, the battle raged. Prince Ostello's Royal Guard was fighting to the bitter end, but were not sustaining their numbers, the mundians and the students were overpowering the superbians. Outside the walls, however, the citizens had gathered but most were not fighting. There were some proud and courageous citizens that were trying to fight. Those that were attacking, the mundians were quickly able to take out. Zeke was happy to see most of the superbians actually joining the mundians. The mundians were keeping the superbians from entering the palace courtyard.

As Zeke continued to circle around Ostello and repeatedly sent attacks at him, Prince Ostello attacked a Mundian flying on a broom, knocking the Mundian to the ground. Ostello took the broom and took to the air and began to chase after Zeke. It did not take him long to figure out how to fly the broom. As Ostello was chasing after Zeke and Longtail, he began sending attacks at them.

Longtail and Zeke dodged the incoming spells and quickly outmaneuvered Ostello on the broom. Zeke was now chasing Ostello, and continued attacking, trying knock the prince off the broom. As he was chasing Prince Ostello, Zeke had a little more time to look around. He noticed that King Sol and Mahdrin were still battling it out on the ground, but Mahdrin was showing signs of fatigue.

The chase between Zeke and Prince Ostello lasted quite a while. Eventually, Zeke hit Prince Ostello with a "rigesco". Prince Ostello went rigid and fell from the broom. Ostello hit the ground with a thud, right beside where King Sol and Mahdrin were still fighting. Mahdrin saw his prince laying on the ground and moved to protect him. Two more of Prince Ostello's most loyal and trusted guards were also close by and went to assist Mahdrin and their leader.

Zeke steered Longtail toward the ground where Prince Ostello had landed. Before Longtail had landed, Zeke jumped to the ground. Zeke and King Sol moved to attack Mahdrin and the two guards. As they approached the prince laying on the ground and his three top guards, the three guards huddled around their fallen prince and all four of them disappeared. Zeke and King Sol looked around the courtyard trying to see where the group of four had went to.

They were gone. They were nowhere in the courtyard. The remaining Royal Guards in the courtyard, after seeing that their leader had abandoned them, one after the other began surrendering. A few moments later, the battle was over. All attacks had stopped. Zeke sent Longtail to begin flying over the city and surrounding forest to locate Prince Ostello and Mahdrin. Others used either the animesco abilities or their brooms to do the same.

While they were searching, others were attending to the wounded. Less than fifty citizens from Cortis Mundi had been killed. A couple hundred had been injured but were able to be healed. Also, about a hundred of Prince Ostello's Royal Guards had been killed by deflected spells, or crossfire. Another several hundred had been taken out of the fight by a less than lethal spell from a Mundian or one Zeke's students.

As those that could be helped were being attended to and the search for Prince Ostello and Mahdrin continued, they bound and restrained Prince Ostello's Royal Guards, and the citizens of Superbia Saltu that had fought. They would be tried and interrogated. Those that could be trusted would be released, those that remained loyal to Prince Ostello would be held in Phylaca Malignus.

In the weeks that followed, Zeke gave his students a much-needed break. Zeke, King Sol, Barmor, Grambine, and others formed a tribunal they called the Guild for Humanity. The Guild would be filled with delegates chosen and elected from all the city states and realms around the world. The Guild for Humanity would oversee the trials for those captured during the battle, and any other future evil doers. The Guild would also help with worldly matters. They would have no control of how the realms or city states operated day to day.

The Guild would devise a plan for world improvement. The things that were now possible because of the use of magic were endless. In a world of peace, the people and their magic would take the world to new levels. However, there needed to be some guidelines. Magic was never to be used to kill or impose one's will on anyone else.

Now, with the worldwide use of magic, goods, knowledge and services could be shared around the world very quickly. There would be the creation of dozens of magical schools in every realm and city state. The schools could then compete in magical tournaments. Travel around the world would be almost seamless.

Although barter was a normal means of trade, the Guild would develop a currency system to be used worldwide. The currency system would be used along with the barter system. It could be used by people who needed to buy supplies without needing anything to trade.

There was no sign of where Prince Ostello and Mahdrin had disappeared to. They must have jumped somewhere far away. Scouts had been sent to find them, but until they were harming people or gathering a large number of followers, they were not much of a threat. Zeke knew that they were evil enough, that it would only be a matter of time that rumors of their whereabouts would start to spread. They would eventually be found.

Everyone knew that although the battle was over, the war was not. They also knew that, for now, there was no impending war, and they would be able to focus a lot more on advancing magic to better themselves and the world. It was only the beginning.

About the Author

James Dellwo was raised on a ranch in Montana. He went to college for diesel mechanic, and later became a truck driver. Wanting to try to make something creative, James began his journey as an author. Zekious Starbo is his first finished work, with more that he is working on.

www.ingramcontent.com/pod-product-compliance
Lightning Source LLC
Chambersburg PA
CBHW031458160726
47994CB00005B/2094